If You Knew

Barbara Meyers

If You Knew

Copyright © 2019 by Barbara Meyers

This edition published by Barbara Meyers, LLC and Sandalstring Productions

First pass edits by Noah Chinn

Cover by Steven Novak, Novak Illustration

ISBN 978-0-9836772-7-7 (Trade Paperback)

ISBN: 978-0-9836772-6-0 (E-book)

1. Contemporary Romance – Fiction 2. Iowa (U.S.) – Fiction 3. Family Relationships – Fiction. 4. Small Town Politics – Fiction. I. Title

Acknowledgments and Thanks

As always, I thank God for every bit of writing talent and ability He gave me, and for the daily inspiration and assistance He sends me.

To Bill for everything he has done for me for the past 38+ years.

To my wonderful beta readers: Alison Nissen, Donna Kelly, Ellen Holder, and Kathy Haffner.

To Cathy, Sandy and Danielle. They know why.

To my editor Noah Chinn.

To my cover artist, Steven Novak, Novak Illustration.

To my Facebook, Twitter, Instagram and newsletter followers for their support and feedback on everything from research to covers.

To Lakeland Writers, Novelists, Inc., Florida Writers Association, and Coffee & Quill friends for their assistance and support.

I hope I didn't forget anyone.

Chapter One

Devonny Campbell pulled into the parking lot of a roadside diner and turned off the car's engine. She sat for a moment taking deep breaths, willing away the cramps and lightheadedness threatening to overwhelm her. She peered through the windshield at the two-lane blacktop she'd just exited. A few cars and pickup trucks dotted the diner's gravel lot.

Still not feeling any better she opened the car door and forced herself out. She dreaded stepping into a restroom stall, afraid of what she might find. Was she losing something she hadn't even realized she wanted?

No. She refused to give up her unborn baby that easily. It was the last piece of Jack she had. His final gift to her. She wasn't ready to let go.

She pulled open the glass door to the diner and glanced around. Her entrance was barely acknowledged by the scattered patrons. A sign invited diners to seat themselves. A long counter ran along one side with round red stools right out of the fifties offering single diners a place to sit. A line of booths with the same red vinyl on the seats offered a view of the parking lot and the two-lane. Tables and chairs were crowded into the open space between the counter and the booths.

Devonny spotted a sign for the restrooms and darted that way. The dingy ladies' room had one of everything: toilet, paper towel holder, soap dispenser, sink.

She wasn't spotting, as she'd feared. The discomfort she'd felt earlier seemed to have eased somewhat once her bladder was empty. She still didn't feel like herself, but she felt marginally better than when she'd pulled off the interstate. She stared at her reflection. Maybe she needed to give herself a break.

She'd been driving for two days. She hadn't slept well at the motel she'd stopped in last night. She was in *Iowa*, for God's sake, which was about as foreign to her as LA was familiar.

"You look like hell," she told the mirror. Tears surged into her eyes, which helped to relieve the dry grittiness. Jack would be so upset with her if he was here. He'd have never let her get this run-down, this exhausted. He'd be fussing over her, making sure she ate right, rubbing her feet at night. She imagined him talking to her tummy even though her baby was barely even formed at this stage.

You're going to be okay.

There was that unpredictable voice in her head again. Sometimes it seemed to be all around her. At first she thought it was Jack. Encouraging her. Calming her down. But it wasn't Jack. No matter how much she wished it was. It was only her subconscious.

Wasn't it?

"Stop it," she warned herself. Jack was gone. It was up to her to take care of herself now. To do what was best for her baby. Jack's baby. She desperately longed for a nap. A bed with clean sheets and heavy drapes to block out the light. Some place where she wouldn't have to think for a while. Some place she could just sleep.

Feeling as good as she was probably going to for a while, Devonny left the restroom and made her way through the dining room toward the exit.

"Everything okay in there, hon?" asked a chubby waitress with overly-bleached blond hair and too-thin eyebrows.

"Fine," she choked out. She pushed at the door and ran straight into the man who was about to open it. Devonny stumbled and he steadied her, his fingers gripping her upper arms.

"Whoa, there. You okay?" She registered sandy hair and kind concern in his brown eyes. And just enough facial scruff to qualify as a beard.

"Fine. I'm fine." She pushed away from him and got into her car. She backed out with a screech of tires and turned away from the interstate she'd been traveling earlier. Moments later, she passed a sign. *"Welcome to Red Bud, Iowa."*

"Well, Dorothy," she muttered. "We're definitely not in Kansas anymore."

The tree-lined two-lane led to a prosperous-looking downtown. She drove around the town square. Shops and offices lined the perimeter and a stately old courthouse surrounded by a grassy lawn took up the middle.

"So this is what the Midwest looks like."

Somewhat enchanted by the view of the park where children played while mothers chatted, Devonny continued to meander. She took note of an ice cream store on one corner and a coffee shop on another. She drove down a few of the streets that branched off the town square and circled back.

This was America personified. Houses that had likely withstood everything that had been thrown at them for the past fifty or hundred years. Bikes abandoned in front yards. Kids shooting hoops at an over-the-garage backboard. Lawn mowers buzzing. Red Bud, Iowa had a kind of sturdy innocence about it, Devonny decided. A solid place where families had probably been neighbors with each other for decades. If a movie director scouted locations for "wholesome town in America's Heartland," he'd start filming right here.

Without a fixed destination, she simply kept driving, taking in the town, until she saw a sign pointing to Twelve Forks Inn. She gazed at the Victorian-style mansion with its wide front porch and peaked roof and turret.

She parked and approached the steps, feeling like Cinderella if she'd arrived much too early for the ball.

Wicker furniture, an old-fashioned swing, and ferns in hanging pots gave the porch a certain dated charm. A sign near the door said, "*Come on in.*" Devonny did.

She stepped into the light of an old crystal chandelier and onto the polished wood floor that creaked with age. A registration desk sat to one side. Another sign said, "*Ring bell.*" Devonny did.

In seconds, footsteps sounded approaching from the rear of the house. A middle-aged woman appeared. "Hello. Need a room?"

"Yes. If you have one available."

"This time of year, they're all available. Take your pick. Just you?"

"Yes."

"How about the green room? It's at the back. Nicest bathroom."

"That's fine."

"Just for the night?"

"I'm not sure."

The woman slid a registration form toward her. "You can stay all summer if you want. Need help with your bags?"

"No. It's fine. I can get it."

"I'm Pat, by the way. Pat Callahan. Place belongs to me and my husband. His grandmother thought she was doing us a favor leaving it to us. But it eats up money like nobody's business."

Devonny smiled politely and introduced herself, hoping she had the energy to drag her overnight bag up the stairs. She slid the registration card back across the desk.

"I'll need a credit card. Or cash. It's sixty for the night."

Devonny handed over her credit card and signed the slip. Pat gave her a keen appraisal. "You look done in, hon. Sure you don't need help with your luggage?"

Let her help you.

Was that Jack telling her what to do? Devonny swayed. She gripped the edge of the desk.

"All right. That's it." Pat plucked the car keys from Devonny's hand. "Tell me what you need and I'll get it."

"It's the red carry-on in the backseat. Thank you."

Devonny sank onto a ladder-back chair near the desk. From there she could see into what must be the drawing room. Sofas and chairs from another century, their upholstery redone in either paisley or floral prints, took up the space. A crystal vase of fresh flowers took place of honor on a pedestal table. She breathed in the scent of them mixed with the fragrance of lemon furniture polish.

Pat returned with her bag. "I locked your car," she said, handing Devonny the keys. "Not that it's necessary around here. But you're not from around here. Come on." She indicated the staircase at one side of the hall. "You first. So I can catch you if you fall."

"I won't fall," Devonny assured her as they started to climb. It didn't seem right that Pat, who looked to be in her fifties, would be more capable of hefting a suitcase than someone in their twenties.

"Uh huh." Pat appeared unconvinced. At the top of the stairs she pulled up the handle on the wheelie bag. "Keep on going, straight down the hall. Last door on the right." Devonny wondered exactly how old the house was. The stairs were covered with a cushioned red runner, but they creaked and groaned as the entry floor had. Obviously the structure was old, although someone had attempted to update the interior twenty-odd years ago, if the striped silver and taupe wallpaper and beige carpet were any indication.

Devonny opened the door and was immediately charmed by the big bedroom with its lacy curtains and moss green walls. The trim was painted bright white. An intricately patterned green and white quilt covered the bed.

"Bathroom's through there," Pat said, pointing to a partially open door. "I don't serve dinner, but you can order takeout from the Chinese place or there's always Petrovanni's. They'll deliver a pizza or anything else you want. Menus are in the nightstand drawer."

"Thank you."

"Breakfast's at eight. It's included in the room price. But if you don't show up by nine, I'll clear it away."

"Thank you," Devonny said again. She wasn't sure if she should tip the innkeeper. Or would that be inappropriate?

"You need anything else, press zero on the phone, there, all right?" She indicated a push-button landline on the nightstand.

"Yes, thank you."

Pat backed out and closed the door.

Devonny wiggled out of her jeans and kicked off her shoes. She yanked the quilt back and collapsed between the clean white sheets. She closed her eyes and dreamed she was in heaven.

Jack was there. But he wasn't the vivid Jack of her waking memory. The Jack with the black hair and laughing eyes. Not the larger-than-life Jack who'd swept her off her feet when she'd been a naïve eighteen-year-old, the one she'd married, the one who'd been her whole world.

This Jack was fuzzy, as if he were behind layers of gauze. She couldn't see him clearly. Yet she knew he was there.

He showed her things. A house on a quiet tree-lined street. The house had a metal roof and forest green siding and a stoop at the front. In the back was an old-fashioned swing set. The swings squeaked, especially one where a little girl pumped her legs, dark hair flying out behind her. *Is that me?* Devonny wondered in her dream.

There was a school and a park. She followed the girl and watched her enter the school and slide down the slide at the park.

She looked happy, that girl. *So not me*, Devonny knew. The girl waved. Did lips press against her temple while she slept? She couldn't be sure.

Chapter Two

Devonny woke to morning sunlight shining through the lacy curtains and a gentle breeze lifting them away from the sill. She vaguely recalled getting up in the middle of the night to use the bathroom and climbing right back into the bed. She'd slept through the afternoon and evening and the entire night. She assessed how she was feeling. The deep fatigue of the previous day had disappeared. She felt...wonderful. And ravenous.

She groped for her cell phone on the nightstand. It was after seven. She had plenty of time for a shower, but she definitely planned to be downstairs and waiting when Pat served breakfast at eight.

She luxuriated under the warm water, washing her hair and shaving her legs. Wrapped in a fluffy white towel, she padded into the bedroom for body lotion, deodorant, and clean clothes. She straightened the bed and folded her things.

You can stay here all summer if you want. She could, she supposed. But she wouldn't. She didn't know what she'd do, exactly. She'd left LA without a plan. Only knowing she needed to be somewhere different. Be *someone* different.

Her old life was gone and she had to create a new one. For herself and her baby. At the moment, a place like Red Bud, Iowa, seemed about as different from LA as she could get.

She picked up her cell phone and looked at her messages. Four were from her mother. She pressed delete without reading them. One was from Cherry. *Miss you already, girl,* it read. Cherry was probably the only person who understood why she'd left LA. Devonny smiled and texted back. *Miss you too.*

It wasn't quite eight, but Devonny ventured down the stairs and found her way to the dining room. A huge table ran the length of the room, ornately carved chairs standing at attention, five along each side and one at either end.

Through a doorway to what must be the kitchen, Pat appeared holding an insulated carafe of what Devonny desperately hoped was coffee.

"Good morning," Pat greeted her, setting the carafe on an antique sideboard.

"Good morning."

"Coffee here, if you'd like some. Help yourself. I've got French toast and sausage on the way." She then disappeared back into the kitchen.

Devonny poured a cup of coffee and sipped as she toured the room. Every piece of furniture was from the previous century. Perhaps even the century before that. Pat lived in a gold mine of lovingly preserved and well-cared for antiques. Paintings of farming landscapes, barns and fields, and one of a covered bridge graced the walls.

Windows looked out onto a gazebo in the back yard, as well as a flower garden. Devonny wondered if she had what it took to create a flower garden. To nurture living things and watch them grow. She smiled, thinking if all went well she'd find out soon enough. Maybe it wouldn't be a bad idea to practice on flowers first.

Pat returned with platters of French toast and sausage patties. "I've got some rolls in the oven. They'll be out in a few minutes." She set the platters on the table. "Usually I put everything on the sideboard there for a buffet. But since it's just you and me this morning, we'll do it this way." She moved the butter and syrup next to the food and set out two plates and silverware.

Devonny took the seat Pat indicated. "This looks wonderful."

"You must be hungry. Have you eaten anything since you arrived? I never heard a peep out of you last night."

Devonny helped herself to the food and dribbled syrup over her French toast. "I slept right through dinner."

"Did you a world of good. You're glowing today."

Devonny smiled and started to eat. Filling her mouth with food would keep her from having to converse.

Pat got up once to refill their coffee cups and retrieve the rolls from the oven. She set them down on a trivet next to the French toast. Orange and cinnamon wafted in Devonny's direction. She'd already eaten three slices of French toast and two sausage patties, but nothing was going to keep her from tasting one of the rolls.

She bit into it and the buttery pastry melted in her mouth. "Oh my God. These are delicious."

Pat nodded. "Clyde's grandmother's recipe. That woman could bake like nobody's business. Never used a recipe, either. She had it all up here." Pat tapped the side of her head. "I watched her and wrote it down as best I could. Had to estimate measurements and it took some experimentation, but mine are pretty close, if I say so myself."

***

After breakfast, Devonny arranged for another night's stay before she stepped outside. Pat had assured her she could walk safely almost anywhere in the town, and there was little danger of getting lost. But if she did, all she had to do was ask anyone and they'd direct her back to Twelve Forks.

The sun held the promise of more heat to come, but for now, it was pleasantly warm. Devonny turned left. There were several old stately homes lining the street, but none quite as impressive as Twelve Forks. In the next block, the homes grew smaller, most were clapboard with porches or stoops at the front. If not exactly prosperous, they looked well cared for, the yards neatly maintained. Many sported flower beds.

At the end of the second block, Devonny turned left again, enjoying wandering the town and getting a feel for it. The neighborhood was quiet. Only a few cars passed by. In one yard, a woman on her hands and knees weeded her garden. In another two children chased each other, laughing and shrieking at their game. Their antics made Devonny smile.

She walked on, determined to burn off at least some of the calories she'd consumed. She wondered if there was a gym in Red Bud. Surely there was. The town was big enough to support one. But then this wasn't body-conscious LA.

Her footsteps slowed a little as she approached a forest-green house with an aluminum roof, a stoop, and a single oak tree in the yard. There was a "For Sale by Owner" sign in front.

It was the house she'd seen in her dreams.

But how? She had not come down this street yesterday, she was sure of it. How had she dreamed of something she'd never seen?

Her feet propelled her forward, as if an invisible hand at her back had given her a nudge. The yard had been recently mowed, and on either side of the stoop the earth had been turned, perhaps in preparation for flower beds.

Devonny stood on the sidewalk and assessed the house. It seemed to be unoccupied. There were no curtains on the windows. A blank slate. Isn't that what she wanted? Somewhere completely different from LA. A place to recreate herself. To start a new life.

She climbed the three steps of the stoop which allowed her to see in the windows on either side. She glimpsed hardwood floors, walls painted white, and a well-proportioned living room. She began to envision the space with furniture and rugs on the floors.

She stepped off the stoop and looped around the one-car garage to the back where she stopped dead in her tracks. There stood the swing set from her dream, an ancient thing made of sturdy metal which had turned a brownish grey from age and weather, but completely intact. Devonny approached it slowly. The swing seats had been replaced fairly recently, as had the chains which were a shiny silver. In her mind's eye she saw the girl from her dream flying back and forth through the air, dark hair winging behind her. Gently, Devonny pushed one of the swings, watching until it stopped moving.

She turned to look at the back of the house. There was a bigger porch here. Devonny imagined having breakfast there on a day like today. Sipping her coffee, watching her little girl on the swing. Fanciful thoughts. She had no idea if her baby was a girl or a boy.

You know.

Devonny whirled. "Jack?" She wasn't sure if she'd said his name aloud or if she'd just thought it. But she was convinced she'd heard his voice as clearly as if he'd been standing right behind her.

She marched up the porch steps and looked in the window. She gasped at the completely upgraded and redesigned kitchen. The cabinets were a golden oak which contrasted nicely with the darker hardwood floors. She wondered if the floors were original. They looked it. There was room for a table and chairs, but there were no appliances. Apparently the seller had decided to leave that decision up to the buyer.

From the window on the other side of the back door she could see through to the front door. This was all the living space: a living room, dining room and kitchen. Based on the small size of the house, Devonny surmised there was probably only one bathroom and two bedrooms. But that would be plenty. One for her and one for the baby.

Wait a minute. Was she thinking that because she was looking for a place to be, this was it? It was *Iowa*, for Pete's sake!

She walked slowly around the far side of the house. The windows there too high for her to see in, but she suspected her earlier assessment was correct. Two bedrooms with a bathroom in between.

As she approached the front yard she glimpsed a man jogging along the street. He slowed when he caught sight of her, then stopped and stared at her. She stared back. He wasn't old by any means. He also wasn't wearing a shirt, just a baggy pair of running shorts and sneakers. A sheen of perspiration shown on his lightly tanned torso. His close-cut beard matched his sandy hair. She had the vague sense that she'd seen him before, but that was impossible.

He started walking toward her calling, "Good morning."

She stopped, ready to run if he made even one move she could interpret as threatening, despite Pat's assurances that it was safe to walk *almost* anywhere in town.

"Good morning." She kept her eyes on him, liking what she saw in spite of her caution. Physically he was nothing like Jack, who'd been broad, dark, sturdy, muscled. This guy was lean and tall and long-limbed. His gait wasn't quite even, as if he slightly favored one leg over the other. He was attractive though, she had to admit.

Why was she thinking this? She was nowhere near over losing her husband.

"Are you interested in the house?" he asked.

"I might be."

"I can show it to you if you like."

"Right now?"

"Sure, if you don't mind my uh, lack of clothes." He grinned. "Or, I can meet you back here later after I shower and make myself look more presentable."

He had brown eyes, Devonny noticed, filled with kindness and humor. He seemed easygoing. Steady. Like not much would ruffle him. Still, to enter an unoccupied house with a barely-dressed man in a town where she knew no one, and no one knew she was here?

She glanced around. There were other houses nearby. Surely if she screamed…

She heard someone snort nearby. A barely-there touch on her back.

Go on.

"You have a key?"

He grinned. "I have one hidden."

"Is this your house?"

"Not for long, I hope. You in?"

She assessed him once more. She'd been protected her whole life. First by her mother. Then by Jack. Shielded from the harsher realities of a big city. Sometimes she questioned her own instincts since she'd never had a chance to utilize them. Yet she'd instinctively been drawn to Jack, over her mother's constantly shouted objections. And that had been the right move, hadn't it? She realized she wanted to trust this man who was so unlike Jack in appearance. On some level, she was certain that she could. "All right."

"Be right back." He strode across the lawn and around the side of the house, disappearing from sight. But not before Devonny got a view of his backside which was just as appealing as the front. Smooth skin and the kind of tan that did not come from a spray or a tanning bed. Muscles that were defined, but not overly developed or the result of daily sessions with a personal trainer. His was a quiet, subtle strength, despite the hitch in his gait.

He soon reappeared and headed for the front door, waving for her to follow. He unlocked the door and pushed it open, making a sweeping gesture as he did. "Madam."

"Would you mind unlocking both the doors and leaving them open?"

"Not at all." He went through and did as she asked, but not before she got a whiff of his scent. Sunshine and sweat layered over the clean scent of soap or a mild deodorant. An odd ripple went through her that she tried to stifle. She didn't want to be attracted to a man who wasn't Jack, even though they'd talked about it before he died. He'd insisted she wasn't meant to be alone. That she'd find someone else. He swore he'd come back and haunt her if she didn't. The dreams, the voice she sometimes heard, the sense of someone touching her she couldn't explain? Maybe he'd already begun. Jack insisted being with someone else had nothing to do with how much she loved him. He wanted, *needed* to know that she'd go on and live her life. But she'd promised Jack she'd treasure what they'd had forever. That was a promise she planned to keep.

She stood in the middle of the living room and turned in a circle, trying to take in the space with not only her own eyes, but Jack's as well. Would he have liked it? Yes. Already she could envision the placement of furniture. "Oh! There's a fireplace." She hadn't noticed it when she'd been peeking in the window earlier. It was tucked into a corner almost as an afterthought, the brick and mantel painted the same white as the walls.

"Does it work?" She looked back at the man. "Sorry, I don't know your name."

"Luke Bradshaw. And I'm sorry I didn't introduce myself earlier. I got carried away by a possible sale. And you are?"

"Devonny Campbell." She moved closer to examine the fireplace.

Luke stepped further into the room. "It does work but it's not wood-burning. I had a gas one installed. At least it will put out some heat. I don't know why they built one so small. But on a cold winter's night, it will be a nice touch."

"Hmmm." In the kitchen Devonny ran her hand along the countertop. It was smooth and cool to the touch.

"That's concrete. It's low maintenance and will last forever."

"Hmmm." She looked out the window at the back yard. Trees and bushes lined the far edge. No way to tell if there was another house behind them.

She continued into the adjoining space. "I guess this is meant to be the dining room."

"Originally, yes. But you can use it however you want."

She eyed him. "If I buy the house." She started down the hall. "Are the floors original?"

"Painstakingly refinished." He said from behind her.

She opened the door on the right into a bedroom with a large window that looked out on the backyard. A child's room. The closet wasn't huge but it was adequate.

"What year was the house built? The windows look new."

"1942. They are." Luke hadn't entered the room with her, but instead leaned on the door jamb and watched as she looked around.

He eased back as she edged past him to inspect the bathroom at the end of the hallway. It wasn't huge, but again, it was adequate and had obviously undergone a recent renovation. She opened a door to discover a water heater and space for a stackable washer and dryer. Next to that was a narrow linen closet.

She was aware of Luke once again loitering in the doorway, giving her space, but watching as she inspected everything. He pushed open the door to the other bedroom. She stopped when she entered.

"Oh!" The room was bigger than she'd expected. Light splattered in from the window that overlooked the front yard shaded by the oak tree. There was another narrow horizontal window set high in the wall. A bed would fit perfectly underneath. Opposite was all closet space.

"Someone put a lot of work into this," she said as she took in the shelves and drawers, cubbies for shoes and plenty of room to hang clothes.

"That would be me."

She shot him a look. "You designed this closet?"

"Trying to make up for lack of a master suite."

"Did you do all the renovation?"

"Yes, ma'am."

"Is that what you do?"

"It's a sideline, I guess you'd say."

"Oh."

"I work over at the high school. We all have a certain amount of downtime. Holidays, summers."

"Fixing up old houses is your hobby?"

"I'm hoping it will be more of a supplemental income kind of thing to being a coach and guidance counselor."

"How much is this house, anyway?"

He named a price so low, Devonny wasn't sure she'd heard him correctly. "You're kidding, right?"

"Too high? It's negotiable."

"No. But where I come from, you couldn't get even one room in this house for that price."

"Where's that?"

"California." Why she didn't say LA, Devonny didn't know. For some reason, she felt the less anyone local knew about her, the better. There were certain things about her past that might not be so acceptable here in small town middle America.

"I want to look around some more, if that's all right."

"Sure." He followed her back to the kitchen and they stepped out onto the back porch.

"This is pretty." The porch flowed out of the foundation of the house and the sides were made of the same sturdy material. Concrete, she supposed, but not the smooth grey like concrete was today. This was a pale brown and chunks of stone were visible in the smoothed surface. Whatever materials were used for concrete in 1942, she supposed.

"That swing set looks ancient."

"I think it's original. Sure looks it, doesn't it? But it's sturdy as can be."

She asked more questions about the neighborhood and Luke answered them all. He'd lowered himself to sit atop the railing, legs splayed out in front, ankles and arms crossed. Devonny did her best to keep her eyes off his chest and well-defined abs, but she couldn't help noticing the scars that crisscrossed his right knee.

"Is it just you that'd be living here?"

"For the moment." Again she decided it best not to divulge too much. He didn't need to know. He was just the guy who owned the house. She might never see him again, even if she did decide to settle down here. Not until her child started high school anyway. Maybe not even then. By then Luke Bradshaw might have moved on.

Tell him you'll take it.

She ignored Jack's voice in her head. "I'd like to think about it," Devonny said as he locked everything up and they were outside on the front stoop again. "Can I get in touch with you tomorrow?"

"You sure can. You're staying at Twelve Forks, right?"

"How did you…?"

He grinned. "Only decent place in town to stay. Plus I ran past there earlier and saw a car with California plates." He tapped the side of his head. "I'm not a math teacher but I put two and two together."

"This is a small town, huh?" Devonny wasn't sure how she felt about that. It seemed much too easy for anyone who cared to know her business. But maybe that was better than big, impersonal LA where it often seemed no one was interested in anything but themselves.

"There's a coffee shop downtown."

"I saw it yesterday."

"We could meet there. Ten o'clock?"

"All right."

"See you then."

Luke took off jogging. Devonny began her walk back to Twelve Forks, watching him until he was out of sight.

***

Her name was Devonny Campbell. Luke could not believe his luck. She was the same woman who'd barreled into him at the diner yesterday before taking off in a rush. Even before he'd noticed her California license plate as she peeled out of the parking lot, he'd known she was not from around here. Now he knew why.

She was like an exotic creature from Mars set down on planet Earth, after taking on the form of a human being. She didn't quite seem to fit in a place like Red Bud. Maybe it was her clothes. Was that what they called California Casual? The well-fitting and strategically ripped jeans, the loose off-the-shoulder top, hair piled haphazardly atop her head.

She'd been upset about something yesterday, but today she seemed more at ease. And she obviously didn't remember him. He refused to be insulted by that. Not like he could attract the notice of every woman on the planet. But there was something about Devonny Campbell that intrigued him.

First of all, California to Iowa? What had brought her here? Not a job, surely. She was staying at Twelve Forks, so not family, either. He'd subtly checked out her ring finger. No wedding ring, but maybe the faintest hint of a lighter indentation where one might have been. Divorced perhaps? She'd been a bit ambiguous as to whether she planned to occupy the house alone. *For the moment,* she'd said. Was there a boyfriend on his way to come live with her?

Probably. A woman like Devonny couldn't be single.

Please, God, he prayed as he sprinted the last quarter mile, *let her buy that house.* He'd gone over budget renovating it, and he hadn't had any serious nibbles since he'd put it up for sale. He was itching to buy another property to keep himself occupied for the rest of the summer. Devonny hadn't balked at the price. He took that for a good sign.

Chapter Three

At ten the next morning, Luke walked into the coffee shop to find Devonny already waiting there. She was sipping what looked like hot chocolate and perusing the classifieds in the *Red Bud Record*. He ordered a coffee and took the seat across from her.

"Job hunting?"

"Just seeing what's available."

"Anything interesting?"

"Apparently there's an opening at the high school for an aide of some sort."

"Ah, yes. Beverly Padgett's job."

"Why'd she leave?"

"She didn't leave so much as she…died."

"On the job?"

"In bed."

"You know this how?"

"Word on the street."

"Natural causes?"

"Sex."

Devonny leaned in. "She died from having sex?"

"I don't think it was the sex that killed her. Most likely a heart attack."

"I guess she died happy."

"Doubtful."

"Why do you say that?"

"She was in bed with Rufus Sylvester when it happened."

"And Rufus Sylvester would be…?"

"An eighty-year-old hog farmer not known for his interest in personal hygiene for one thing—"

Devonny held up a hand. "Let's change the subject, shall we?"

"I can put in a good word for you with the principal if you like. He'll make the final decision about who gets hired."

"You don't have to do that. Besides, you hardly know me. Maybe I'm not even qualified."

"To be an aide? If you can read and operate a copy machine, you're qualified. And I'm betting you've got better sense than to let ole Rufus have his way with you."

"Ugh. Now I really do want to change the subject."

"You want to buy the house, don't you?"

"You're awfully sure of yourself."

"I've been told it's one of my most attractive traits."

"Have you had it appraised?"

"My self-assuredness?"

"The house."

"Nope."

"How did you come up with the price?"

"Looked at what similar houses in the area sold for in the past couple of years. Took into consideration what I put into it and the fact that it's completely renovated. You can call in an appraiser if you want. You'll have to in any case to qualify for a mortgage. But the price is fair."

"I don't need a mortgage."

Luke's eyebrows shot up and he sat back. "You don't?"

"Do you have a problem with that?" Devonny asked.

"Not at all. Should I call my attorney and have him draw up the papers?"

"It will take me a couple of days to transfer some funds, but you can go ahead and start the paperwork if you want."

"Full asking price?"

"Unless you want to give me a welcome-to-town discount?"

***

Back in her car, Devonny used her phone to find the nearest branch of her bank. There was one in Shenandoah, some thirty miles away. She got on the road, ideas already forming in her head. Shenandoah also had a mall with a couple of department stores and hair salons. Apparently, Operation: Start a New Life had begun.

As she drove through virtually nothing but farmland, Devonny assured herself it wasn't too late to back out if she changed her mind. But she knew she wasn't going to. She'd spent some time yesterday driving around the rest of town. She'd checked out the schools and the supermarket and the business district. All the essentials were there. She'd paid for another night's stay at Twelve Forks and taken her laptop to her room to do more research.

Centerville was a slightly larger town twelve miles east of Red Bud. The city of Shenandoah was north and west of Red Bud. If she needed a movie theatre or a mall or a supermarket with a better selection of produce, she might have to travel a bit. But travel on these flat, nearly deserted roads in rural Iowa was likely to be less time-consuming than similar distances in LA.

After visiting the bank, Devonny headed to the food court in the mall for lunch. A stylist at one of the mall's two hair salons could take her right away. Devonny watched as much of her hair fell to the floor. But when the stylist was finished, she smiled at herself in the mirror, happy with her decision.

Next were the department stores. She hadn't gained much weight yet, but her figure had changed, expanding to make room for the baby. She found several outfits, choosing long loose tops and slacks and skirts that would give her room to expand. They'd do for the next couple of months. Then she'd have to shop for fall and winter.

As she passed an eyeglass display she paused at the poster featuring a woman about her age, peering out from behind a pair of oversized horn-rimmed glasses. Devonny had been a home-schooled geek, and she'd never stopped seeing herself that way. She'd never needed glasses, but wearing them would indicate who she was on the inside: A math and science nerd who'd read just about every book she'd come into contact with.

Why not?

She wasn't sure if the voice she heard was hers or Jack's, but the idea of glasses to further change her look simply appealed to her. She didn't have to wear them all the time. She was starting over. She could be whoever and whatever she wanted to be.

But she wasn't sure who she would be without Jack. Missing him was like a dull ache around her heart that never went away. Before he died they'd discussed her future, though it was the last thing Devonny wanted to do. She tried to be brave for him. To be strong. But the reality of losing him was killing her inside.

"Being with someone else doesn't mean you'll forget me, you know," he'd said.

"I can't." Can't talk about it. Can't think about. Won't do it.

"Dev." His arms came around her and she buried her face in his shoulder as she gave in to her sadness. He pressed his lips to her temple. "Dev. I'll always be with you. You know that, right?"

She nodded, unable to speak. Her tears were soaking his shirt.

"This was my time. Our time together on this plane."

She pulled back. "Stop giving me your New Age-y wisdom."

He gave her that half-grin she loved. He chucked her gently under the chin. "I'll haunt you if I find you curled up in a corner crying your eyes out for the next twenty years."

She raised an eyebrow. "Twenty? You're pretty sure of yourself." And just like that he'd teased her out of her sadness.

"Even one. Live your life, Dev. Find someone to share it with. Be happy. I need to know you'll do that so I can be at peace."

She'd do anything for Jack. That's the way it had always been. Anything that was hers to give. "Okay." If this was the last, the final thing she could give Jack, so be it.

"Promise?"

"Promise."

She pulled back from reminiscing and perused the rows of eyeglasses through the store window. All her life she'd been appreciated for the way she looked and, she supposed she'd capitalized on it to a certain extent.

Certainly her appearance was what first attracted Jack, but if that had been all she'd had to offer, he wouldn't have stuck around.

Thank God her mother had always encouraged her to read. And because she'd been fairly isolated during her formative years, she'd done just that. Being with Jack had given her an outlet for all the theories and ideas she'd formulated. They'd had lively discussions and debates about almost everything. Even though Jack hadn't gone to college he was smart and widely read, although his tastes in fiction tended to run to the classics. And he'd probably read thousands of scripts. He was also fascinated by mysticism and spirituality. And toward the end, he'd been comforted by books about angels and the afterlife.

She stepped into the eyeglass store and tried on several pairs before she found what she wanted. If the sales clerk found her request for clear lenses odd, she didn't comment.

Devonny returned to her car swinging her shopping bags, looking forward to the drive back to Red Bud while nibbling on the big chocolate chip cookie she'd bought.

"Corn, cows, and soybeans," she marveled as she drove the four-lane highway. "That's all they grow here." She'd never seen such huge flat fields or so many pastures dotted with cows.

She thought back to LA with its snarled freeway traffic and the houses stacked almost on top of each other, everyone fighting for a bit of space or a parking place. She felt how she imagined an alien might when it arrived in a foreign world. But she was determined to fit in, to make a new life. If indeed she would soon have a daughter to raise, Devonny wanted more than anything for her to have the kind of childhood she hadn't. Go to school, play sports, have sleepovers with giggly girlfriends, and eventually a boyfriend. To attend school dances. The prom.

Devonny sighed. How she would have loved that. To dress up and dance with a boy. To have a wrist corsage.

Again, she smiled remembering that she had danced. With Jack on their honeymoon in Las Vegas. On the balcony of their hotel room with the lights of the city below. That had been the beginning of her life with Jack.

And this? This was the beginning of her life without him.

Chapter Four

Two days later she arrived at the attorney's office with a bank check in hand. Luke was already there. Introductions were quick and they got down to business. Signed lots of papers. Devonny handed over the check. Luke gave her the keys.

They stepped outside. Devonny wasn't sure what to do. Shake hands and go on her merry way? She needed to call the storage facility in LA and have her belongings shipped to her new address.

The thought struck her. "I have a new address!" She laughed. Buying a house on her own was perhaps the most adult thing she'd ever done. A wave of sadness hit right in the middle of her delight. The ink had barely been dry on the mortgage papers for the house she and Jack had finally been able to afford in LA before he got sick.

Luke's smile faded. "What's wrong?"

"Nothing. I just thought of something."

"Something that made you sad."

"It's nothing. Thank you. For the house, I mean." She stuck out her hand.

Luke took it in his, but he didn't shake. He just held on. "Can I buy you coffee or lunch to celebrate?"

"I can't." Devonny tugged her hand away. "I've got some calls to make and appliances to shop for."

"Oh. Sure. Of course."

"Another time," Devonny said, knowing she didn't mean it. Luke probably knew it too.

"Of course. If you need help with anything, give me a call."

"I will. Thanks." She turned toward her car.

"I like the haircut, by the way."

She swiveled to walk backwards for a few steps and called, "Thanks," before she turned back around.

She drove to the house, periodically eying herself in the rearview mirror the whole way. She liked her haircut, too. It was a drastic change from wearing it long as she'd always done. But this was shorter and sassy and messily layered. It made her feel more adult. Jack had loved her long hair. More memories of him surfaced. How he'd tangle his hands in her hair when they made love. Twirl strands of it around his finger afterward while they held each other close.

Would he like this house, she wondered as she sat in the driveway staring at it. Would he like my haircut?

***

A week later, Devonny sat across from Principal Nicholas Foster while he perused her resume and the paperwork from the school system's HR department.

He glanced up. "You come highly recommended, Miss Campbell."

Devonny didn't correct his assumption that she was a "Miss." "I do? How is that even possible?"

"Luke Bradshaw said you might apply. Said I'd be a fool if I didn't interview you, and an even bigger fool if I didn't offer you the job."

Devonny wasn't sure how she felt about that. "That was very kind of him, but I'm not sure he knows me well enough to make a recommendation. We've only met a couple of times."

"I know." Foster sat back in his chair and smiled. "He told me you bought the house he renovated over on Maplewood Avenue. You must have made quite an impression on him."

When Devonny didn't respond, the principal went on. "Truth is, this isn't a particularly difficult position. Mostly you're doing work the teachers don't have time to do. Making copies. Helping them keep their classrooms organized. Entering grades into the computer system. Handling requests for supplies. That kind of thing.

"The aide usually oversees ordering supplies for the concessions at the athletic events and chaperones dances if need be. You'd keep track of tickets for school plays, concerts, social gatherings like prom and homecoming. You'd also be in charge of keeping the money straight, making deposits and turning in sales reports. Think you could handle that?"

"Of course." Devonny had practically run Chemistry's office single-handedly, once Claire had trained her. Devonny was exceptionally good with numbers.

"I see you worked for a film company in Los Angeles. Chemistry Films?"

"Yes." Devonny reminded herself she had nothing to hide.

"Meet anyone famous?"

"We did specialized projects. Nothing with big motion picture stars."

"I'm a big Tom Hanks fan myself."

"He's a wonderful actor."

Foster asked her a few more questions before the interview was over. He said he'd be in touch in the next day or two. He followed her into the front office. The secretary who had been there before, casually dressed because school wouldn't start for another two weeks, was absent. But Luke Bradshaw had taken up residence. From a row he had laid out along the counter, he was assembling papers and stapling them together.

He looked up and there was that smile again. "Hi, Devonny." His gaze slipped over her to Principal Foster. "I was right, wasn't I? But I won't say I told you so."

Foster gave him a pained look.

Devonny glanced from Luke to Foster and back. "Right about what?"

"About you," Luke said. His gaze went once again to the principal. "She's perfect for the job, right?"

"Fine. Yes." Foster turned to Devonny. "There's no point in keeping you waiting. Provided you pass a background check, of course, I'd like to offer you the job."

"It's not because of him, is it?" Devonny asked, indicating Luke.

"No, I'd have offered you the job anyway. You're the most qualified candidate from the applicants we had. Over-qualified, if I'm being honest."

Something loosened in Devonny's chest. She didn't want to owe Luke Bradshaw for anything, but she didn't know why.

Liar. She knew exactly why. She was attracted to Luke, and she was on the verge of putting herself in a position where she'd be in constant close proximity to him. Widowhood coupled with Operation: Start A New

Life was triggering all sorts of emotions she didn't know how to deal with. Guilt was just one of them.

She was aware Luke had stopped stapling and was listening to the two of them.

"It usually takes about a week for the background check. I'll call as soon as they give me the all clear and we'll schedule a time for you to come in and complete the paperwork. That way you'll be ready to start the first day of school."

"Thank you." She shook hands with Foster and nodded in Luke's direction. "Nice to see you again," she said.

She was ready to push open the door to the outside when Luke called to her. "Devonny, wait up."

Her stomach did that odd flip-flop again as Luke hurried over.

"I'm sorry if I was out of line."

"It doesn't appear that you were." She wanted to keep some kind of formal distance between them.

A faint frown formed between his eyebrows, as if he wasn't certain how to respond.

"Have a good day," she said. She pushed the door open and walked away, aware that he watched her the whole time.

***

"First frost will kill those, you know."

Devonny looked up from her newly planted flower bed to see the owner of the voice. Her next-door neighbor, apparently. The old lady limped carefully down the steps of her front porch, leaning heavily on a cane and holding onto the railing. She made slow progress across her driveway and onto Devonny's property.

"You're planting too late in the season," she went on.

"I know." Devonny patted the dirt around a purple petunia.

"Who sold you those? They've got a fool for a customer."

"The nursery off the highway," Devonny replied. The fact that she'd just been insulted by her neighbor did not bode well for their future relationship.

"Must have been Russell Melburn. Well, he should have told you—"

"He did," Devonny said. She reached for another petunia and determinedly dug another hole with her brand new trowel. Why must this old lady ruin what had started out as a perfectly pleasant pastime? It was something she had been looking forward to from the moment she'd taken possession of the house.

"Oh." The woman seemed to ruminate on that bit of information while Devonny silently planted the petunia. "Those mums might do well enough. For a while, anyway. They like the fall weather."

The nursery proprietor had told Devonny that as well. In fact, he'd tried to discourage her from buying the petunias. They were overgrown and scraggly-looking, but Devonny had fallen in love with their bright purple color. And they were already priced at a deep discount.

Devonny had been beyond excited to plant her first flower garden, such as it was. She'd chosen the area beneath her bedroom window so she could look out and see the fruits of her labors when she woke up each day.

But this nosy neighbor with her unwanted advice was ruining it for her.

"I suppose like most young people you don't want any advice from an old lady. Doesn't do anybody any good getting old. Every bit of knowledge you've accumulated doesn't have anywhere to go. Nobody wants to listen."

"I never had a garden before," Devonny told her. "But I love flowers, and everyone here seems to grow them. I'm having fun practicing right now. Next year, I'll plant early, which is what the man at the nursery advised." She sat back to view her efforts. The sun was warm on her back, and she wiped the perspiration from her forehead. She was happy with her efforts even if her neighbor found them lacking.

"You're going to water them, I guess. Probably won't get much rain for the next week or so, though that's a good thing this time of year."

Devonny got to her feet, remembering the hose with the spray attachment she'd left in the trunk of her car. "I will water them, yes."

"Do it in the evening or early in the morning," the woman advised. "Otherwise, the water dries right up."

"Yes, ma'am. I'm Devonny Campbell, by the way. I just moved in."

"I've got eyes, don't I? I've seen your car and the delivery and moving trucks."

Devonny was taken aback by the sharpness of her tone. Did getting old give one a license to be rude in Iowa? "If you'll excuse me," Devonny said stiffly.

"Oh, get off your high horse," the woman said. "All I meant was I've still got all my faculties. And there's nothing wrong with my eyesight or my hearing. If it weren't for this bum hip I'd have a flower garden, too. I'm Loretta, by the way. Loretta Herman." She stuck out her hand.

Devonny took it. The woman had a firm grip in spite of her gnarled fingers. Her skin was surprisingly soft. "Nice to meet you."

Loretta cackled. "I doubt that. But it's nice to see somebody taught you manners."

If Loretta only knew. Devonny's mother had been a stickler for etiquette and decorum. She'd made Devonny read Emily Post from cover to cover when she was a girl.

Loretta looked at the plants. "You'll want to give those some water now, too, seeing as how they're newly planted. Otherwise they'll be wilted from this heat. If you want to come over when you're cleaned up, I'll give you a glass of cold tea. I've got banana nut bread just baked this morning."

Devonny's stomach growled at the mention of a cold drink and carbs. "I'd like that," she said.

"All right." Loretta turned and marched away with as much dignity as her hip would allow.

She's lonely.

She recognized another Jack thought in her head, and knew it was likely true. Well so am I, she reminded herself. Maybe she and Loretta could find some common ground — unlikely as that seemed. In fact, that was one of the reasons she'd interviewed for the job at the school. Having no routine and nothing to do once she got the house in order did not appeal to her. If she was going to make Red Bud her new home, she needed to meet people and become involved in the community. Working at the high school seemed ideal.

She would, she realized, have to tell Principal Foster about her pregnancy, assuming she passed the background check. Perhaps he'd withdraw the job offer. But she hoped he wouldn't. She looked forward to being in the high school, since her mother had seen to it that she hadn't attended as a student.

You're looking forward to seeing more of Luke Bradshaw.

Surely that was her own thought and not one of Jack's. It was a bit disconcerting to have Jack, or who she thought was Jack, in her head so often. But sometimes, she talked to him, so she thought this was his way of responding. Sometimes it was hard to tell. In this case, she could admit to herself that she did like seeing Luke. As different as he was from Jack, something about him appealed to her.

It's too soon, she thought.

Says who?

Devonny groaned in frustration as she screwed the nozzle onto the hose and the hose onto the spigot. "I do."

Who are you, your mother? That's what she said about getting married. It was too soon. You don't know him well enough. You're too young. You'll live to regret it.

But her mother had been wrong, and until her dying day Devonny would be glad she hadn't listened to her, that she'd followed her heart. Even if it meant her mother no longer spoke to her.

Well, that wasn't technically true. Her mother called and texted, but Devonny ignored her. Devonny wouldn't trade what she'd had with Jack for anything.

She could still hear her mother's parting words after the memorial service. "You got what you deserved. And so did he." Devonny had wanted to slap the satisfied look off her mother's face, though she'd never raised a hand to her before. Instead, she'd turned her back on the woman who'd raised her and hadn't spoken to her since.

She twisted the handle on the spigot and a stream of water shot out, hitting her in the face. She put her hand out to try to stop it before she realized how good the cool water felt on her heated skin. She'd forgotten to screw the hose on tight enough. Eventually, she turned the water off and made a few adjustments. But when she turned the water back on, it shot out at her again. She laughed. Either the spigot was defective or her hose handling was to blame. Perhaps she'd ask Luke about it.

She finally gave up and retrieved the watering can she'd purchased at the nursery. After filling it several times, she decided her flowers were sufficiently damp and that they'd survive the afternoon, no matter what Loretta might say about her technique.

***

"So, you've met Luke," Loretta said, once she and Devonny had settled at her kitchen table. Glasses of tea and a plate of banana bread sat between them. The table was old and scarred. A genuine antique, Devonny would be willing to bet. Nothing in Loretta's house looked like it had been updated for half a century, except the plasma TV mounted on the wall across from a well-worn recliner.

"Yes." Devonny slid a slice of the bread onto the plate in front of her. It looked delicious and smelled like heaven.

"That was his grandmother's place, you know."

"No, actually, I didn't. He never mentioned it." Devonny took a bite of the bread. It was as yummy as she'd expected it to be.

"She was a good friend and a good neighbor. Left the place to him when she died."

"I'm surprised he didn't live there," Devonny said.

"He did for a while, when he first got to town and the whole time he was fixing it up. Maybe there were too many bad memories there for him."

"Bad memories? Why? What happened?"

"Oh, lots of things, I expect. It was a long time ago. But he came to Red Bud after—he was staying with Mary Lee when she passed."

"Didn't he grow up in Red Bud?"

"Nope. His mother did, though. That'd be Mary Lee's daughter, Pamela. But she married right out of college and never came back except to visit. Brought those boys with her. Not the husband, though."

Devonny reached for another slice of bread. "You must miss your friend."

"Ain't hardly got any friends left." Loretta's tone was one of resignation without self-pity. "That's the other thing about getting old. Everybody my age gets sick and they start to die off. Only socializing I do now is at funerals and doctors' offices."

"You can socialize with me."

"Ha! Why'd a young girl like you hang around with an old lady like me? You're just being polite. But don't think I don't appreciate it."

"I just moved here. I don't know anyone. Well, except for Luke. And now you. And if you want to bake banana bread and invite me over, I'll be happy to come."

"So, it was the banana bread that got you to come, huh?"

Devonny laughed. "I came because I wanted to. Because you invited me. The banana bread was just added incentive."

"Well, in that case, go on." Loretta pushed the plate closer. "I can see you're itching to have another slice."

***

Devonny had finished filling the watering can the next morning when Luke jogged by. When she waved to him he made a beeline in her direction, stopping a couple of feet away. "Good morning." He didn't try to hide his pleasure at seeing her.

His upper body was covered with a sheen of perspiration that trickled down the line of hair that disappeared where the low-riding shorts began. Devonny blushed, suspecting she'd been caught looking. She yanked her gaze back to his. He looked amused. "You said if I had any problems with the house to tell you."

The amused look went away. "Problems?"

"It's the spigot." She waved the full can in that direction and some of the water sloshed over. "I can't get the hose attached to it properly. Water shoots out."

"Ah." Luke came over and bent to examine it. Devonny stepped over to her flower bed and let the can tilt to soak the ground, while she watched him. He had well-developed calves and a hell of an ass she couldn't help but notice, especially when he bent to take a better look at the spigot. Her mouth went dry about the same time the watering can did. Luke straightened and she adjusted her attention as quickly as possible. He still had a hint of that knowing, amused smile on his face. "Threads are shot, that's why the hose doesn't fasten properly. I can put an attachment on here. That will be the simplest fix."

"All right."

"I'll pick one up and stop by later if that's okay."

"Sure."

"Everything else okay with the house?"

"Yes. It's perfect."

Luke's smile returned. "Maybe after I fix your spigot you'll go for that coffee with me?"

"Oh. Um…"

Go.

Shut up, Jack.

Go on. You want to have coffee with him. Admit it.

"No!"

Luke held up his hands. "Okay, okay. Can't blame a guy for trying."

"Sorry." Devonny clenched her jaw. "I didn't mean for it to come out like that. My mind was elsewhere."

Luke tilted his head to one side waiting for further explanation. Which Devonny didn't know how she could give without sounding like a total loon. "But thanks for inviting me."

"Sure. Another time maybe."

***

When Luke returned a couple of hours later, Devonny stayed inside. She saw him park a complicated-looking racing bike behind her car. From a canvas backpack he removed a bag with the local hardware store's logo on it and a compact toolbox. He wore a baggy pair of khaki shorts and a tee shirt.

He didn't knock. Probably didn't want to set himself up for more rejection from her. She didn't like the way Jack seemed to be pushing her toward him, either. She'd tried to tell Jack she wasn't ready, but he hadn't replied.

Luke was attractive, sure, and she was definitely attracted to him.

But…

She always came up against the but. But she'd have to explain about the baby. About Jack. About their life together in LA. That's the part she wasn't ready for.

If Jack were alive, if he were here, he wouldn't have liked Luke's obvious interest in her at all. Jack hadn't been the jealous type exactly, but he had been possessive. But now? Jack wasn't acting jealous or possessive. She supposed in death he'd moved past the negative components in the human psyche. All he seemed to radiate now was positive energy and encouragement.

Chapter Five

"Excuse me, Devonny? Could you come into my office for a minute?"

"Sure."

There was someone else in Principal Foster's office when Devonny followed him in. Mr. Sylvester, if she wasn't mistaken, one of the math teachers.

"Have you met Bob Sylvester?" Nick asked. "Devonny Campbell."

Bob reached a hand over to Devonny from where he was seated. His other hand held an ice pack to his jaw.

"Bob's had a crown come loose during lunch. He can see his dentist this afternoon, but he's got an Algebra II class last period. Normally we'd get a sub, but since it's only one class, would you mind covering it? Bob's got an assignment prepared, which the kids can work on for the first half hour and a quiz you can hand out for the last twenty minutes, right Bob?"

Bob nodded, then groaned.

"Happy to help," Devonny said. "I've been thinking about getting my teaching certification." Excitement bubbled inside of her at being in a classroom, interacting with the students, helping them learn. Math had always come easy to her.

Nick said, "That's great, but you won't have to do any actual teaching today. Just hand out the assignment and the quiz and be the adult presence in the room. If any of the students give you trouble, I want to hear about it, all right?"

"All right."

"Good. Report to Bob's classroom after the fifth period bell so he can show you what to do. Thanks, Devonny."

***

Devonny was a bit nervous as she stood by Bob Sylvester's desk while his class found their seats. There was the usual chatter before the second bell, but once it rang, they quieted. Most looked at her expectantly.

"Mr. Sylvester has to be somewhere else this afternoon," she began. "I'm Devonny Campbell, the teacher's aide."

"We know who you are," one of the guys said loudly. Several of his buddies chuckled and high-fived him.

Devonny narrowed her gaze on him and his cheeks turned pink. He ducked his head and stared at his desk.

"As I was saying, Mr. Sylvester left an assignment for you." She picked up the stapled pages and handed them to those in the first row to pass back. "You'll have thirty minutes to work on it." There were multiple groans and a rising chorus of murmurs. "In silence," she added. "You can take the assignment home with you and turn it in tomorrow if you don't finish it in class today. And I'll be handing out a quiz."

More murmurs of dissent. Again, she waited for them to end. "Any questions?"

"Have you got a date for homecoming?" This came from one of the guys. Not the same one who spoke up before, though.

"As a matter of fact, I don't," Devonny said, deciding to play along. "Nor do I wish to contribute to the delinquency of a minor." There was some good-natured ribbing amongst the group of guys and she saw several of the girls roll their eyes. She winked at one of them who smiled back.

"All right, begin your assignment. Remember you've got thirty minutes before the quiz."

The class settled down and all that could be heard was the scratch of pencils and the shuffle of paper. Devonny had no wish to sit behind Bob Sylvester's desk, so she strolled slowly around the room, looking at the bulletin boards which were unimaginative at best and boring at worst. Bob Sylvester clearly had no wish to make the subject of math interesting to his students.

If this were her classroom, she'd brighten it up. Maybe post some kind of easy way to remember equation rules or steps for breaking down a problem. Maybe some jokes. What did Y squared say to X to the seventh power? Or "Two quadratic equations walk into a division sign."

She turned away from the bulletin board when she heard whispering from the center of the room. Two of the girls were engaged in a discussion, although to give them credit, they were trying to be quiet about it. Devonny came up behind them. "Is there a problem here, girls?" she asked, keeping her voice down so as not to distract the rest of the class.

One of the girls, a blonde with big blue eyes, looked upset. "I don't understand factoring polynomials." She picked up her assignment paper. "I'm not asking for any answers, just help."

Devonny frowned. "Didn't Mr. Sylvester already cover this?"

The girl looked even sadder. "He did. But I still don't understand it."

"What about you?" Devonny asked the other girl, a bookish-looking brunette with glasses.

"Not really."

Nick had told her she wouldn't have to do any actual teaching today. But he hadn't said she couldn't. "What about the rest of the class?" she asked the girls. "Do most of them understand it?"

They shrugged.

Devonny made a decision. She strode to the front of the class. "Class, stop working for a minute, please." Pencils stilled and heads came up. "I'm going to give a quick lesson up here on factoring polynomials. It may help those of you who are having trouble with the concept. If you already understand it, go back to your assignment. Anyone who needs help, come up here now and bring your assignment sheet."

Devonny watched as half the class came forward. She doubted their lack of understanding had anything to do with not studying. Perhaps that would be true if only one or two of them didn't get it, but not half the class.

She took an assignment sheet from the girl nearest her and studied it for a moment before picking up a marker and turning to the whiteboard.

***

"Ms. Campbell! Wait up." Devonny had been strolling across the rear parking lot after school, something she often did because it took her past the football field. That was where the coach, one Luke Bradshaw, and the team practiced almost every afternoon. She turned to see the two girls from the algebra class hustling to catch up with her.

"Mind if we walk with you?" the blonde said.

"No, not at all."

"I'm Allie. That's Kelly."

"Devonny."

"You mean we don't have to call you Ms. Campbell?"

"You can if you want. At school, certainly you should. But when I'm not at school, I'm Devonny."

"That's a pretty name."

"I had nothing to do with choosing it. But, thank you."

Allie giggled. "Kelly and me, uh, Kelly and I wanted to thank you for helping us in class today."

"No problem."

"If Mr. Sylvester explained things the way you do, algebra wouldn't be so hard."

"I'm sure Mr. Sylvester is a very good teacher," Devonny said diplomatically. "But some concepts are harder to grasp than others."

"If he was a good teacher, half the class wouldn't have wanted extra help," Kelly put in. She had a huskier voice.

Devonny decided it would be best not to discuss Bob Sylvester's effectiveness as a teacher. "Well any time you girls need help, let me know. I've always liked math."

"I didn't think anyone liked math," Allie said.

Devonny laughed. She glanced around and lowered her voice. "Can I tell you girls a secret?"

"Sure," they said in unison.

"I'm a total science geek, too."

"No way!" Kelly said. "I hate biology. We're going to have to dissect a frog this semester."

"And a pig embryo next semester," Allie put in. "Yuck!"

Devonny's eyes widened. "Really? I'm so jealous."

"Wow, you really are a geek if you're jealous of that."

"I was home-schooled. I never got to dissect anything. It sounds like it would be interesting."

"To me it sounds gross."

"But you'll get to see the nerves and the organs and the blood vessels. The way a human body works is similar to an animal's. Everything's connected and everything has a purpose. I'd be fascinated to see how it all works."

"I never thought of it like that," Kelly said.

"If you girls ever need help with your assignments, I don't have much going on during the lunch break. I could help you then."

"Maybe we could meet in the media center," Allie said. "If Mrs. Jefferson doesn't mind us eating in there. Because I know I'm going to need help to get through algebra."

"And biology," Kelly added.

"I can ask Mrs. Jefferson about it," said Devonny. "If we can't meet there, maybe there's another room available. I should probably make sure it's all right for me to do this, though."

They walked on. The sun was already beginning to slant into late afternoon. The heat of the summer was rapidly dissipating, and some of the leaves on the trees were starting to show signs of red and gold. Devonny was looking forward to her first fall in the Midwest.

"Are you going to the homecoming dance?" Allie asked.

"Yes. I'm supposed to chaperone." Devonny was looking forward to that. She'd never been to a high school dance, either.

"Good. We'll see you there," Allie said. "This is our street."

They waved and turned at the corner.

Devonny continued on, feeling good about the contribution she'd made today. She'd check with Principal Foster and Mrs. Jefferson about setting up study sessions during lunch. And she was definitely going to look into what it took to get a teaching certificate. And then, Bob Sylvester, you better look out.

***

"Devonny, could I see you in my office, please?"

Devonny turned from the copier to see Nick waiting. She'd seen Bob Sylvester go into Nick's office a few minutes ago.

"Close the door," Nick said, as he rounded his desk and took his seat.

Devonny took the chair next to Bob. He did not look happy. "I hope you're feeling better," she said.

"I'm fine."

Nick folded his hands on top of his desk. "Devonny, a few of the students told Bob you helped them with their assignment yesterday. Is that true?"

"I explained a couple of things to them, yes. They were having trouble understanding some of the concepts and were struggling to complete the work."

"Bob says he'd already covered the information in a previous class. Right, Bob?"

"That's right. They didn't need any extra help."

"Except they did." Devonny looked at Nick.

"I don't appreciate you thinking you can do my job better than I can," Bob said.

Oh. That was it. Bob's fragile ego couldn't handle the fact a mere aide had explained something to his class in terms they could understand.

Devonny decided to ignore Bob Sylvester and addressed Nick. "Is there a problem here?"

Nick turned to the teacher. "Bob?"

"What I just said."

So he'd got his nose out of joint. After seeing over half the class taking up her offer of extra help, she had little sympathy for him. However, she had no wish to make an enemy in her new home.

"I'm good at math," she began. "It's always been easy for me, but it isn't easy for everyone. I asked if anyone wanted extra help and those who did joined me for about five minutes. Then they went back to the work Bob assigned them. I didn't think it was a bad thing if I could help some of the kids. Isn't that what we're all here for?" She looked from Nick to Bob and back.

"Of course it is," Nick said.

In for a penny, in for a pound, Devonny decided. "A couple of students approached me after school actually, and I offered to help them during lunch if they needed it. They suggested we could meet in the media center. That is, if Mrs. Jefferson approves."

"Now wait a minute," Bob said, at the same time Nick said, "You'd be willing to do this on your own time?"

"Of course."

"I'll talk to Mrs. Jefferson about it."

"I don't know what you think you can teach them that their teachers can't," Bob grumbled.

"Maybe nothing," Devonny conceded. "But at the very least, they'll be using the time trying to learn."

Nick looked pointedly at Bob as if daring him to disagree.

When he didn't, Devonny decided to be the adult in the room just as they'd asked her to do yesterday, although there she'd been surrounded by fifteen-year-olds. "I certainly don't intend to overstep." That was as much of an apology as Bob was going to get from her if that's what he'd come looking for.

"Good," Bob said. He got up and walked out.

***

"Mind if I join you?"

Devonny looked up, up, up into Luke Bradshaw's dark brown eyes, before her glance darted around the crowded Shenandoah coffee shop. The extra chair at her tiny table was literally the only open seat. No matter how much she didn't want to sit at the same table with him, to tell him no would be beyond rude. But she couldn't make herself say yes, either.

"Wow," he said. "If you won't let me sit with you, could you at least tell me what I did to deserve that cold shoulder you always aim in my direction?"

Nothing. Except interest me. Except be the best-looking, single guy in Red Bud, Iowa. Except run by my house almost every day with your shirt off so I can see what a great body you have. Except have a career encouraging teenagers, reinforcing my belief you're a great guy. Who do you think I've been fantasizing about for the past couple of months? Why do you think I walk past the football field on my way home? It's not because I have to. It's so I can get a glimpse of you coaching those kids. Those kids who adore you, by the way.

Luke took a sip of coffee while he waited for her to answer his question. Not that she had any intention of giving him one. But she could sit across from him for a few minutes. She could be polite. Pleasant, even. And when he asked her out, which she was about a hundred and ten percent sure he was going to do, she'd gently decline. Without an explanation of course. An explanation wasn't required, thank God. A simple, "No thank you," would suffice. And if he kept asking, she'd use that same reply. Even if she had to practice it in the mirror. Even if everything in her wished she could accept such an invitation.

"Please." She gestured to the other chair and moved her things closer to her side of the table, relocating her coffee.

Luke set his own coffee and muffin down, angled his way into the chair and shrugged out of his jacket. "Never seen it so crowded here before," he said.

"You come here often?" Devonny asked carefully. If he did, she'd have to find another place to spend part of her monthly Saturday morning sojourn to Shenandoah. It had become a ritual. Bringing along her mail and her laptop. Reviewing the statements that coincided with each direct deposit while sipping her coffee. Sometimes she balanced her checkbook or paid bills. Other times she simply sat and sipped her coffee and gazed out the window.

"If I'm in the area and I have time," Luke said. He bit into his muffin and studied her while he chewed.

She sort of didn't like the way he looked at her, yet she sort of did. She pushed her glasses up her nose even though they hadn't slipped. She took a nervous sip of her coffee.

"How about you?" he asked.

"Occasionally," Devonny hedged. He didn't need to know her routine.

"Astigmatism?"

"Excuse me?"

"The glasses." He gestured in her direction. "I see someone as pretty as you and I wonder why no contacts. But some people can't wear contacts."

"Oh, right."

"That was a compliment, by the way," Luke said before he took another bite of muffin.

"Inferring I have astigmatism?"

He laughed. Choked. Coughed. Covered his mouth with his hand until he could swallow. Took a drink of coffee and swiped at his lips with a napkin before he grinned at her.

"The 'someone as pretty as you' part. But speaking of glasses, there's definitely more to you than meets the eye."

"Why do you say that?"

"Just a general impression."

Luke's eyes bored into hers. She was afraid he could see all the way through her and know all the thoughts lurking inside her head. Which was the absolute last thing she needed.

"You weren't wearing glasses when we first met," he said.

"I should get going." Forget that she hadn't finished her paperwork. Hadn't even unpacked her laptop or looked over the statements. Staying here with Luke sitting across from her was dangerous.

At the exact moment she scooted her chair back a few inches, someone got up to leave, bumping into her table hard enough to tilt it sideways. Luke grabbed it before it overturned, but not before every piece of paper on it slid to the floor, followed by Devonny's coffee. The lid popped off and the remaining contents spilled in a slow creamy ridge across her mail.

She scrambled to pick everything up. Luke was right there with extra napkins, blotting at the wet pages. He picked up the damp envelopes. Was it her imagination or did he take a second to get a glimpse of the return address?

Great. All he'd have to do was Google "Chemistry Films" and if he was interested and diligent enough, he'd figure out what that more than meets the eye entailed.

Luke helped her dry everything off. It wasn't so bad. She'd already drunk most of the coffee in the cup. Some of her papers and envelopes bore damp coffee stains, but they'd survived. She gathered them up as quickly as she could, shoving them back into a pocket of the folder, which had remained completely dry.

She and Luke walked outside together, but she wasn't going to give him a chance to converse further.

There was no point. "Thanks," she said, waving to him. "See you around."

She knew he watched her as she made her way to her car. She wasn't dumb and he hadn't disguised his interest in her from the first day she'd met him. He'd been biding his time, she supposed, waiting for some encouragement from her. Which hadn't come. That cold shoulder she'd aimed in his direction hadn't been his imagination.

***

Luke watched Devonny drive away. He'd never met a woman so elusive.

He started toward his Jeep. There could be lots of reasons why she'd want to hide. He knew that, better than most, because he'd been hiding who he'd once been for years. If he hadn't, he probably wouldn't have a job. No one wanted a former junkie counseling their kids. Not in a public high school in the heart of the Midwest. Not in a private school, either. Maybe he could get a job in a juvenile detention center somewhere, but even that was iffy.

Luckily, he'd never been busted. He had no criminal record. The gaps in his college attendance had never been questioned. All that mattered to the county school board was that he had a degree and a teaching certificate. And that he was also willing to take on the role of football coach for a few thousand extra dollars a year.

Devonny didn't have the look of a former junkie, though, if there even was such a look. But she was definitely hiding something about herself.

Then again, wasn't everyone? He bet if he dissected the lives of every family in Red Bud some extremely unpleasant secrets would come oozing out. He had no desire to do that, of course. He wasn't interested in the secrets of the families in Red Bud. He was interested in Devonny Campbell.

And she was doing everything in her power to convince him she wasn't interested in him. What, he wondered, would it take to change that?

Chapter Six

Devonny was falling in love with the town of Red Bud. She walked to and from work most days, reasoning that fresh air and exercise were good for the baby. Sometimes she took alternate routes home so she could get to know the town better.

Generally, she left from the school's rear entrance and cut through the student and teacher parking lot. The football field was on the opposite side of the lot and a couple of times she'd even stood outside the fence to watch a practice. Sometimes the cheerleaders were gathered near the bleachers practicing.

On those afternoons Devonny had eyed them wistfully. She wasn't all that much older than some of the seniors, but when she looked at them she felt ancient. She'd been married and widowed and had a baby on the way. She'd never been a cheerleader or attended a high school football game. There were no pictures from a homecoming dance or a prom.

Slow down, she wanted to tell them. Don't be in such a hurry to grow up. Enjoy high school while you can.

On one occasion, early in the football season, she'd been so caught up in her musing she hadn't noticed Luke approach until he was right in front of her.

"Hi."

Devonny had jumped. "Hello." She yanked her gaze away and focused instead on the teenagers.

"You know you're welcome to sit in the bleachers and watch if you want. Maybe later we can go for that coffee we never did have."

"What coffee?"

"After the lawyer's office. You had to go buy appliances or something. You said you'd give me a rain check."

"I don't remember that. The rain check part."

"Okay. You didn't exactly say that. I think what you said was, "Some other time maybe.'"

She narrowed her eyes. "I don't remember saying that, either."

"Oh." He seemed to be trying to think up another line, which gave her time to study him. His eyes were kind but there were hidden shadows in their depths. She wondered about the beard. Was he following a trend or did it cover a weak chin? She studied what she could see of his jaw line. Nope. No weak chin. And it wasn't one of those crazy long I-never-want-to-shave-again beards, either. It was…just enough she decided. More than scruff but much less than the average Santa Claus.

"I think what I said was 'another time.'"

His eyes brightened. "Perfect. This is another time, isn't it? And may I say, what a good memory you have. I'll be done here about six. How's six-fifteen at the coffee shop on the square?"

She grinned at his puppy-like persistence. But something held her back.

It's okay. Go. Have fun. It's just coffee.

I can't.

"I can't," she said aloud. "Another time perhaps. See you."

She'd turned her back on him that day and walked away, feeling a weird, double kind of sadness. Here was this perfectly decent man showing interest in her and she couldn't allow herself to return it. She'd turned him down again. His disappointment was so obvious she felt it.

The next day, she'd sought him out, poking her head into his office. He'd looked up and once again his eyes brightened. She'd never have to guess how he felt because he didn't even try to hide his interest in her. That was a good thing. Wasn't it?

"About your invitation for coffee…"

He waited expectantly.

"I'm…going through something."

He didn't say anything. Why couldn't he let her off the hook? Tell her it was okay or not to worry about it? Why was he letting her bumble her way through this? She blew out a breath. "Look, it's not you, it's me."

That got an unwilling chuckle out of him. Maybe he didn't believe her. Or more likely he'd heard that line before. Which made her feel worse. But didn't change the fact she didn't feel ready. Not even to willingly have coffee with him.

"When I said 'another time,' I meant it. But…not right now."

"Okay. Consider it an open invitation."

"I will." She couldn't think of anything else to say, so after another few uncomfortable seconds she went back to her desk. Football season had ended. She'd had that awkward encounter with Luke in the Shenandoah coffee shop. But 'another time" still hadn't come.

This afternoon, although there were still several cars in the lot, most of the students had left an hour ago. The football field was deserted. She picked up her usual brisk pace, looking forward to getting home. She'd made chicken and vegetable soup with noodles yesterday and looked forward to a steaming bowl for dinner, along with some creamy Havarti cheese and crackers. And maybe one of the muffins she'd baked over the weekend and stuck in the freezer. She'd have that with some chamomile tea later. A bubble bath. A book. Bed. Heaven.

"Hey, Miss Campbell."

She drew up short when Miles Winston stepped from between two parked cars. She hadn't been paying attention to her surroundings, which, for someone with an ever-vigilant LA background, was unforgiveable. She'd been lulled into a false sense of security, she supposed, after only a few months in this rural town.

Devonny knew Miles was considered a gifted quarterback, the star of Red Bud High's football team. Devonny had met his mother, Petula, a couple of times. She taught girls' P.E., coached several of their teams, and preferred the nickname, Petty. Miles's father was head of the school board.

Something about Miles's demeanor put her on alert, however, although surely he wouldn't try anything, not here, in sight of the school. Still, prickles of unease teased their way down her spine. She'd noticed the way the boys tended to ogle not just her, but also a few of the other females on staff.

"Hello." What do you want?

"I just wanted to talk to you."

"About what?"

"A couple of things, actually. Like your movie career."

Devonny stiffened. She wanted to ask how this, this boy knew about that. But, she reminded herself, the internet was everywhere. Even a company with a niche market like Chemistry Films made their wares widely available. All anyone needed was an internet connection and a credit card. She'd been naïve to think that here in this small Midwestern town no one would ever visit the Chemistry site. That none of them would recognize her. What she hadn't expected was to be approached directly about it. By a student.

"I have no idea what you're talking about." She made to move past him, but he wrapped his fingers around her elbow. She glared at him in warning. "Get. Your. Hands. Off. Me." She didn't have to work a chill into her tone. She felt like she was spitting ice in his direction.

"Okay, okay. Relax." He held up both hands in a placating gesture. "Maybe we can make a deal. Tawny."

His use of her screen name sent prickles of dread down her spine. "A deal?" In spite of herself she was curious. Curious, but suspicious. She had a pretty good idea what kind of "deal" this kid had in mind.

"You do me a favor, maybe a couple of favors. I keep my mouth shut."

"Favors, huh? I don't think so."

She took a few steps, but he kept pace with her. "Seriously? It's nothing you haven't done before. All you gotta do is suck my—"

She whirled on him so fast he couldn't get out of the way in time. Her knee missed its mark, but it came close enough that he had to back away. He started toward her again.

"Get away from me," she growled.

"Come on." He leered. "A whore like you? I figured you'd be an expert at making deals."

She itched to slap him as hard as she could. "With a grown man, maybe. Not a pimply-faced child. I imagine your—" She gave his crotch a withering glare. "Equipment is as small as your mind."

"What's going on here?" They turned to see Luke coming toward them from the school.

Devonny stared at Miles and took a gamble. "Care to explain?"

Miles looked at Luke, then at her. His lip curled slightly. "No. It was nothing. I wanted to ask Ms. Campbell a question is all. See you around." He got into his car and peeled out of the parking lot, spraying gravel behind him.

"What was that all about?"

"Nothing."

"It didn't look like nothing. If your knee had connected he'd be walking funny for a week. Nice move, by the way."

"Yeah, but I missed. I must be losing my touch." She tried to smile, but Miles's threats had shaken her up more than she wanted to admit. Her earlier happiness evaporated like a puff of steam in a snowstorm.

"Can I walk you home?"

He sounded so hopeful. She could see it in his eyes, how much he wanted to. And truthfully, she wouldn't mind a companion because it was always possible a now thoroughly pissed-off Miles might circle around and approach her again.

"Sure, if you want."

They fell into step together. Luke shortened his stride and let her set the pace. Again, she was aware of the slight hitch in his gait. "Everything at the house still okay?" he asked once they were off school property.

"I love it. In fact, I was thinking how much I like living here."

"There are definitely pluses. Like, for example, you can walk pretty much anywhere. Minuses, too, though."

True. I just had a run-in with one of them. But Devonny wasn't going to bring up what had happened with Miles. If he wanted to tell every single citizen in Red Bud about the films, there was nothing she could do to stop him. She'd brazen it out, somehow. There'd be talk, but just like in Hollywood, some new scandal would come along and eventually, she hoped, hers would be old news.

"You're awfully quiet," Luke said as they turned the corner.

"I was thinking."

"About Miles?"

"No. Not exactly."

"About having coffee with me sometime?"

She laughed. "Not about that either."

"The invitation still stands," he said.

"Thank you. And thank you for not pushing me."

"Not my style. Persistence. That's my style." They walked a bit further before he said, "Don't you love this time of year? Between seasons? Fall's almost over. You know winter is coming. But not yet. It's like it's waiting. Watching. Ready to pounce when the time is right."

Laughter bubbled out of Devonny. "You realize you just described your own behavior, right?"

They were already at her driveway. They faced each other. "Thanks for walking me home."

"Let's have that coffee sometime, okay?" He grinned and backed off with a wave before he turned and loped back the way they'd come. She watched until he turned the corner.

***

Miles Winston's behavior toward Devonny troubled Luke. He'd watched the two of them from the steps of the building where he paused to check his voice mail. At first he hadn't noticed anything unusual, but something about Miles's aggressive stance had put him on alert. He was in the middle of a call when he saw Miles grab Devonny's arm. They were some distance away from him, but when he saw Devonny try to knee Miles in the groin, he stepped up his pace and called to them.

Devonny was radiating more than one emotion, while Miles appeared to be both pissed off and sheepish at the same time. Luke couldn't figure out the cause of the undercurrents between them.

***

Petula Winston watched her sophomore girls P.E. class jog around the track. How she envied them their youth, their shiny hair, their untapped futures. She stared at her clipboard and her stopwatch, blinking furiously, pushing away the unwelcome thoughts that unrelentingly dogged her these days.

So many mistakes, the first of which was denying who and what she was. The second was marrying, compounded by vowing to love, honor and cherish a man, especially one like Doug. And the third, her biggest regret, was giving in to Doug's demands and giving birth to a child she hadn't wanted.

So many regrets. So many mistakes. So much denial. And the fear. The fear was the worst. "What will people think?" Her mother's refrain echoed in her head nonstop. She'd been hearing it all her life, for every choice she made which could be viewed as inappropriate. Everything from not attending her cousin's wedding to choosing to wear white shoes after Labor Day.

Through her jacket, she felt a chill run through her that wasn't caused by the brisk air of the late fall morning. "Okay, girls, that's time," she called, shaking herself out of her dismal mood. She resisted the urge to hug herself, because certainly no one else was going to. "Last lap before we head inside."

Chapter Seven

Devonny pulled open one of the double glass doors that led into the main hallway of the school, rubbing her arms against the chilly air outside. She'd had to step outside to let the maintenance man into the storage facility. The keys on the lanyard around her neck jingled against each other. The hall was nearly empty, since second bell had just rung.

But as she made her way down the wide corridor with its gleaming floors and walls lined with lockers, she saw some movement. She couldn't quite make out who they were; her eyes were still adjusting from the glare of the bright sun outside. But she could tell it was two students who should be in class by now.

She picked up her pace, deciding she'd remind them of that if she had to, although it wasn't her job. They hadn't seen her, more focused on whatever it was they were doing. They exchanged something. Devonny sucked in a breath. Even from this distance, it was obvious what was happening. Cash went into one hand and a small bag into the other. A locker, which had been slightly open, shut with a loud click. One kid had his back to her, but the other looked up and saw her.

She stopped when she recognized him. Their eyes met. He tugged on his companion's sleeve and muttered something to him. They took off down the hall toward the gym.

Devonny stepped back into the office. Janet glanced up over the high counter, then went back to staring at her computer and clicking on her keyboard.

The other office assistant, Lauren, was on the phone, shuffling files from one side of her work space to the other. The history teacher was at the copier, waiting patiently while the machine spit paper into its tray.

Luke's door was closed, as it often was, but she could hear the murmur of his voice. He was probably on the phone. Principal Foster's door was ajar. He had an open-door policy, but his door was rarely open all the way. He liked his privacy and the partially closed door shielded him from unnecessary distraction, while allowing him to keep his ears alert to any situation that might require his attention.

Devonny sank into her chair in the corner and began sorting requests from the teachers by priority. As soon as Mr. Hannibal was done with the copy machine, she could start on the copy requests. In the meantime, she filled out a requisition for thirty-five copies of Jane Eyre for the freshman English teacher.

But while she worked, her mind kept straying back to what she'd seen in the hall. She hadn't been close enough to see what was in that plastic bag. Pills or pot, most likely. God, she hoped it wasn't heroin. Or cocaine. She wasn't sure exactly what she'd seen. Perhaps it was nothing and it had only looked like a drug deal to her. But that boy's reaction indicated he'd been caught doing something he shouldn't have, and he knew it.

Perhaps she could ask Luke about it. Surely he would know what the drug situation was like in the area. In the school. She didn't have to say anything about what she'd seen. She could keep it general.

As if she'd conjured him by thinking about him, Luke appeared next to her. She hadn't heard his office door open or his approach.

"Hi."

She jumped, startled. "Hi"

"Sorry. Didn't mean to sneak up on you."

"It's okay. My mind was somewhere else."

He smiled at her. God, she liked that smile. Liked everything about him, actually. It didn't hurt that she could tell he liked her too. What woman didn't like getting attention from an attractive man? Even if she had no intention of returning that interest. At least not right now. But maybe someday, if he was still available. He probably wouldn't be. She wasn't sure how a guy like him wasn't already attached.

He truly seemed to have it all together. He was confident, intelligent, well-liked. He worked out. He had a good job. He was obviously caring or he wouldn't be a guidance counselor and the kind of coach the kids admired. Plus, he was…hot. There was no other way to put it.

Devonny's mind drifted back to the first day she'd met his shirtless self, jogging down the street. The chest, the abs, the ropy muscles in his forearms and the obvious strength of his biceps. She liked the facial hair, too, she decided. It worked for him, which couldn't be said for every guy who sported it. In Luke's case, it made him hotter. To her, anyway.

Working in such close proximity to him gave her a lift every weekday morning. Because she knew he'd see her, she wanted to look her best. Even as she chose an outfit and did her makeup and hair, she insisted to herself she wasn't ready to date. Attempting to attract him but ignoring his interest was a bit twisted of her and not particularly admirable. But she couldn't seem to help it, either.

Today he looked particularly good. He always wore a shirt and tie in the office but as the weather had turned cooler, he'd added a navy vee-neck sweater. Somehow he managed to look both rakish and preppie at the same time.

"Is that a problem?" Luke asked.

"What? Oh, no. No. Not at all." She had to hit the rewind button on the last few moments. While she'd been musing, Luke had asked her a question about the disciplinary forms he was out of. "I'm sure they're in the supply closet. I'll bring you some if that's okay?"

He was still grinning and Devonny could feel herself getting flustered. Did he know what she was thinking? She frowned as she scooted her chair back.

Luke stepped aside. "Thanks. I appreciate that."

Devonny unlocked the supply closet and turned on the light. There was a form for everything that went on in the school. She'd organized them in a way that was logical to her and in seconds she found the ones Luke needed. She picked up a sheaf of them and brought them to his office. His door was open now. She handed them across the desk.

"That was fast. Thanks."

Devonny peeked behind her to make sure no one was paying any attention to them. She eased Luke's door closed. He leaned back, his curiosity aroused. Devonny sat on the edge of the chair across from him. "Can I ask you something?"

"Sure. Anything."

"Um…is there a drug problem in this school?"

Luke sat forward. The humor wiped from his face. "Why?"

"I'm…just asking, is all."

His lips set in a thin line. "Devonny, if you have any knowledge of —"

"No, it's not like that!"

Luke held her gaze. "But you suspect."

"Yes." She could admit that much.

"There are pockets of drug use, yes. I wouldn't say it's an epidemic, but we're certainly not immune to it. Any incident on school property is cause for concern."

"Of course."

"If you see something, or you know something, you can tell me. You know that, right? No one has to know it came from you. Our job is to protect these kids to the best of our ability."

"Of course." Devonny stood. "Sorry. I should get back to my desk."

"Close the door on the way out, if you don't mind," Luke said. He picked up his phone.

***

"What's going on?" Devonny asked Janet, shortly after the lunch break. Through the office windows she could see Nick and Luke in a huddle with a couple of men in uniform. One had a German shepherd on a leash.

Janet followed Devonny's gaze. "Sheriff's office is doing a sweep."

"Sweep?"

"That's a drug-sniffing dog."

"Oh."

Janet swiveled her chair toward Devonny. "We've had a couple of incidents over the years. It's amazing how that dog can sniff out anything. Had to expel a kid last year. It's a shame, because he had a full ride to ISU. Now he's working over at the feed store. Going to the community college."

"That is too bad," Devonny agreed. She returned to her desk. She hadn't been all that subtle when she talked to Luke earlier, but she hadn't expected this. She wouldn't be surprised to learn that he called the Sheriff the moment she left his office.

But she couldn't dismiss the look Miles Winston had given her before he hightailed it down the hall. And she couldn't forget the way he'd accosted her in the parking lot and threatened her that day. She'd heard rumors Miles was in the running for an Iowa State football scholarship. Sometimes people got what they deserved, as she well knew. And sometimes…they didn't.

***

Miles would not admit he was scared. Not when Coach Bradshaw had knocked on the door of the science lab and pulled him out of class. Not when he'd seen Sheriff Grady waiting for him in the hallway. Not when they'd escorted him into Coach Bradshaw's office.

He wasn't scared, he insisted to himself; he was pissed off. Big time. Especially when he saw the uppity teacher's assistant who'd turned from her desk to watch his walk of shame. It didn't take a genius to figure out who had squealed on him. That damn bitch. He didn't know how, but he was going to make her pay. For blowing him off. For turning him in. For making him so hard every time he saw what she did with that guy in those movies.

***

An hour later, Devonny put her hands over her ears so she wouldn't have to listen to Doug Winston's tirade at full volume. He'd arrived with his lawyer in tow fifteen minutes ago. Unfortunately, the thin walls and Principal Foster's closed door did not create much of a sound barrier.

Janet, Lauren, and Devonny exchanged looks with each other as Doug's voice rose and fell.

"This whole thing is ridiculous," Doug exclaimed. "So you found a few seeds and leaves you claim are marijuana in his locker. That doesn't constitute possession, Sheriff. Who's to say that stuff wasn't in there when he was assigned the locker at the beginning of the year? Tell him, Charlie."

The attorney spoke in a reasonable tone that didn't penetrate the walls the way Doug's indignant tone did. There was another low murmur, this one probably from the sheriff.

Devonny gathered the copies she'd made and put them in an envelope for Mrs. Phipps, the art teacher. She began to sort mail and messages to put into the various teachers' boxes. All the while she wondered how nothing more than seeds and leaves had been found. Students were not allowed to leave during school hours. Which meant, if what she'd seen was Miles buying weed, he'd moved it from his locker before the sheriff showed up. So where was it?

It could be in his car, she supposed. Which would probably be off limits unless the sheriff got a search warrant. Which he probably wouldn't do. Doug Winston was not without influence in this town. Not only was he head of the school board, she'd heard he planned to run for mayor. In which case the sheriff would have to deal with him quite a bit. Making trouble for Miles with so little evidence was probably not a smart political move.

Devonny would be wise to steer clear of both Miles and his father, she decided. Somehow Miles knew about her films. Did his father?

"What's going on? Where's Miles?" Petula Winston blew in through the office door, dressed in sweats and running shoes, her hair held back by a thick headband. Her face was ruddy from the cold.

Janet tilted her head. "In Principal Foster's office. You can go on in."

Petty did, hustling around the counter and pushing open the door without knocking.

"For God's sakes, Petty. Couldn't you have combed your hair and put on some lipstick? Do you always have to look like such a jock?"

Devonny cringed at Doug's tone. She couldn't make out Petty's reply. For that she was grateful.

***

"What's the matter?" Devonny asked Loretta the following afternoon. She'd taken to popping in on her neighbor a few afternoons a week. Loretta always seemed glad of the company and Devonny secretly looked forward to whatever homemade treat Loretta had to offer. They were ensconced at the table with cups of tea and a plate of chocolate chip cookies between them. Devonny was warning herself not to go for a third cookie and instead focused on Loretta's manner.

"Oh, it's nothing, really. Just that Vi Goodwin's daughter had her baby." Loretta sighed.

Devonny frowned. "I'm...sorry?"

"Why would you be sorry? She had another girl. Eight pounds, eleven ounces."

"Oh. Well, you don't seem happy about it."

"Vi's gone to Ames to help out, is all."

"I still don't understand. You seem a bit down about that."

"Vi's been my ride to church ever since I had to give up driving. She's been good about picking me up and bringing me home every Sunday."

"Surely there's someone else at your church who could fill in?"

Loretta lifted her shoulders and let them drop, which Devonny took to mean Loretta was too proud to ask for help.

"What church do you go to?"

"Christ Community Congregational, over on Fifth Street and Elm."

"What time is the service?"

"Ten."

Devonny considered the timing. "I could take you if you like. Until Vi gets back." Surely Vi wouldn't be gone too long, a week or two at most.

Loretta peered at her. "I'd need a ride home, too."

"It's fine. Maybe I'll sit in on the service."

"Sit in?"

"I've never gone to church. Not regularly, anyway. I'm curious."

"If you're sure you wouldn't mind," Loretta said, pushing the plate of cookies closer to Devonny. "I'd appreciate it."

Devonny didn't need any further urging to grab another cookie. "I don't mind."

☐

Chapter Eight

"Cherry!" Devonny wrapped her best friend in a huge hug, ignoring the cold air and snow flurries whirling into the warm living room.

"My nipples are about to fall off, they're so cold. Can I come in already?" Cherry asked, her mouth muffled against Devonny's shoulder.

"Yes! Come in. Come in. Let me take your jacket. Is this all you're wearing?"

"You are not getting my jacket," Cherry told her, hugging the hot pink blazer around her slender frame. "And yes, this is all I wore. You didn't tell me I'd need a parka and fur-lined boots to maintain my body temperature."

Devonny giggled. "Sorry. I figured you'd know Iowa's weather is nothing like southern California."

"I wasn't thinking. All I could think about was getting on that damn plane to come and see you." Cherry reached in for another hug. "God, I miss you. I miss Jack too—" She pulled back and looked into Devonny's eyes. "I'm sorry. I probably shouldn't have said that. I'm here to make you happy, not sad."

"It's okay. It's not like I don't think about how much I miss him all the time anyway."

Cherry followed Devonny into the kitchen and watched her open a bottle of wine.

"It's getting easier, though. I think getting out of LA has made it easier." She handed Cherry a glass of Merlot.

"Yeah, but Iowa? It's kind of the last place I ever thought you'd land. I thought you'd end up in New York. There's nothing here. I know that because on the drive here that's all I passed. A whole lot of nothing. I still can't believe Omaha is the closest airport. Nebraska. That's definitely a first for me."

Devonny led her into the living room where the gas fire burned bright.

"The fireplace!" Cherry set her glass of wine on the coffee table and held her hands out toward the welcoming heat. She turned around and put her hands behind her. "I have to say, your place is adorable."

"Thanks. I like it." Devonny curled a leg under her on the couch and glanced around the room.

"And you? You look fantastic. I think I'm starting to hate you. You don't even look pregnant."

"I've learned how to disguise my ever-expanding waistline with long tunics and loose sweaters. Trust me, there's a baby in here." She patted her tummy.

Cherry picked up her wine and sat on the opposite end of the couch. She took a sip. "Mmm. Nice choice. I approve. So, what are we doing?"

"Well, there's the party I told you about."

"Oh, yes. A hoe-down with the locals." Cherry grinned and flipped her platinum blond hair over her shoulder. "I should fit right in."

"Of course you won't fit in, but you're only here for the weekend. You might as well liven things up and give them something to talk about while you can."

"It could be interesting." Cherry considered. "And I do love being the topic of conversation. Any cute girls I might like?"

"There are a few around town, I do believe. Although my gay-dar isn't as precise as yours."

"That's because a) you haven't had as much practice, and b) you're distracted by hetero men."

"True." Devonny thought of Luke and smiled before she took a sip of her sparkling water.

"Uh huh. What was that smile?" Cherry wanted to know. "Have you met someone? Already?"

"No. No. Well, yes, I have met someone. But not like you're thinking."

"I saw that smile. It's exactly like I'm thinking. Spill. Every single juicy detail."

"There aren't any juicy details."

Yet.

Not now Jack.

"Then spill the non-juicy ones. Name?"

"Luke Bradshaw."

"Traditional. Strong. I like it. Age? Occupation?"

"If I had to guess he's thirty-ish. He's the guidance counselor at the high school."

"So that's where you met him."

"Actually, no. He renovated this house. I bought it from him before I got the job at the school."

"So he's good with his hands." Cherry peered over the rim of her wineglass, silently urging Devonny to continue.

"I'm assuming so. He also runs. With his shirt off."

"Is he a member of the Polar Bear Club?"

"When it's warm," Devonny amended. "He wears sweats when it's this cold."

"Good looking?"

Devonny thought of Luke's light hair, his scruff, the warmth of his eyes, that lean, hard body.

"Okay. You don't even have to answer. He's so hot just thinking about him has you practically drooling."

"I know. But Cher, it doesn't make any sense. I mean Jack died, what, six months ago? I can't move on to some new guy."

"Why not? You know Jack didn't want you to sit around and cry for years before you even think of dating again. He told you he'd hate that."

"I know. I just…" Devonny looked down at the slight pouch her tummy made beneath her sweater."

"What, hon?" Cherry asked gently.

"I don't want to forget him. Or what we had. And there's a baby. And…"

"You'll have to tell this Luke fellow about the films you and Jack made. And the ones you and I did."

Devonny nodded.

"That is a lot to pile on a guy, I guess."

"But on the other hand, if he can't handle it, I need to know now, right? So I can kiss him goodbye and not waste my time. I've got nothing to hide and nothing to be ashamed of, and if he's too provincial to understand, then hasta la vista, baby."

"Right on, girl." Cherry grinned and they bumped fists. "Is he going to be at the party?"

"Probably. From what I understand it's kind of a command performance for everyone who works at the high school. The head of the school board and his wife throw a big party after football season ends and before the holiday season officially begins. His wife is the girls' P.E. teacher and track coach."

"Oh, yeah?" Cherry's eyes lit with interest. "Is she cute?"

"She's…athletic."

"What's her name?"

"Petula. But everyone calls her Petty."

"Maybe she'd like to be my pet."

"Cherry, I swear. Didn't you hear me say she's married?"

"Which means nothing," Cherry informed her.

"Maybe not in LA. But here it's a bit different."

"It's not as different as you probably think. Are you forgetting I've got a PhD in psychology and that I've made a career out of studying human behavior?"

"Well, that's one of your careers."

"No better way to study people's reaction than to take your clothes off in front of them. At any rate, an 'athletic' female P.E. teacher is a cliché, whether you're in LA or Iowa or Bora Bora."

"Are you saying she's gay? You haven't even met her. You haven't even seen her."

"True. And I could be wrong. She could be straighter than a Donald Trump tie. But I have to do something to keep my gay-dar humming while I'm here."

"Your gay-dar's always humming."

"Hey, a girl can dream, right? I wouldn't want to pass up an opportunity while I'm in town. Life is short. Uh, sorry."

Devonny sighed. "Are you going to apologize every time you make a reference to life or death? I am always going to miss Jack, but I know I have to go on with my life. So stop thinking you have to walk on eggshells around me."

"Okay. Sorry." Cherry held up a hand. "I'm going to stop apologizing, starting now. This is new to me, so cut me some slack. I'm not sure of the protocol."

Devonny stood. "The protocol for right now is we go get dressed in our party clothes so you can check out the school teachers of Red Bud, Iowa, and see if there are any you want to do while you're here."

Cherry followed her to the bedroom. "I'm telling you right now, this Petula sounds promising."

***

The Winston home was ablaze with hundreds of tiny white lights. They dripped from the eaves of the broad front porch as well as from the roof of the second story. They surrounded every tree and bush in the front yard. A group of delicately carved deer were gathered on one side of the walk, and a nativity scene took up the other.

"Impressive," Cherry said as she and Devonny made their way toward the door. They'd had to park half a block away. A glimpse through the picture window showed the party was already in full swing.

A rush of warm cinnamon-scented air and a blast of music and conversation greeted them inside. Miles Winston's parents had recruited him to be the official greeter. He eyed Devonny and Cherry with obvious interest and offered to take their coats. Devonny introduced Cherry, doing her best to keep her tone neutral. "Miles is quarterback of Red Bud High's football team."

"Lovely," Cherry said. Only Devonny was aware of her adverse reaction to Miles.

"Your coats will be in my dad's office." He pointed to an open doorway off the wide hall. "Drinks are set up in the kitchen. Buffet table in the dining room."

"Thank you." Devonny herded Cherry toward the kitchen.

"Smarmy," Cherry hissed in her ear.

"That he is."

Cherry chafed her arms. "He gives me the willies."

"You don't know the half of it."

Devonny was one of the few people who knew that, as a child, Cherry had been molested by two teenage cousins. The abuse had gone on for years before it was discovered. Cherry had been traumatized. Therapy had helped, but she often still had strong reactions to teenage boys. She and Jack had gone to high school together and he'd always been protective of her. Jack was the big brother looking out for her that Cherry had never had, and one of the few men she'd become close to. It struck Devonny again how much Cherry must miss Jack.

Devonny put her arm around her and squeezed. "I'll protect you."

Cherry giggled as they stepped into the crowded kitchen. Devonny wasn't an interior design expert by any means, but she could tell that the original details had been lovingly restored and enhanced with modern updates. The cabinets were a distressed shade of cream with old-timey hardware. The large breakfast area was surrounded on three sides by paned windows. The professional chef's six-burner gas range, with a custom designed hood, took place of honor. Devonny was impressed. She and Cherry were greeted by several of Devonny's coworkers and Devonny made the introductions.

She saw Luke look up from the far side of the room. His gaze swept over her with undisguised appreciation. Devonny smiled and wiggled her fingers at him.

"Is that him?" Cherry whispered as they moved to the counter for cups and ice.

"Yes," Devonny whispered back. "Be subtle."

"You don't have to be straight to tell he's by far the hottest guy here."

They poured drinks and circulated into the dining room where Petula broke away from the group she was with. "Devonny. I'm so glad you could make it. And who's this?" Petula took in Cherry from top to bottom.

"This is my friend, Cherry Pickler, from LA. She's visiting for a few days."

Petula took Cherry's hand in both of hers. "Cherry. It's lovely to meet you in person."

"Thank you."

Petula wore a red holiday sweater, dark slacks and low-heeled boots. Her make-up was minimal and her hair was in its usual no-nonsense style. Devonny took in her reaction to Cherry and wondered if her friend was right about Petula.

"What do you do out there in LA, Cherry? I must say, you remind me of someone I've seen on TV or in the movies. Are you an actress by chance?"

Cherry tried to hide a smile. "I have done a few films. Nothing you'd have seen, I'm sure."

"Oh, you might be surprised."

Devonny wondered at the confidence in Petula's tone. A flutter of warning tickled its way up her spine. "Your home is beautiful," Devonny said, hoping to change the subject.

Petula looked around, as if seeing it for the first time. "Thank you, but I have to give Doug most of the credit. He's the one who wanted a big house. Thinks it will impress everyone. You know how men are. Always trying to make up for their shortcomings."

"Did I hear my name mentioned over here?" Doug Winston said, joining their group. "I'd love to know what all you lovely ladies are saying about me." His gaze slithered over Devonny and Cherry much like his son's had. Devonny could almost feel Cherry's shiver of revulsion.

"I was telling them how you like having such a big house." Petty's gaze remained on Cherry's. "This is Devonny's friend Cherry. She's visiting from California."

"Very nice to meet you, Cherry," he said. "Good of you to come, Devonny."

"Thanks for having us," Devonny said, all too aware of the undertone of that remark.

Luke edged his way into the group, positioning himself between Devonny and Petty. "Is this a private conversation or can anyone join in?"

"You're always welcome to join in," Petty assured him, patting his arm. "Have you met Devonny's friend from LA?"

"No, I haven't."

Cherry held out her hand. "Cherry."

"Nice to meet you, Cherry. I'm Luke."

"Nice to meet you too," Cherry said. "I've heard a lot about you."

Devonny subtly elbowed Cherry.

Luke looked amused. "Oh? I can't imagine how that could be."

"Dev here mentioned she bought her house from you. She told me you flip houses in your spare time. And that you work at the school."

"All true."

"Speaking of houses," Petula cut in, "Cherry, would you like the grand tour? We recently redid the master suite. I'd love for you to see it."

"Thank you, Petula. I think I'd enjoy that very much."

"Please, call me Petty. Everyone does." Petty took Cherry's arm and led her away.

Doug looked displeased with the way the group had re-formed. "Well, if you'll excuse me, I need another drink. Enjoy the party."

Devonny raised an eyebrow at Luke. "Separating me from the herd?"

He laughed. "That wasn't exactly my intention, at least not this early. But what can I say? I'm not displeased to have you all to myself."

Devonny took a sip of her drink, thinking what it would be like to be part of a couple again. To attend this party next year as Luke's…what exactly?

Her musing screeched to a halt. No, it was still too soon.

Why?

Because I'm not done mourning. I'm not done missing you, she answered back.

That doesn't mean you can't entertain the idea of loving again. Go for it. See where it leads.

Devonny frowned.

"Too possessive?" asked Luke.

"I'm not ready."

"Not ready for what?"

Devonny had been speaking to Jack but she'd said the words aloud. Again.

"Not ready to leave without checking out the buffet." As if in sync with her statement, her stomach rumbled.

Luke followed her. They said more hellos to the other guests. Devonny took small portions of everything that appealed to her, and they found a relatively quiet corner to set down plates and cups.

Miles had given up front door duty and joined his girlfriend of the month in the living room. Devonny was pretty sure they were both consuming more than soft drinks. The girl giggled at everything Miles said and his hand crept further up her thigh with each comment.

"Nothing like being young and drunk, is there?" Luke asked.

"I suppose not." She stared into her cup which was empty except for a few ice cubes.

"Need a refill? What are you drinking?"

"Club soda."

"Really? Me too. What do you know? We have something in common."

Devonny watched as he went to the kitchen with her cup in his hand.

Doug Winston sidled up next to her. "Enjoying yourself?" Devonny stiffened. He stood much too close, purposely invading her personal space.

"I'd enjoy myself more if you'd back up a couple of steps," she said, looking directly into his eyes.

"Spunk. I like it. Up to a point." He did, however, back off half a pace. "What's with that friend of yours?"

"What do you mean?"

"She looks like a high-class call girl."

Devonny's jaw clenched at the insult to her friend. Doug Winston knew nothing about "class." High or otherwise. Still, her palms itched with the urge to slap him.

"Does she charge by the hour, do you know? Or—"

Devonny reacted without further thought. Her hand connected with Doug's cheek with all the strength she could muster behind it. He grabbed her wrist, enraged. "Listen, you. I don't know what kind of game you're playing—"

"Let her go." Luke was right behind Doug. "Now."

The hum of conversation around them stopped. All eyes turned in their direction. Doug dropped her wrist.

Devonny saw Cherry coming down the stairs. Her hair was a bit mussed and her lipstick had rubbed off. She had a satisfied gleam in her eye until she took in the scene in the corner. She streaked toward them.

"What's going on?"

Devonny stared at Doug, daring him to explain. His gaze went from her to Luke to Cherry. His jaw set and a vein throbbed in his forehead. "Nothing. A misunderstanding, is all. If you'll excuse me."

Devonny watched his retreat and saw Petty coming down the stairs. Petty's gaze zeroed in on Cherry, but she turned toward the kitchen. Petty wouldn't want to start any gossip. But it was a little late for that.

"Are you okay?" Luke asked Devonny.

"I'm fine. I think Doug's had too much to drink and I...overreacted."

The other guests began to talk again, mostly about what they'd seen or overheard, Devonny was sure. She looked down at the remaining food on her plate and realized she'd lost her appetite.

"I think I'm ready to go," she said.

"Oh. Are you sure?" Cherry said. "Petty told me she has a pottery studio out back. She offered to show it to me."

They'd come in Cherry's rental car since it was parked behind Devonny's. "It's fine," she said. "You stay. I can walk home. The exercise will do me good."

"I'll walk with you," Luke said.

"You don't have to."

"I want to. I'll get our coats."

"Having fun?" Devonny asked Cherry the moment Luke was out of earshot.

Cherry grinned. "Let's just say I was right about Petty. The poor woman. She's starved for the right kind of attention."

Over Cherry's shoulder, Devonny saw Doug with a refreshed drink in his hand watching them with a brooding expression. His face was red, and not just from the imprint of her hand. She chafed the wrist he'd held in that bruising grip. Apprehension twisted in her gut.

Luke appeared with his coat already on and Devonny's in his hand.

"Just…be careful, would you?" Devonny hugged her friend.

"Always," Cherry assured her.

"Ready?" Luke asked. He helped Devonny on with her coat. Under the circumstances, she didn't feel the need to thank her host.

☐

Chapter Nine

The moment they were off the Winston's property, Luke took her gloved hand in his and squeezed. "Are you okay?"

She didn't answer right away, lingering on how nice it was to hold hands with him on this cold night. Their breaths left puffs of frozen air and their boots crunched against the thin layer of snow.

"It was nothing," she said. "Doug was out of line and he knew it. I probably shouldn't have slapped him, though."

"Actually, from what I know of him, he was probably overdue."

Devonny giggled.

"I can't believe you're letting me hold your hand."

"We're wearing gloves."

"Still, it's progress. Does this mean the cold shoulder is thawing?"

Say yes.

"Maybe."

They walked on in silence. Devonny looked at the lights and decorations people had begun to put up for the holidays, even though it wasn't even Thanksgiving. In a few of the houses Christmas trees were visible in windows.

Devonny hadn't given much thought to decorating for Christmas yet. The few decorations she'd accumulated were packed away in one of the boxes still in the garage. It had seemed silly to decorate the place just for herself. Maybe she'd buy a tree and put it up in front of her window.

But what would she be celebrating? Her first Christmas without Jack? Jack had never cared about holiday lights or trees or cards. But even that first year, when they'd been newly married and money was tight, he'd presented her with a tiny wrapped package. The diamond studs were less than a quarter of a carat, but Devonny loved them. She wore them all the time.

Next year, she decided, she'd decorate big. Lights outside and a tree and garland everywhere. Her baby wouldn't even be a year old, but they'd start making their own holiday traditions, just the two of them.

She hadn't been paying attention to where they were walking but when Luke turned, she realized they were at her house. They climbed the steps and stood by the door facing each other. "Thanks for walking me ho—"

Luke kissed her. His mouth was warm and tasted faintly of cinnamon. He'd caught her off guard, but she didn't even need Jack's voice in her head to ask why not? If she were honest with herself, she'd admit she wanted Luke to make a move. To take the decision out of her hands and start something so she could stop plaguing herself with what ifs and I can'ts or I shouldn'ts. And if Luke turned out to be a lousy kisser or a crummy date, she could tell him now and mean it, for a better reason than her own uncertainty.

She parted her lips and Luke made a low sound of encouragement. His hands slid into her hair the way Jack's used to. She reprimanded herself. No, not exactly the same way. But in a way she definitely liked.

The stoop's railing pressed against her back and Luke's body pressed firmly against her front. His beard was soft. Kissing Luke was different from kissing Jack. But definitely in a good way. She could, she realized, stand out here all night like this. She slid her arms around his waist. He smelled fresh and clean, like the winter air with something woodsy underneath.

She ended the kiss with a surprised, "Oh!"

Luke lifted his head.

"Oh, my God!" Devonny tore at the buttons on her coat and yanked off her glove. She pressed her hand beneath her sweater and the waistband of her slacks. She felt it again and laughed. "Oh, that's incredible."

"What's incredible?"

"Here. Feel." She grabbed Luke's hand and pressed it in place. "Feel that?"

"Yes. But what is it?"

"The baby."

"Baby?"

"She's kicking."

"You're pregnant?"

"Yes!" Joy spilled out of Devonny. This was more than those flutters and ripples she'd felt before. This was a heel or an elbow or a foot. Her baby was definitively making its presence known.

"Lucy? I think you've got some 'splaining to do." Luke hadn't moved his hand. Devonny could feel the baby still kicking against it. She studied Luke in the porchlight. He'd uttered one of the names she'd been considering for the baby. It seemed like an omen. A good one.

"It's a long story. Want to come in?"

"Uh, yeah."

Luke started the fireplace while Devonny brewed chamomile tea. Once they were seated she said, "I was married back in LA. Jack passed away in June."

"Oh. Oh. Jesus. I am so sorry."

"Thank you."

"Now it all makes sense."

"What does?"

"The cold shoulder. The arm's length. The way you seemed interested but—"

"I kept backing off," Devonny said. "I know I gave you mixed signals."

"God, if I'd known. I wouldn't have been such a jerk about asking you out."

"You weren't a jerk. You were just…persistent."

"I appreciate you telling me, because like I said, now it all makes sense."

"Does it? I'm not sure it makes sense to me."

"That kiss made sense, didn't it?"

"It was a good kiss."

"It sure was. But I'm willing to see if we can top it."

"That's it? I don't have any 'splaining' to do?"

"Well, I do have questions. The baby. It's your husband's, I presume."

"Of course."

"Can I ask what happened to him?"

"A brain tumor. Aggressive. Inoperable. Our last time together, well, I didn't think anything would or could happen, but Jack…" Her eyes misted over. "It was so tender and beautiful and…peaceful. So…"

"Loving?"

He gets it! She could almost hear Jack crow in delight.

"Yes."

"He must have been crazy about you," Luke said. "It must have killed him knowing he was going to die. Er...no pun intended."

I like this guy.

"Hush."

"Sorry. That was out of line."

"Not you," Devonny corrected. "Sometimes — this will sound stupid — but sometimes I hear Jack's voice in my head."

"Oh? What's he saying that you had to tell him to hush?"

"Unh-uh. I've already got one guy in my head. I don't need another one."

Luke scooted closer. "Okay. I'll settle for being the guy in your life, if you think you're ready for that. What do you think?"

"I think I want you to kiss me again." When he kissed her Devonny couldn't think about anything except how much she liked the idea of him in her life. The baby kicked as if in agreement as they slid down so they were lying on the couch.

The kissing went on for a while. Hot and slow, and Devonny started to feel all those feelings she used to feel with Jack. Her nipples hardened. She listened for Jack's voice to tell her to knock it off, or how dare she let another man touch her like this. But all she heard were their sounds of arousal and heavy breathing. Her breasts, which were fuller than they used to be, reveled in the feel of Luke's chest as he pressed against them. And Luke was very turned on. So was she, but going further didn't feel right. Jack might be quiet, but her own inner voice wasn't.

She tore her mouth away. "Luke."

"Yes." His lips traced their way along her jawline to her ear. His tongue trailed a path below and behind her earlobe and her eyes rolled back in her head. He'd found that sensitive spot that drove her crazy.

"Stop." She gasped.

He did.

"I can't, um, I can't sleep with you."

"Okay." He kissed her again.

"Just like that? 'Okay'?"

"Maybe okay was the wrong word," he allowed.

"It's not because I don't want to," Devonny assured him.

"Good."

"But it would be too weird."

"Because of the baby and your husband's voice in your head?"

Devonny nodded over the lump in her throat.

"We can still kiss and stuff, though, right? That's not weird, is it?"

"Not at all."

"Good."

"We'd be more comfortable in the bedroom, wouldn't we?" Devonny said a short time later. "With our clothes on," she felt compelled to add, just so Luke didn't think she'd changed her mind.

"Can I take my shoes off?"

"Yes, but leave your socks on."

"Why? Do you have a toe fetish? Tell me now."

She slapped his chest. "No. I'm pretty sure I can control myself around your naked toes."

Luke turned the gas off in the fireplace and followed her into the bedroom. They pulled the covers back and got comfortable, her head on his shoulder, his arm curled around her.

"I can't believe you're pregnant. I think I'm still in shock. But it can't be easy for you. With the way things are now."

"When I first got here, to Red Bud I mean, I was afraid I was going to lose the baby."

"Wait, was that the day you came running out of the diner all upset?"

"Yes. How did you know?"

"Because you ran straight into me."

"I did?"

"You did. I asked if you were all right and you said you were fine. But you obviously weren't."

"No, I wasn't. I was alone and exhausted and confused. But I drove around town for a bit and came across Twelve Forks. The next morning everything looked different. I felt better. I felt…ready."

"Ready for what?"

"For whatever was going to happen next. I didn't feel so lost any more. I went for a walk and I saw this house."

"And I happened along."

"I didn't remember you from the diner. But I dreamed of a house like this that first night. There was a swing set like the one out back and a little girl swinging on it."

"So it's a girl?"

"In my dreams, she is." Devonny hesitated. "I think Jack knows."

Luke paused, as if wondering how to proceed. "Tell me about Jack. How'd you meet him?"

"In a coffee house where I was working. Jack was a regular. The first time I saw him, I had a crush on him. He was an actor. Of course, in LA, who isn't?"

"You, apparently."

Devonny decided not to correct that assumption. "I was eighteen. My mother was strict. She home-schooled and was pretty over-protective. I was also incredibly naïve. But she had to let me go sometime and she wanted me to go to college that fall. She figured working in a coffee shop not too far from home was safe enough."

"Who was being naïve then?" Luke said.

"Exactly. She hated Jack."

"Which only made you more crazy about him, I bet."

"I couldn't have been any more crazy about him, I don't think. I was seriously, madly in love with him. The sweep-you-off-your-feet kind of love. He was twenty-five and way more sophisticated than I was, but he fell for me, too. I felt like the luckiest girl in the world when he asked me to marry him."

Luke squeezed her. "He was lucky to have found you. That kind of love doesn't happen very often."

"It doesn't bother you to hear this?"

Luke scooted down and turned on his side so he could face her. "I want to know about you. I want to know you, better than I already do. It certainly doesn't bother me to know what kind of love you're capable of."

"Oh. Good. Well, Jack and I adored each other. We made everyone else sick with how crazy we were about each other."

Luke chuckled. "They were jealous."

"Probably. And we probably were obnoxious, too. Anyway, at first Jack's acting career was not going the way he wanted it to. He'd take other jobs between gigs and he did some modeling. A few commercials. I worked, too. He got a couple of bona fide roles in movies. We were building a life; we'd bought a house and talked about having children. The normal stuff married people do. We were close to having it all…" Her voice trailed off.

"Then he got sick."

Devonny nodded, the movement barely visible in the dim light of the bedroom. "They told us three to six months. It was almost six."

"That had to be tough."

"I didn't believe it. This was Jack. Healthy, strong, good-looking Jack. Love of my life. We'd only had seven years together and been married for five. It couldn't be true."

"Denial. The first stage of grief," Luke said like he knew what he was talking about.

"Jack went on like nothing had changed, right up until the end. Only he started talking about how it would be when he was gone. What I should do. I wasn't to sit around and mourn him. It was okay if I was sad but I had to go on with my life."

"And that's what you're doing."

"Trying to," Devonny said. "I'm trying to."

***

Devonny came awake at the muffled sound of the front door closing and footsteps in the living room. She half sat up to listen, and Luke's arm dropped from where it had been draped across her side.

They were both still completely dressed except for their shoes. While she stealthily moved to get out of the bed, a shadow appeared in the bedroom doorway.

"Dev?"

"Cherry!"

Even though they spoke softly, Luke woke up. "Huh? What? What's going on?"

Devonny turned on the bedside light and they all blinked owlishly at one another. "Sorry to interrupt." Cherry leaned against the doorjamb, a knowing smile glinting across her features. "I'll take the couch."

"Time is it?" Luke asked, running a hand through his hair, messing it up even more.

"Two-thirty," Devonny said after a glance at the bedside clock.

Luke sat up and reached for his shoes. "I should get going."

"Hey, don't leave on my account." Cherry's smile was broad. She winked at Devonny.

"'S okay."

Cherry disappeared into the bathroom and Devonny followed Luke to the door. "This is going to go down in history as one of the best nights of my life. And I think it's going to win for most unusual." He kissed her tenderly, but it was a kiss full of meaning.

"Goodnight."

She locked up behind him and watched from the window as he loped down the street.

Cherry pounced while Devonny straightened the covers on the bed. "You said this was a sleepy town where nothing ever happened."

"Until you got here," she said dryly, shooting her friend a look. "You certainly had a busy evening."

"I did indeed. And I'm exhausted." Cherry had changed into a too-big flannel nightshirt. As usual, she looked adorable with her blond hair and kittenish features. "But not too exhausted to hear about you and Luke."

"The baby kicked."

"It did? Is it kicking now?"

"No. It's sitting on my bladder. Be right back."

When Devonny returned from the bathroom, Cherry said, "I'm not asleep. Tell me everything."

"He kissed me."

"Well, duh. How was it?"

"Wonderful." She turned so she and Cherry were face to face. "He kissed me when we got here. He didn't ask or anything. He just…kissed me. And we kept kissing. Then the baby kicked and I got so excited I told him. I had to invite him in so I could explain."

"I'm guessing there was more kissing after that."

"There was. Lots more. But I told him I couldn't sleep with him because that would be, you know—"

"Weird."

"Exactly. We came in here and talked some more and kissed some more and… I guess we fell asleep."

"He likes you," Cherry said, her eyes shining in the near darkness.

"I know."

"Did you tell him? About your previous career?"

"No. I will. But I thought…"

"Baby steps," Cherry whispered.

"Right." Devonny closed her eyes. She tried to imagine Luke's reaction when she told him.

Show. Don't tell. He'll understand.

She opened her eyes and stared hard at the shadows in the room. A grayish blur seemed to be lounging near the window. She stared hard and squinted. Jack? She blinked and didn't see anything except the way the room normally looked at night. She fell asleep smiling, with the words He'll understand running through her head.

***

"I think Petty's husband's got a screw loose or something," Cherry said late the next morning. She was leaning against the counter watching Devonny sprinkle shredded cheese into the giant vegetable omelet she'd created.

"Doug? Why, what happened?" Devonny peeked at the biscuits in the oven. They were starting to brown nicely. She turned her attention back to Cherry.

"He walked in on us."

"Oh my God! Why didn't you say anything last night?"

"Because you had happier news. I didn't want to spoil it."

"What happened?"

"Well, we had our clothes back on, so I guess it could've been worse," Cherry said. "Still, he barged in on us in Petty's studio. We were sitting on the couch talking, but…"

Devonny waited. She turned her attention back to the omelet and flipped one half over the other, then turned off the heat. Breakfast was almost ready.

"He said some nasty things and basically kicked me out."

"I'm sure it was an unpleasant situation for everyone," Devonny said carefully.

"She hates being married to him, you know."

Devonny hadn't seen Cherry look so sad since Jack died.

"Why does she stay?"

Cherry took her mug of tea to the window and gazed out at the back yard. "Why do you think? She's afraid of what people will think. That small-town mentality, you know?"

"Nothing says she has to stay here," Devonny said. She took the biscuits out of the oven and turned it off.

Cherry sipped her tea. "It's her home. It's familiar. I can understand. I think you can too."

Devonny divided the food onto two plates and set them on the table. "Come and eat."

"Petty recognized me. She has every one of my films. Some of yours, too."

"Ah. That explains why she said it was nice to meet you in person. I couldn't figure it out before."

"Me neither."

"Still. I didn't think anyone here would have seen our films."

"Why not?"

"I don't know. I guess I equated small Midwestern towns with wholesomeness or something."

"You said wholesome." Cherry started to giggle. Devonny didn't know why it was funny but she joined her.

"God," Devonny said, when she stopped laughing. "I guess I'm as judgmental about them as they might be about me if they knew."

"Well, Petty's not."

"Oh, my God." Devonny's fork clattered to her plate. She stared at Cherry wide-eyed.

"What? What is it?"

"Petty's son, Miles."

"What about him?"

"He threatened me."

"What? When? Last night?"

"No. Several weeks ago. He recognized me. I was surprised because teenage boys aren't exactly Chemistry's target market. But it makes sense if Petty had them."

Cherry frowned. "I doubt she'd leave them lying around in the open."

"Maybe he snoops through his parents' things when they're not around."

"What did he threaten you with?"

"Exposure, if I didn't give him a private performance."

"Ick."

"Exactly."

"What'd you do?"

"Told him to back off. When he didn't I went for a knee to the groin."

"Which he so richly deserved."

"Yeah, well, I missed. Then Luke showed up."

"Our dashing hero." Cherry grinned at Devonny over the rim of her mug.

"He was. He walked me home." Devonny looked at her food, but she couldn't stop the heat that crept into her cheeks. And she knew Cherry would notice.

"Aww. You guys don't just work at a high school, it's like you're in high school. Did he carry your books, too?"

Devonny gave Cherry a look of exasperation. "No, he didn't carry my books," she said, mocking Cherry's tone.

"You know there's nothing wrong with liking him."

She's right.

"Shut up."

Cherry looked hurt. "Okay, but all I'm saying is—"

Devonny squeezed Cherry's wrist. "Not you. Jack." She pointed to her head. "Agreeing with you."

"He's here? He's still talking to you? Hi, Jack!"

Cherry waited expectantly.

"I don't think it works like that," Devonny explained.

Cherry looked crestfallen. "Oh."

"I'm not saying he can't hear you or doesn't know you're here. I mean, I don't know. Is it even really him? Sometimes I'm sure it's his voice I'm listening to, and sometimes I think maybe it's my own inner voice."

Cherry's smile was back. "Maybe it's you agreeing that it's okay for you to like Luke."

When Devonny didn't say anything, Cherry said, "Besides, whether or not you think it's okay, the fact is you do like him. A lot. Right?"

Devonny ducked her head without answering. Once they were finished eating, Cherry said, "I still can't believe you ended up here of all places. Tell me again. Why here?"

"I can't explain it. I started driving without knowing where I was going or what I was going to do. I was exhausted and I wasn't feeling well, so I stopped at that diner out on the highway. I thought I was going to lose the baby. I figured I had to rest for a bit, so I spent the night at a B&B." Devonny took a moment to gaze out at her backyard, at the empty swing set and the leafless trees. "The next morning everything looked different. I had a dream that night, Cher. About this house, the baby, that swing set out there." She jutted her chin toward it. "I was poking around the property when Luke showed up. He let me look around and it all fell into place. I can't explain how it happened. It just felt right, you know?"

"Serendipitous," Cherry said.

Their eyes met. "It was Jack, wasn't it?" Cherry asked, her voice almost a whisper. "He was looking out for you."

"I like to think so," Devonny answered just as softly.

Cherry's eyes began to mist. "I miss him. I miss you. Nothing's the same anymore. LA. Chemistry. My research project. Nothing."

"Oh, Cher." Devonny squeezed Cherry's wrist.

"You guys were like my family. My best friends." She tried to shake off her mood. "I'm being silly."

"I know it feels like I abandoned you, but I needed to start a new life. A different life. I couldn't do that in LA."

"I know. I understand. It's just I've missed you guys so much. I don't think I realized how much until I saw you. I mean, holy shit, I'm going to be Aunt Cherry!" She made an attempt at a smile.

"You sure are." Devonny knew that Cherry didn't have to stay in LA any more than Petty had to remain in Red Bud. It was up to them to make a change.

Chapter Ten

Emmaline Sanchez listened to the purr of Doug's breathing. The sheets were a tangled mess. She needed to pee and clean up a little. But she didn't move. Instead she watched the play of light on the walls caused by the streetlight coming through the lace curtains. Shifting patterns danced along the wall, mesmerizing as always.

Doug shifted in his sleep. She'd have to rouse him soon and send him home. To his big fancy house and the wife he didn't love. To his son who needed a father.

Emmaline's affair with Doug had begun as revenge. He'd dumped her after high school. She didn't have the right pedigree or connections. She didn't have the right skin color. That was most of the reason. Doug's father had finally gotten through to him. And Doug had broken Emmaline's heart.

She'd moved in with her aunt in Des Moines, continued her education and worked as a massage therapist. She married a few years later, but it hadn't lasted. Her visits to Red Bud had been rare but when her father fell ill, she'd returned to nurse him until his death last year. He'd left her his house on the outskirts of town. She had some savings. She decided to stay. After remodeling part of the downstairs and the attached garage, she opened her own spa. She offered massage, aromatherapy, facials, waxing and eyelash extensions.

The first time Doug came in for a massage Emmaline had been professional and polite. She acted like she didn't know him even when his bare skin, which she remembered well, was beneath her hands.

He'd groaned with pleasure as she dug into the knots of tension in his shoulders. When he rolled to the front, his erection tented the drape. Emmaline blushed. She knew he was watching her. She didn't look at him but worked on his scalp, arms, feet, calves and thighs using increased pressure as she worked her way up each leg.

She remembered how he'd wanted her once. Remembered their first time together. She'd loved how much he needed her, and the power that gave her.

"Take your time," she said coolly, after she finished the massage. "Come out when you're ready."

She left him there with his hard-on and smiled to herself. If he'd expected a different outcome he could think again. Doug tipped her generously that first time and he kept coming back.

Over time her anger dissipated. She still wanted him and that surprised her. But this time it was on her terms. This time she vowed she'd keep her power.

Something had been eating at him tonight. He'd shown up unexpectedly in the wee hours of the morning, and the last thing he wanted to do was talk. She knew he and Petty'd thrown their annual pre-holiday party. Emmaline had heard all about it from several of her clients. But all Doug was interested in was sex. He made love to her roughly, passionately, just the way she liked it. She needed to know he needed her.

Her favorite part of the time she spent with Doug was waking him up. Poking his shoulder none too gently, listening to him resist giving up his sleep, shoving at him until he left her bed. It was part of her revenge. Her power. You should have married me. She never said the words aloud, but they were never far from her thoughts. And this is what you get for not doing right by me twenty years ago. Go home to your wife who hates having sex with you. To your big house that doesn't sound like much of a home. To your child. One of your children, anyway.

Emmaline snuggled down in the covers, and pretended to be asleep while she listened to Doug get dressed. She smiled knowing he'd be out in the cold, starting his car, waiting for it to warm up. Served him right. He'd left her out in the cold all those years ago. He pressed his lips against her temple. Brushed back a lock of her hair. She made herself continue to feign sleep. But what she wanted to do was wrap her arms around him and beg him not to leave.

***

Luke watched coffee drip into the carafe. He was going to need lots of caffeine after his night with Devonny. He smiled as he recalled her walking into the Winston's kitchen. Ever since he'd met her, he felt incredibly lucky if he so much as caught a glimpse of her at school or anywhere else. If they had a conversation, if she even said hello to him, his joy increased ten-fold.

He'd told himself repeatedly it was ridiculous to have this kind of a crush. He was an adult for Pete's sake. Yet he felt like a character from a Victorian-era story, hungering for nothing more than to be able to touch her sleeve.

He'd tried to tell himself for months to move on. Devonny Campbell was not interested. She was polite about it, sure. She'd discouraged him from day one and

Luke hadn't pushed it. But he hadn't given up hope that her feelings would change over time.

After walking her home last night he'd decided to risk it. He kissed her, almost without thinking. He had wanted to for a long time, and part of him was sure she felt the same, but had been holding herself back. When the opportunity presented itself, he figured it'd be easier to ask for forgiveness rather than permission. But it turned out he hadn't had to do either.

Might as well admit it, he told himself as he poured coffee into a mug. He was at least half in love with her. He stood at the kitchen sink and stared out the window at the frozen back yard, mulling over what to do about it. Wondering what would happen when he laid it all on the line, told her about his past, about the struggles he had, even now, with the demon that had almost killed him.

He'd worked hard to build a meaningful life, to give back. But would Devonny understand? Or would she only see his weakness and despise him for it?

He knew it was a chance he'd have to take. But the thought of losing her because he'd decided to bare his soul was almost more than he could bear.

He poured a cup of coffee and fired up his laptop. As soon as he got online he typed "Jack Campbell actor" into the search engine. He read down the list of possibilities. He had no idea if Devonny's husband had used a stage name or if Jack Campbell was his real name. There must be thousands of actors named Jack Campbell in the world and at least a hundred or so in Hollywood.

Well, there was one in Australia. None in the U.S. At least none came up on Luke's search. He tried John

Campbell, but that wasn't it either. He tried a series of middle initials with Jack and John as the first name. What the hell? He had nothing better to do this morning. He'd go for a run later, in spite of the cold. He needed to clear his head after last night. Inside he felt all jumbled and not sure what to expect because so much had happened with Devonny so fast.

He refilled his coffee, frustrated with the lack of results. Devonny said her husband modeled. A search for "Jack Campbell model," provided him with a few promising results. He scrolled through them. He found bios for some of the likely candidates, doing his own exclusions based on what he knew about Jack. He slapped himself on the forehead for overlooking the obvious. Obituaries.

A Jack Campbell who had died in June in LA. Two minutes later he was looking at a professional photo of Devonny's late husband. Luke was pretty sure if he looked up tall, dark and handsome in the dictionary, there'd be a photo like this one.

The guy appeared to be in excellent physical condition with the sturdy build of an action/adventure hero. His eyes and smile drew you in with the kind of warmth that rarely translated in photos, especially online. Luke could only imagine the impact he must have had in person.

Luke wondered why a guy like that hadn't been more successful as an actor. But he'd read about actors like Tom Selleck, for example, who weren't wildly successful early on. Sometimes they had to mature or find the right vehicle to showcase their talent. Sometimes they just needed a lucky break. Maybe Jack Campbell had died waiting for his big break or the right role. The thought made Luke sad. To be cut down in one's prime, never to see his own child…

There was a link to an interview with a Claire Reddington, head of Chemistry Films. Luke clicked on it. Claire extolled the virtues of Jack Campbell, calling him a natural and bemoaning his early demise. "Though he starred in only a few films, they are, and will continue to be considered classics in the world of adult entertainment."

Luke sat back, frowning. Adult entertainment?

Intrigued, he did a search for the Chemistry Films web site. A quick search of the offerings led him to a list of several short films with DVD covers starring Jack Campbell. Always with his shirt off. The guy was physically gifted, Luke would give him that. And always with the same dark-haired female who seemed unable to keep her hands or her mouth off him.

Luke stared at the DVD covers. Even though her face wasn't completely visible in any of them, her head always turned to the side, her clothes mostly off, Luke couldn't believe what he was seeing. Though the name on the cover was Tawny Devon, the woman looked an awful lot like Devonny.

***

Luke's cell phone buzzed. His brother's likeness lit up the screen.

"Hey, Paul, what's up?"

"I was just going to ask you that."

"Nothing. I'm having coffee, trying to wake up, screwing around online. You?"

"Just got back from a run. I'm meeting Julia later for brunch."

Luke snorted. "Brunch."

Paul chuckled. "That's what she likes to call it. I think of it as a second breakfast."

"Julia's a snob."

"Maybe, but she's a hot snob."

"You're so superficial."

"I know. It's a curse."

Even though he'd been compared to him and found wanting his entire life, Luke adored his older brother. The man was unflappable. It was virtually impossible to get under his skin.

"How's things going with the hot teacher's aide?"

Luke hesitated. "There's been progress."

"Oh yeah?"

"I spent the night with her."

"That sounds like more than progress."

"Yeah, well, there's a bit of an unexpected development."

"Go on."

"She's pregnant."

"Sorry. I think my reception faded out. Did you say she's pregnant?"

"Yes." He told Paul about Jack.

"Huh." Was all Paul said when he finished.

"I looked up his obituary."

"Why?"

Luke shifted uncomfortably. He and Paul never flinched from asking each other the tough questions. "I was curious. If you heard the way she talked about him… I might be competing with a Greek god."

Luke's gaze shifted back to the laptop screen, to the picture of Jack and a woman he strongly suspected might be Devonny.

"You're getting into murky waters here, pal," Paul said. "A dead husband? A baby on the way? That's a lot of baggage. This one does not sound like relationship material."

"What if I told you her husband was an adult film actor?"

"Porn? Are you kidding me? Wait? What are you saying? That she—That they—"

"I don't know about her."

"Did you sleep with her?"

"Yes." Luke grinned when he heard Paul sigh. "But we didn't have sex."

"Yeah. Because that would be weird. Look, if she was doing porn, you don't know what you might catch from her."

"That's unfair!"

"Take some advice from your slightly older, much wiser brother, for once, would you? Walk away, Luke. Walk away now."

"I can't." I like her. "Nor do I want to."

Paul sighed. Neither of them said anything for at least a minute. "Don't you think you've been through enough?" Paul asked quietly.

"What's that supposed to mean?"

"After the accident, the surgeries and the lawsuit, all the rehab..."

"Go on."

He heard Paul sigh again. "It's like you look for ways to make your life harder instead of easier. You move to this town in the middle of nowhere. You're coaching high school football when you could have been coaching college. You start flipping houses even though you didn't have the money — "

"Hey, I paid you back," Luke cut in.

"Yeah, you did. But instead of dating some, I don't know, sweet kindergarten teacher or something, you find a widowed, pregnant, possibly former porn star. What's up with that?"

Paul sounded so genuinely baffled Luke started to laugh. Pretty soon, Paul joined in. Because when his brother put everything he knew about Devonny so succinctly, it did sound rather bizarre. Out of all the towns in Iowa, she'd arrived in his and had literally run into him her first day here.

"God, I don't know," Luke said. "I'll call you back when I figure it out. In the meantime, go have your second breakfast with Julia the Snob."

"That's Hot Julia the Snob thank you very much." He paused. "Hey, you're still coming to Dad's for Thanksgiving, right?"

Luke's jaw clenched and acid backed up into his throat. Thanksgiving was next week. He'd promised Paul he'd be there this year, but it was the very last thing he wanted to do. Already his father's voice was in his head, listing his many shortcomings and reminding him of how he'd screwed up big time. Still, this was his family. It was as hard for Paul, he reasoned, as it was for him.

"Yeah. I'll be there Thursday morning."

"Great. Talk to you later, bro."

Reluctantly, Luke turned back to the laptop. He took a sip of his now lukewarm coffee and hit a few keys. He extracted a credit card from his wallet. Maybe, as Paul had said, he did have a tendency to make things harder on himself than they needed to be. But knowing, he had learned, was generally better than not knowing. And because he didn't want to believe it, he had to know whether the woman on the poster was Devonny or not.

So today was the day he'd be paying to download an adult film. Because short of asking her point blank—which meant having to admit to digging into her husband's past—he couldn't think of another way to find out what he didn't want to, but had to know about her.

Chapter Eleven

Miles jumped when his father pushed into his room without knocking. He'd lost the privilege to have a lock on his door several years ago for some infraction which had long since been forgotten. But the lock had never been replaced and since his parents never seemed to notice he was around he hadn't pushed the issue.

He slapped his laptop closed and tried not to squirm, hoping his father wouldn't notice his hard-on.

Unfortunately, when the old man did decide to pay attention to him, his sharp gaze missed nothing.

"What are you doing?"

"Nothing. Just homework."

"If it's just homework why'd you close your laptop so fast?" Doug held out a hand. Miles shoved the laptop away from him and crossed his arms behind his head, acting like he didn't care. But of course, he did. All he'd ever wanted was his father's approval. Maybe even his love, although that was a sappy sentiment he'd never willingly admit to anyone.

Miles might not have minded as much, if his mother had ever been there for him. But she wasn't the maternal type. Mostly he felt like he was in her way, somehow. He was an afterthought, like a dress on sale she'd decided to buy, even though it didn't fit and she now regretted the purchase. He suspected she regretted ever having a child. Or getting married. Or coaching high school girls and teaching PE. Miles suspected his mother had a lot of regrets, though, of course, they'd never discussed the subject. They never discussed anything.

Doug flipped the laptop and woke up the screen. Miles knew his dad was in for a surprise. He probably thought he'd hidden his stash of porn pretty well, in a shoebox that supposedly housed one of his wife's many pairs of athletic shoes.

Miles often explored his parents' bedroom and closet looking for clues to who they were. What had made them the way they were? From his perspective they appeared to be two people living under the same roof who despised yet tolerated each other. He didn't think they were staying together because of him, because he didn't think he was important to either one of them. Only when he scored a touchdown or made a basket, did they seem to notice he belonged to them.

"What is this?" Doug asked, staring at the screen.

Miles smiled to himself. He knew exactly what part of the film Doug was looking at because he'd watched it numerous times. It was that chick, Devonny Campbell, the hot teacher's aide at school, going down on some guy. The first time he'd watched this particular disc, she looked familiar but he couldn't place her. Maybe she was one of those actresses who did bit parts on TV shows or commercials or something. He knew he'd seen her before, but he couldn't remember where.

Then one day he'd seen her walking past the football field after school. She glanced over to where Coach Bradshaw was explaining a new defensive play. She wasn't wearing her glasses that day. And it clicked. Devonny Campbell had made porno flicks. Soft core, sure, the kind that might appeal to chicks. But still, they turned him on. Hers and a bunch of other ones. Girls with girls. That had surprised him. That two girls getting it on got him hard. But most everything got him hard these days.

Miles didn't answer his dad's question. Surely even a supposedly straight arrow like Doug Winston knew what he was looking at.

"Where did you get this?" Doug's gaze was still fixed on the screen. Of course it was, because Miles knew he was imagining what it would be like to have a hot chick doing to him what she was doing to the guy on the screen. Miles had some success in that area. But the girls who'd been willing weren't experts. Still, the end result had been satisfactory.

Miles continued to watch his dad. He was kind of enjoying the old man's reaction. He was getting turned on and frustrated at the same time. His face was red, his eyes were bugging out, and he was starting to perspire. Miles chuckled. He hadn't meant to. It just came out.

Doug's head snapped up and he slammed the laptop closed. "Where did you get this filth?"

"Duh. Where do you think?"

"I asked you a question, smartass. I expect a proper answer."

"It's okay, Dad. You're secret's safe with me. As long as you don't mind sharing."

"I swear to God, Miles, if you don't answer me right now, I'm going to beat the crap out of you."

"You can try."

Doug back-handed him across the face.

Miles glared at his father. "What the hell you'd do that for?" He hated himself at that moment. He should stand up for himself, fight like a man. Instead he cradled his jaw in his hand and fought back the tears surging into his eyes. He was five years old again and he'd knocked his cereal bowl over. Milk had splashed on Doug and the newspaper he was reading. He'd slapped Miles so hard he'd knocked him off the chair. Miles had raced to his room and cowered under the covers, terrified his father would come after him. But his father never came. He never apologized. Just one of the many incidents swept under the rug in the Winston household.

"I'll ask you one more time." Doug's face was beet red. He clenched and unclenched his fists. "Where did you get this?"

Miles looked away. "Your closet." He didn't even try to hold back the tears, but let them fall. He'd be in trouble for two things now. Poking through his parents' things and watching porn.

"What did you say?"

You heard me. "Your. Closet." Miles looked back at his dad. Miles was angry now, even though he didn't want to be. He didn't want to be anything like his dad, but he couldn't stop the surge of rage bubbling up inside him.

"Don't add lying to your other transgressions," Doug warned.

"I'm not lying!" Miles yelled. Didn't the man know what he had in his own closet? Didn't he remember how cleverly he'd hidden it amongst his own wife's things? "There's a whole freaking box of these." He gestured at his laptop. As if you didn't know.

The anger seemed to seep out of Doug like air from a leaky tire. A nugget of comprehension dawned in his eyes. He extracted the disc. He looked around and found the case tossed on the desk. He picked it up and left the room.

Miles rubbed his jaw again. "Nut job." He wondered how much more trouble he'd be in if his dad knew he'd hit on the hot teacher's aide. Well, that really wasn't the right word, was it?

Miles had started out all cocky and sure of himself, but when she'd fixed him with a look that hardened her soft features and erased the usual warmth in her eyes, something inside of him had shriveled. Then Coach Bradshaw showed up…

Fortunately, Miles comforted himself, he wasn't as dumb as people sometimes assumed he was. Devonny Campbell was way out of his league, and if he was honest with himself, he'd have been terrified if she'd actually agreed to blow him. Though not too terrified to act on it, he reminded himself smugly. He'd still like to give her something to remember him by. He promised himself he would if he ever got the chance.

***

Petty sat for a moment looking at her home while listening to the tick tick tick of her car's cooling engine. This beautiful Victorian house was her prison, Doug and Miles her keepers. Until Cherry Pickler had blown into her life.

Cherry had pointed out that Petty had chosen to imprison herself this way, to be a slave to other people's expectations. Their judgment. Petty had tried to make Cherry understand. The woman had a PhD in psychology, for Pete's sake. Truth was, Cherry did understand, but she was fast losing patience with Petty.

Wearily, Petty pushed open the car door and got out, dragging her oversized bag crammed with paperwork with her. She was drowning beneath the forms and documentation required for every move she made, every field trip she wanted to offer, every tiny injury that occurred during class or competition.

The house was dark. Usually by this time of the evening Doug had all the lights turned on, including the porch lights. Inside it was just as quiet. The kitchen looked like no one had touched it since this morning. Petty crept through the empty rooms downstairs. Something wasn't right.

She padded up the carpeted stairs, feeling them creak under her weight. She pushed open Miles's bedroom door and found him sound asleep fully clothed on top of his covers. He stayed up far too late most nights but Petty had long ago given up arguing with him. Teenagers required a lot of sleep and as long as he wasn't doing it in class, she didn't care when he got it.

She closed the door and continued down the hall to the master suite. A light shown under the closed door. Ugh. That meant Doug was there. Usually he'd be downstairs with the news on while he scrounged around for something to eat. The bedroom was for dressing and undressing and sleeping on opposite sides of the king-sized bed.

Petty couldn't wait to get out of her work clothes, put on her favorite pair of sweats, and find something mindless on TV while she tackled the work she'd brought home.

The bedroom was empty, but the closet light was on. "Doug? What's going on?"

She pulled the partially closed door open and Doug turned around with a shoebox in his hand. Not just any shoebox, she realized. *The* shoebox. The one where she kept her stash of porn.

She should have known better. She should have hidden it in the studio. Except Doug never looked through her things. He had no interest in her or her possessions. As long as they maintained the veneer of a "happy couple," Doug mostly left her alone.

"What are you doing?" she asked, refusing to be embarrassed by her collection. Doug had his entertainments. She had hers.

"Quite an assortment you have here," he said, lifting one after another up so he could read the titles. "Pirate's Booty; Screwing the Board; Pink-tipped Ladies."

"Give them to me." Petty held out her hand.

"Then there's the one I caught our son watching: Executive Action."

"Miles?"

Doug stared her down.

"Miles was watching these?"

"Well, that one, anyway. I've no idea how many he's seen. Possibly all of them."

"That little sneak," Petty said.

"Well, at least we know which side he gets it from."

"Oh, get down off your high horse," Petty snarled. "Not like you're up for Parent of the Year any more than I am."

"Touché."

Doug held the box out to her and she grabbed it, daring him to say anything more.

"Put this somewhere he won't find it, for Chrissakes. The last thing I need is for it to become common knowledge that my son has access to pornography."

"Even if they are pornographic, these films are also beautiful and touching."

"Oh, I'm sure there's lots of touching."

"Get your mind out of the gutter," Petty snapped.

"It goes there to keep yours company, dear wife."

"You disgust me."

"That's rich. I disgust you? And while we're at it, what do you think is going to happen between you and your friend Cherry? You don't think she's taking whatever happened at the party seriously, do you? A woman like that—"

"You don't know anything about her, so why don't you shut up?"

"She's not going to take you seriously, Pet."

"Don't call me 'Pet.' I'm not your pet."

Doug unbuttoned the top button of his shirt and began loosening his tie. "But you used to be, didn't you? Back when we first met? You loved the way I petted you, remember?"

"Things were different then," Petty said.

"Not so different. Take your clothes off."

"No."

Doug sighed. "Do you want me to have another talk with your mother? Tell her I'm concerned you might have been influenced by those dykes you call friends? Explain to her that you refuse to do your wifely duty."

"You wouldn't."

"We made a deal. Or have you forgotten? You give me what I want when I want it. And the rest of the time, I leave you alone."

Petty fought the tears surging behind her eyes, the stomach acid backing up into her throat. "Please..."

"What did you say?" Doug asked. He'd unbuttoned his shirt and was undoing his pants. "You want to please me? Right now?"

"Doug..." Petty knew she'd give in. He'd found so many ways to make her life miserable, not the least of which was discussing his concerns with her pious, God-fearing mother. And he wasn't above using them to get what he wanted. He stepped out of his slacks and reached for the box she still held. He set it aside. "The DVD Miles was watching gave me some ideas," he said, his voice husky, his eyes glinting at her. "Of course, it will require you to be on your knees."

Exhaustion swamped her as Doug stood there in his boxers. Not from her long work day, but her entire life. The hours and days she'd spent doing things she didn't want to do. Doing what her mother told her to do, what her family expected her to do, what her husband demanded she do. Or else.

She was tired of the "or else" hanging over her head. Or else...what? What will people think? Did she care about the opinions of others? She certainly didn't care what Doug thought. She already knew he despised her and had for a long time. She knew about his mistress. Emmaline. He should have married her after high school. But she knew why he hadn't. Because he'd done the same thing she had. What his father told him to do, what his family expected of him. And it hadn't brought him happiness any more than it had her.

Why are we doing this? Why are we making each other miserable? And Miles...what is this sick relationship between us doing to him?

"No." The word came out of her mouth before she realized she'd said it aloud.

Doug stared at her as if he'd never seen her before. Perhaps he hadn't. Not the real her, anyway. "No?"

"I don't want to do this anymore."

"This being?"

She gestured at him. "This. This game we play. This sick, ridiculous relationship we call a marriage."

"Really? We'll see what your mother has to say about that." He started toward the nightstand where the phone was.

"Go ahead. Tell her everything," Petty said. "Tell her I'm gay. While you're at it, tell her about Emmaline. Tell her we never loved each other and that our marriage was a mistake. Tell her I want a divorce."

Doug stopped. Petty turned. He didn't pick up the phone. He seemed frozen in place as if he didn't know what to do. "Doug, please. You're as miserable as I am. Let's end this. We could both be happy."

He turned and gave her an icy glare. "A divorce? Do you know what that will do to my mayoral campaign? I'm running on a family values platform and my wife divorces me in the middle of it? I'll be a laughingstock."

"How do you know you aren't already?"

Doug strode toward her. "How dare you?" He'd never hit her. Not once. No, she thought sadly. He takes his rage out on Miles. Always has. And she'd let him. God she was pathetic.

"Maybe you should shift your platform. The face of the American family has changed in case you hadn't noticed. It's the twenty-first century, for God's sake."

"Don't be naïve. This is Red Bud. Things haven't changed that much."

"You could drop out of the race."

"Now you're being ridiculous. Old Bart Carmichael's had a stranglehold on the town council for too long. No one's challenged him in years. It's time for someone younger to step in and shake things up. With enough finesse, he might see the wisdom in announcing his retirement. If he does, I can run unopposed."

Typical Doug. Bullheaded. Stubborn. It was either his way or the highway. Was he any different with Emmaline, she wondered? It was hard to understand the attraction.

"That's your choice." She stepped around him. She wanted to escape into her bathroom. Take a long hot shower. Try to wash away the remnants of this nasty day.

Doug grabbed her elbow as she tried to pass. "Petty." He didn't sound angry. She looked into his eyes. He was calm. Calculating. "Could you not do anything right away? Give me some time to absorb this? Figure out a way to make it work?"

His change of tone and tack made her suspicious. "How much time?"

"A few weeks? Until after the holidays?"

Her eyes narrowed. "I don't see what difference it makes. I won't go public with it or anything. But you need to know, I'll spend that time making arrangements as I see fit."

He released her. "All right."

She closed the bathroom door and locked it. She leaned against it for a moment contemplating a future she'd never imagined. So close. She was so close.

Chapter Twelve

Luke retrieved his mail, sorting through it as he made his way to the house. There was never much beyond junk mail and bills. Today there was a square flat cardboard envelope addressed to him with a discreet Chemistry Films logo and return address.

He glanced around, but of course there was no one to see what was in his mailbox or to show interest even if they'd known. The mailman, Art Wentzler, had been on the job for as long as Luke could remember. He could care less about what he delivered where. Everyone in town knew for the last three years Art had been counting the days until retirement.

Enough with the overanalyzing paranoia.

Inside, Luke dumped his backpack and the rest of the mail on the kitchen table. He held the package in his hand, debating whether he wanted to see what it held. He'd decided not to download one of the films, but instead had purchased the DVD. Somehow, he'd thought that would be less traceable as the headline, "Porn discovered on school guidance counselor's computer" had flashed through his head during the ordering process. Of course, getting caught with a physical copy wasn't any better, but at least he felt more in control of preventing accidental exposure this way.

If anyone cared to delve too thoroughly into his past, he'd be skating on thin ice as it was. Nick would stand up for him, he supposed, but not even Nick knew all the details about him. Pornography possession by the high school guidance counselor and coach would not be viewed lightly by the good citizens of Red Bud even on the best of days, but added to his earlier transgressions? He didn't like to think about how easily he could lose everything he'd worked for.

Luke thought briefly of how he'd like a good stiff drink before he watched the movie. That was bad. It wasn't the movie, per se. It was how easily the fear of exposure triggered those old responses. He could call his sponsor, but there was nothing alcoholic in the house and Luke had no intention of walking the mile or so to the nearest convenience store. The weather was gloomy and a cold rain was expected later this evening.

Instead, Luke set the package on the counter and headed into his bedroom. He'd get comfortable, he decided, as he pulled an ancient pair of sweats from a drawer. Make himself something to eat. He'd indulge in a big glass of sweet tea with it, something he didn't allow himself too often because of the sugar content.

If he still felt the urge to drink before he started the movie, he'd call his sponsor. Otherwise, he'd make himself watch at least the beginning. See if it was Devonny. And if it was? He wasn't sure how he'd react.

***

An hour later, knowing he was being ridiculous, Luke made sure all the curtains were drawn and the doors locked. He loaded the DVD into his laptop. The introductory credits were short and sweet, well done and of high quality. The opening theme fell somewhere in the Irish folk music genre. Whatever else this film company was about, the movie did not appear to be amateurish or low budget.

Jack filled up the screen, dressed in what looked like pirate garb. He was in a seaside pub drinking with his mates, brooding a bit as he stared down into his glass of ale. It looked like a professional movie set, rather than a high school production.

A serving wench entered, her manner demure as if hoping she wouldn't be noticed and leered at. Luke studied the actress. The bodice of her costume bared an exceptional amount of cleavage, and though most of her hair was tucked up under a cap, he had no doubt it was Devonny.

His gut clenched when one of the customers made a grab for her, throwing her off balance. She cried out, but the men's companions grabbed at her. The men were all youthful. Their costumes fit well enough to define hard abs and biceps and chests, but they were a rough-looking bunch nonetheless.

A free-for-all ensued, with the men at the table deciding they could take turns with the virginal-looking serving wench. Who got her first became a bone of contention and a fight broke out, with Devonny being shoved in Jack's direction. He caught her easily, and the camera caught the smoldering look that passed between them. Jack whispered something in her ear. Devonny looked back at the fighting men before she slid her hand into Jack's. They slipped away leaving the melee behind.

In the next scene they were in a room. A fire burned merrily and Devonny was bent over, helping to get Jack's boots off, which allowed the camera another delicious view of her cleavage. The sleeve of her top slid down over one creamy shoulder. Her cap had been removed and tendrils of dark hair curled around her neck. She thanked him for getting her away from those men. He told her he wasn't interested in taking anything from a woman that wasn't freely given.

Jack reached out and tugged the other side of her top down, baring her other shoulder, causing her breasts to nearly spill out of the remaining material. His gaze burned into hers. She appeared more hesitant but just as interested in what was to come.

The dialogue between them was sparing, but the chemistry was real. As were Devonny's nearly bare breasts. She got the boots off and tossed them aside.

Jack quirked a finger at her and she sauntered back to him, straddling his lap and looping her arms around his neck. "You don't have to do this, you know," he said, his hand curving around the back of her head and tangling in the hair tumbling enchantingly down from her topknot.

In answer, she kissed him.

What followed was a love scene nothing like what Luke had expected. Luke somehow felt like he'd intruded on a very private moment between these two, then realized that's exactly what the film maker wanted him to feel. Devonny and Jack seemed to care nothing for the camera watching them. They didn't even appear to be acting. If they were, Luke decided, they should win some kind of award for their performance. It was that real.

The pacing had Luke enthralled. Surely no man had ever taken this much time to undress a woman. Clothes came off bit by bit, and Jack's hands were never still, caressing her bare breasts and everywhere else. He had to admire Jack's discipline, if that's what it was.

Although Jack, being Devonny's husband, might have made love to her an hour before filming started. Which would certainly make it easier for him to control himself.

After watching it all the way through, Luke took an emotional step back and studied the film from a more detached stance the second time he watched it. The focus wasn't on the genitals, although viewers were treated to Jack in full frontal nudity and also a long shot of his backside when he went to add fuel to the fireplace.

The actual lovemaking scene was intense, but it was by no means raunchy.

Luke got what Chemistry Films was doing. They were making love films, for lack of a better term. He understood the name of the company now. These were not actors screwing each other just for the titillation of the audience. This was a demonstration of love, reverence, and protection.

In the next love scene, it was early morning, and Devonny did most of the work, rewarding Jack for the way he'd treated her the night before. But the camera angles were kind and part of the scene was shot from a distance so the viewer could get the idea without being hit over the head with close-up after close-up of Devonny's mouth and Jack's cock.

The ending showed Devonny bringing Jack a steaming mug, while he steered his ship out of the harbor and toward the horizon.

Luke stopped the disc and stared at the film's cover which filled his laptop screen. It looked like a romance novel, and in some ways that's how the movie felt as well. Bodice ripper? Was that the term he'd heard somewhere? Chemistry Films wasn't selling porn, not the way most people thought of it, anyway. They were selling passionate romance to women who wouldn't mind leaving some bits to the imagination, instead of blatantly crude and graphic detail.

Chick flick porn.

And the Jack on the screen was giving Luke a lot to live up to. Keeping a woman like Devonny happy in and out of the bedroom and protecting her from would-be predators at the same time. Luke recalled the day he'd interrupted Miles and Devonny in the school parking lot. He hadn't imagined Miles's threatening stance and Devonny hadn't explained. But now he was beginning to wonder whether Miles knew about Devonny's films.

Based on what Luke had observed, Miles was the classic example of a boy who had everything except the love and attention of his parents. Doug was only interested in Miles's athletic achievements and Petty, well, Petty didn't seem interested in Miles at all, which was a shame. If Miles spent time watching adult films, it would be easy enough for him to discover Devonny's secret. What if Miles had shared her secret with his friends?

The thought made Luke uneasy. He replaced the DVD in its case, silently wondering if he was man enough to deal with the fallout, should the good citizens of Red Bud become aware of Devonny's past.

***

Thinking about Devonny at school the next day, Luke was surprised to discover watching the film had done nothing to change the way he felt about her. He'd somehow compartmentalized her past and current life. She hadn't lied to him about anything. Certainly not about the way she felt about Jack. He'd seen evidence of that "big love" on the screen. Not about Jack's film career or the fact she'd worked for a film company. He'd never asked her in what capacity. Neither, he supposed, had Nick when he interviewed her.

To Luke, she was still Devonny Campbell, the woman who'd run into him outside the Red Hen diner, and who'd later bought his grandmother's house. A woman trying to make a new life for herself and from what he could see, succeeding.

She'd even befriended crotchety old Loretta Herman, and somehow Loretta had convinced Devonny to drive her to church on Sundays. He'd heard Devonny had also been recruited to help out in the nursery during the morning services. Luke chuckled to himself. If the parents of those toddlers knew about Devonny's films, they'd find her background just as objectionable as parents of high schoolers would.

Likewise, if the parents of the teenagers he counseled and coached knew of his history with addiction, they might not be so inclined to allow him to keep his job.

What he'd become, what he was now, would factor into their opinion of him, maybe even save him. But what kind of chance would they give Devonny, if those films she'd done became common knowledge? It was hypocritical, yes, but true nonetheless. Most of the people around here worked hard, and their lives revolved around family, church and community. Chemistry Films was obviously targeted toward a selective niche market but anyone with an internet connection could access their site. And most everyone in Red Bud had internet access. Devonny used a stage name, but would they still recognize her? She'd cut her hair and often wore glasses Luke suspected she didn't need. Even her clothes were different. She'd also gained a little weight due to her pregnancy. Very few people besides him had seen Devonny as she'd looked the day she blew into town. All in all, he thought it unlikely she'd be recognized. She'd picked the perfect hiding place, if indeed, hiding was what she was trying to do.

Still, those films were out there. Luke was glad he'd found out about Devonny's past before she told him. Eventually, he hoped she'd trust him enough to tell him herself. And, maybe, when she did, he could share his own secrets with her. And hope it wouldn't make any difference in how she felt about him.

With that thought in mind he carried a spring in his step as he negotiated the long main hallway of the high school. Class was in session and the hallway was deserted. The gleaming floors shone under the fluorescent lights.

He'd had to have another talk with Regan Marx about texting during class. He'd confiscated her phone and planned to call her parents about the problem later today. Regan had tried to manipulate him with tears and empty promises, but this was the third time in two weeks he'd had a conversation with her, so it was time to take things to the next level. One of her parents would be required to pick up the phone and it would be their decision whether to return it to Regan.

Knowing the Marxes, Luke didn't have much hope that Regan wouldn't have her phone back by this evening. But he had at least made them aware of the problem.

Devonny stepped out of the media center as he approached.

138

"Hello." He was unable to stop the smile that always seemed to be on his face whenever he saw her. She was juggling a box overflowing with office supplies. "Let me take that." Before she could object, he'd hefted the box. "What are we doing with this?" he asked, glancing at the contents.

"They're going into the supply closet so we can keep it under lock and key," Devonny said. She held up the ring of keys at the end of a lanyard around her neck. "Office supplies have to be requisitioned in the future and inventoried regularly."

"That sounds very official."

Devonny slanted a look up at him. "Evidently there have been abuses."

"Ah, yes. I recall the Great Highlighter Shortage of 2016. And there was that ghastly overflow of copy paper last spring."

She pulled the door open to the administrative offices and Luke preceded her in. She unlocked the supply closet and the door shut behind them once they were inside. "You can put that down here," she said, indicating an open area on the floor. "I have the fun job of retrieving everything the staff isn't currently using and organizing it all."

Luke set the box down. When he straightened and turned, Devonny was so close to him, he bumped into her. He touched her elbow to steady her. "Sorry. You okay?"

"I'm fine."

Luke didn't let go of her until she looked up at him with a question in her eyes. He could smell whatever subtle scent she wore. Something with lemons and honeysuckle, he thought, like a breath of spring air. Clover blooming. Honeybees buzzing. A green meadow.

"Are you okay?" Devonny asked.

He snapped out of his fanciful reverie, but almost immediately another one took its place. Devonny. Naked. Making love to a man amidst tangled sheets. Only this time it wasn't Jack Campbell she was with, it was him. And he was wearing a pirate hat. The red heat of embarrassment suffused his faced as a result of his wayward thoughts.

He dropped his hand and edged away from her. "I'm fine. See you later."

He got out of the door and back to his own office where he collapsed in his chair and stared at the pile of work on his desk. If he wanted a starring role in Devonny's life, he had a couple of things he had to work on.

☐

Chapter Thirteen

Devonny was brushing her teeth when someone knocked on the front door. It wasn't Luke. She'd just had a goodnight text from him. It wasn't late but no one else she knew would stop by at this time. She rinsed her mouth and padded down the hall and put an eye to the peephole before she opened the door.

"Petty!" Devonny couldn't hide her surprise so she didn't even try. Petula Winston was the last person she expected to see.

"Devonny. Hi. Could I come in for a minute?"

Devonny looked over Petty's shoulder. She was alone. "Uh, sure."

Once inside, Petty paced around the living room as if she couldn't decide whether she was going to stay now she was here, or bolt back out of the door.

"Can I take your coat?" Devonny asked.

"No. I'm not staying long." Contradicting her own words, Petty tossed her coat over the back of the sofa.

Devonny waited, wondering why Petty was here. She knew from Cherry that she and Petty were still in touch, so that couldn't be it. Was it something about Miles? Or Doug?

"Can I make you some tea — or —"

"No." Petty stopped her pacing abruptly. "Look, I know this is awkward, but I need you to talk to Cherry for me."

"Oh."

"I did something stupid and now she won't speak to me. She won't answer my calls or my texts or my emails. I'm going crazy."

"Petty, why don't you sit down? Are you sure I can't get you something to drink?"

Petty sank onto the edge of the sofa. "No. No thank you. You must think I'm such a fool."

"I don't think anything," Devonny said. In truth, except for her conversations with Cherry, she hadn't given Petty's situation much consideration at all. The two of them would either work it out or they wouldn't. It wasn't any of Devonny's business except for how it affected her closest friend.

"We were talking about being together. For real. Out in the open. I thought she meant in LA. I could do that. Away from here. Away from my family and where everyone knows me? Sure. But that's not what Cherry wants. She wants to come here. Can you believe that? Find a place in Red Bud or Shenandoah. Move in together." Petty shuddered. "I...I can't do that." Her gaze slid toward Devonny in a search for understanding.

Devonny wasn't sure Red Bud was ready for Cherry Pickler. Even though Cherry had floated the idea of relocating nearby, Devonny hadn't taken her too seriously. She tried not to smile at the thought of her feisty friend barreling into town. One thing Cherry wouldn't put up with was pretending to be something she wasn't. If Petty wanted to be with her, she'd have to accept that.

Devonny went with the simplest question she could think of, because she wanted to understand where Petty was coming from. "Why not?"

Petty turned tormented eyes on her. "What would people think?"

"What people?"

Petty gestured helplessly. "Everyone. People at school. My family. I've lived here my whole life."

"It's your life, though, Petty," Devonny said gently.

"You don't understand," Petty sulked. "I thought you would. Isn't that why you're here? To give yourself a fresh start?"

Devonny knew her reasons for settling in Red Bud had little to do with what anyone else thought. "What is it exactly you believe people will think about you?"

"That I'm — that I'm…"

"Gay?"

Petty nodded.

"Your sexuality doesn't change who you are."

"Try telling that to the average citizen of Red Bud." Petty said. "What changes is everyone will know it if I leave Doug and move in with Cherry."

"So what you're afraid of is that everyone will know you've been living a lie?"

"No! That's not it!" Petty slumped back as the outrage drained out of her. "Oh, maybe you're right. Maybe that is what I'm afraid of."

"Let me ask you something. Are you happy, Petty?"

Petty shook her head. "I haven't been happy for years."

"Don't you want to be?" Petty looked at her as if the idea had never occurred to her. "Don't you think you deserve to be?"

"Of course I do, but…"

"Petty, nothing worth having comes easy. You know that, right?"

Petty nodded.

"Then you know what you have to do."

***

Long after Petty left, Devonny lay awake. Had her journey been easier than everyone else's? She hadn't consciously set out to rebel against or hurt her mother when she met Jack. But she had been more than ready to see what else was out there besides the world her mother had shown her.

Her mother had made it easy for Devonny to desire escape, by trying to control her. Devonny had known she'd eventually have to rebel against her mother and cut those strings that had tied them to each other. Maybe she could have found a more acceptable way to do that, a way that would have kept their relationship intact. Instead she'd found Jack.

What had happened with Jack wasn't anything she could have predicted. He'd never forced her to do anything, hadn't even encouraged her to go against her mother's wishes. All he'd ever done was reinforce what she already knew. It was her life. Every decision she made from the moment she first saw him until the day he died had been hers and hers alone.

Her mother made choices too. She didn't have to approve of every choice Devonny made. She still could have loved me, Devonny often thought to herself. She missed her mother. The woman had been her whole world for eighteen years. She hadn't expected to lose her so totally and completely. But she couldn't forgive or forget her mother's cruelty—or the way she'd almost seemed glad Jack was dead and Devonny was suffering.

***

Since the Winston's party, Devonny and Luke had fallen into a routine, sharing an evening meal together most nights, which sometimes meant Luke stayed over.

They were like a couple of teenagers, responsible teenagers anyway, lying in Devonny's bed, kissing deep and slow, their limbs tangled together, but knowing they weren't going to go all the way. They held each other and talked about everything and nothing.

The long Thanksgiving weekend began tomorrow and Luke was not looking forward to it. He was quieter than usual, his fingers playing through Devonny's hair.

"Don't you want to see your family?" Devonny asked.

"My brother, yes. His girlfriend, I can tolerate. My father? I can't say I'm looking forward to seeing him, no."

Devonny distanced herself, finding her own pillow so she could face Luke. "Why?"

Luke sighed. "We were never close. Never had a very good relationship. He adores Paul. Everyone does. Including me. But, I guess in my father's eyes I never reached the bar my brother set. Nothing I ever did was good enough."

"This probably won't make you feel any better, but even without any siblings, I'm pretty sure I'm a big disappointment to my mother."

Luke smiled and turned to face her. "Then she's a fool."

"So is your father."

"He has his reasons for feeling the way he does."

"What does that mean?"

"Remember at the Winston's party, we were both drinking club soda?"

"Uh huh."

"I caused him some problems back in college. Remember when we met at the coffee shop in Shenandoah and you asked me if I came there often?"

"Uh huh."

"I'm usually in there every Saturday. Before an AA meeting."

"Oh."

"I've been clean and sober for eight years, but I can't say there aren't moments when I'd like a drink. Or two or three or ten."

"Wait, didn't you tell me your mom died when you were in college?"

"Yes."

"Did that have anything to do with your drinking?"

"A lot of stuff happened that I didn't handle very well around the same time. Drinking gave me an excuse not to deal with any of it."

"Almost everybody in LA's been through rehab for something."

"You?"

"No. But a lot of Jack's crowd."

"Jack?"

"Jack experimented a bit when he was younger. Drugs are literally everywhere. But he realized he couldn't do drugs if he wanted a career. He decided to go in the other direction. Eat clean. Work out." Sadness seeped out of her. "All that and he got sick anyway."

Luke slid his fingers into her hair and leaned forward to kiss her lightly on the lips. "Life's not fair, is it?"

"No, it's not."

***

With each mile he drove the next day, Luke's dread of reaching his childhood home outside Des Moines grew stronger. While he looked forward to spending time with his brother, putting up with his father's constant digs did not sit as well.

He'd tried talking to his father about it, but nothing changed. He'd tried ignoring the barbs launched his way, the comparisons made between him and Paul. Everyone knew he'd messed up. His father, however, seemed unable to let it go and move on. He seemed to believe Luke hadn't suffered enough for what should be in the past. Luke often wondered if that was true.

At least the roads were clear, which helped him to relax a bit during the two-hour drive. But still he drove cautiously with both hands on the wheel. He wondered if he'd ever be able to relax while driving. Sometimes, on an especially nice summer day when there was no threat of rain and the roads were clear and dry, he came close to enjoying the experience. But avoiding getting behind the wheel had become second nature to him. Red Bud was small enough he could walk almost everywhere. Sometimes in the summer he rode his bike on errands downtown. He'd become used to shopping in quantities he could carry home easily.

Only his weekly trip to the AA meeting in Shenandoah forced him into his Jeep, regardless of the weather. He told himself his discomfort behind the wheel was stupid. The accident had been just that, an accident, the details of which he couldn't remember. The car sliding, somebody screaming, the impact and then...nothing. Just a black hole where his memory should be, until he woke up in the hospital. And the three-year nightmare began.

He forced his mind away from the memories, eased his grip on the steering wheel, and made himself think of more pleasant things. Devonny. Definitely a more pleasant topic. Seeing his brother. Maybe they could sneak away from the house for a while. Even a walk around the old neighborhood after dinner would be welcome. Just him and Paul, like it used to be.

Paul would like Devonny, Luke decided. He wouldn't judge her, even if he knew her history in the adult film industry. But his father? No way would Luke subject Devonny to his father's judgmental attitude. If he said anything even remotely offensive to her, Luke decided, that would be it. He'd cut off all ties to him then and there.

If he'd do it for Devonny, why hadn't he done it for himself? He didn't have to subject himself to his father's insults anymore. He'd never had to. He'd done it all these years because...why? For Paul? For his mother's memory? Or because, deep down, he believed he deserved it?

But he didn't. He didn't have to keep paying for the accident for the rest of his life. If his father wanted to wallow in painful memories, that was his choice. But Luke didn't have to keep him company.

Today was the day, Luke decided as he approached the city limits of Des Moines. If his dad was going to use him as a verbal punching bag again, he would get up and walk out. Paul would understand. Maybe Paul had been waiting for such a day. Maybe, Luke, thought with surprise, so had his father.

***

Luke put the Jeep in park and stared at his childhood home. The tall two-story white clapboard with the peaked roof hadn't changed in years.

His father, with nothing better to do in his spare time, diligently maintained the house's exterior and the yard. Because, that was what was on the outside. That was what people saw.

But inside? The carpet and furnishings were dingy and dated. The curtains clogged with dust. Cobwebs hung in corners. His mother would be appalled, but it didn't seem to matter to Russell Bradshaw. Every once in a while he ran the vacuum around the four rooms he used: kitchen, bathroom, bedroom and den. The rest of the house could deteriorate around him and he wouldn't notice.

But all most people saw was the outside, Luke mused as he opened the Jeep's hatch and grabbed the food he'd promised to bring. What they hid on the inside didn't reveal itself until you scratched the surface. Sometimes, he supposed, you got more than you bargained for. You found out things about people you didn't want to know. Things they'd been trying to hide. For years.

Like me, he admitted as he approached the front steps. He'd been hiding his past, his shame, afraid of the judgment, afraid...of everything, he supposed. So he couldn't judge his father or anyone else for doing exactly what he'd been doing.

He juggled the bags of food and opened the storm door. But the inner door was locked. He knocked awkwardly, trying not to drop anything, but a bag of frozen peas slipped out and hit the ground. He left them.

After a few minutes he heard footsteps, the lock turned, and his father greeted him. "Oh. It's you," he said, and bent to pick up the peas. "You dropped something."

"Nice to see you too, Dad," Luke said, wondering if the sarcasm would go right over the old man's head.

"For chrissakes. Don't start with me. I thought it might be your brother at the door, is all," his father grumbled as he followed Luke down the hall to the kitchen. Russell tossed the bag of peas on the counter where they ricocheted off the toaster and slid to the floor.

Luke refrained from comment although ten comebacks popped into his head. Maybe, for the first time in about ten years, they could have a pleasant holiday meal together. But if the beating the peas were taking was any indication, this holiday would be like all the others. He wondered if Paul had a recipe for pea puree.

Luke began to unpack the bags. "How have you been?" he asked, glancing at his father who frowned at every item he set on the counter. He scowled at the package of Parkerhouse rolls Luke had brought.

"We're not having the good rolls from Dennison's this year?"

"Not unless Paul's bringing them." He forced a cheery note into his tone. "You got the turkey going, I see."

"Ain't that hard. Read the directions."

"Great!" Luke made himself smile at his father. "Want to peel some potatoes?"

"You and Paul and Julie are cooking."

"Julia's coming?" Paul hadn't mentioned that.

"Isn't that what I just said?"

"Technically, no," Luke muttered as he turned to the sink and tumbled the potatoes into a colander.

He'd met Julia the Snob a couple of times the previous summer. Once, when they'd taken his father out to his favorite steak house for a birthday dinner. Luke had tagged Julia as high maintenance from the start. Appearances seemed to be everything to her and she'd found fault with everything that day. The table location, the menu, the wine. Luke couldn't figure out why Paul put up with her. But his brother didn't seem to mind her whining at all and even appeared amused by it. Appearances, Luke thought again. Julia's exterior would rate a ten, but her personality? In the low threes, at best.

He could imagine Julia's reaction to the house. She'd be dressed in one of her designer label outfits. Nails, makeup, hair. Done, done and done. He wouldn't be surprised if she insisted on dusting the chairs before she sat on any of them. He grinned just thinking about it.

"What's so funny?" his father grumbled.

"Nothing. Nothing's funny." Around here.

He wished he'd invited Devonny. She'd planned to spend the day with Loretta and a couple of her widowed friends, but Loretta had developed a cold. Devonny insisted she didn't mind spending the day alone. And, Luke admitted, he wasn't ready for Devonny to meet his family, see the way his father lived, or have subjects he'd rather not discuss brought up at dinner.

Coward. Luke shied away from the description of himself that popped into his head. He knew he had a long way to go before he became the kind of man worthy of Devonny.

"How's work?" Luke asked. Forcing small talk was like pulling teeth. They had nothing to discuss with each other, nothing in common. Except his brother.

"Never changes," Russell informed him. "'Cept I work harder for the same money, seems like."

"I think a lot of people feel that way."

"Course they do. You watch the news? We got a damn fool in the White House."

"That's what I hear," Luke said, knowing there was nothing he could do to placate his father.

"Damn politicians. Taking money out of our pockets to line theirs."

Luke was content to let his father ramble on in this vein while he peeled the potatoes. About the time Russell wound down, Paul and Julia arrived. They didn't have to ring the bell. His father went to meet them and Luke could hear much more enthusiastic greetings than he'd received.

Luke pulled a towel from the kitchen drawer to wipe his hands. The towel was old and worn and faded. One surely his mother had chosen. He wished with all his heart that she was there. She'd always been able to soothe his father, shush him whenever he became overly critical. She'd gone to bat for Luke on more than one occasion. It made Luke sad she'd felt she had to. But he'd sensed his father's disappointment in him long before the accident.

The three of them, laden with bags, bowls and bottles, arrived in the kitchen. "Hey, little brother." Paul set his things down and man-hugged Luke, clapping him on the back. They were almost the same height but Paul was sturdier, stockier.

"Happy Thanksgiving, Luke," Julia said, with what looked like a genuine smile. She had the put-together style of the advertising executive she was. Her green sweater complimented the blond highlights in her hair and the sparkle in her dark blue eyes.

"Happy Thanksgiving, Julia. Nice outfit."

"Thank you." Luke suspected this was usually the best compliment he could give Julia. He knew from Paul that compliments made her happy. Temporarily, anyway.

"We have pie." She extracted two boxes from one of the bags. "Pumpkin and apple. And real whipped cream." She proudly set the container next to the pies.

Russell looked over her shoulder. "Why didn't you bake pies? These are store-bought."

Julia looked up at him. "I don't bake." Her haughty tone implied such a task might be beneath her.

Paul looked up from where he was rummaging in a drawer for a corkscrew. "They're from Dennison's, Dad," he said. "You like their stuff."

"Did you bring rolls? Your brother didn't."

Paul looked at Luke. Luke sighed. "I did. But not from Dennison's. Hell, I live two hours away." He looked at his father. "If you wanted Dennison's rolls so badly, you should have mentioned it to Paul. Or better yet, picked them up yourself."

"I got the damned turkey, didn't I? I even got your mother's china out. Too bad she isn't here. Bet you wouldn't be talking to me like that if she were."

Paul cut in. "Come on, Dad. He didn't mean anything by it."

"The hell he didn't," Russell said. Luke held his father's gaze waiting for the next arrow.

"I'm gonna see what time the game's on." Russell pushed away from the counter and went into the den.

Julia's gaze went from Paul to Luke and back. "Should I go talk to him or something?"

"Sweetheart." Paul looped an arm around her neck and kissed her hair. "You might as well. You're useless in the kitchen."

She didn't take offense, but instead giggled. "You know me so well." She accepted the glass of wine Paul poured for her and went to join Russell.

Paul rolled up his sleeves. "Okay, what've we got?"

Luke pointed. "Potatoes. Dad's got the turkey in, but you might want to check on it. I'll do the sweet potatoes next. You brought the green bean casserole?"

"Sure did. Just needs to bake."

"And the cranberries?"

"Yeah," Paul whispered loudly. "Don't tell anyone, but it's from the deli near my office."

"So now all we need is for Dennison's to open up and give us some rolls and we can have one big happy family Thanksgiving."

"That's pretty much all it will take."

***

"How come you never bring your girlfriend around?" his father asked after they sat down to eat. "Don't you have one? Or can't you find one as nice as Julie here?"

Julia beamed, even though he'd gotten her name wrong. When had the two of them become such good friends? Over beer and wine and the game? Julia had made at least two appearances in the kitchen for refills.

Luke looked at Paul who was busily addressing his plate of food. "Actually, I have met someone."

"Really?" Julia cut into a slice of turkey. "Is this the adult film actress? What's she like?"

Paul choked on his food. Julia's knife froze. She gave Luke an apologetic look.

Luke's gaze clashed with Paul's. "Her name's Devonny," Luke replied "She works at the high school now. She no longer does adult films."

His father stared at Luke. "What did you say?"

"She works at the high school—"

"I heard that part," his father snarled.

"But she used to be an adult film actress." Luke held his father's gaze. These people, well, except for Julia, or so he thought, were intimately familiar with his shortcomings, his failures, his entire history. Paul had never held any of it against him, but his father held it all against him. For years. He'd set himself up as Luke's judge and jury and condemned him. Maybe joining forces with Devonny was a way out. Maybe that's why he felt something like relief that Julia had blurted out her history. It would give his father something else to hold against him, so he could finally once and for all say, "I'm done." Done being judged. Done being put down. Done being reminded.

His father started to laugh. And once he got started, he couldn't seem to stop. But he was the only one. He laughed until his face was red and tears dampened his eyes, before finally getting hold of himself. He picked up his fork again. "You three. How'd you come up with that? You sure had me going there for a minute."

"Also, she's pregnant," Luke said, warming to the subject.

"What in the hell are you talking about?" his father nearly shouted.

"You asked," Luke said, feigning innocence, wondering what in the devil had gotten into him. He never told his father anything about his personal life because to do so would to be welcome even more criticism. "You wanted to know about the woman I've been seeing."

Russell looked around the table in consternation before he turned back to Luke. "This isn't a joke?"

"Nope."

"A pregnant former porn star, huh?" His gaze went to Paul before it moved on to Julia. Paul had his game face on. Julia's expression mixed embarrassment with guilt. She'd stopped eating. "That's about what I'd expect of you." His father put his head down and started shoveling food into his mouth.

"Glad to know I've finally met your expectations," Luke muttered, his appetite for the subject and the food on his plate dwindling.

"Is she...does she...?" Julia, bless her heart, was clearly out of her depth, and trying to cover her faux pas with polite conversation. She looked at Paul hoping for some help.

He, in turn, looked at Luke. Luke couldn't tell if Paul was amused or exasperated.

"The baby's due in February," Luke said to no one in particular. "It's not mine, in case you were wondering."

"How…nice?" Julia dropped her gaze and toyed with her food.

A few moments of silence ensued when the only sounds were the clatter of utensils against plates and chewing. From the corner of his eye Luke saw his father darting glances at him. But apparently he had no wish to pursue the subject.

"Hey, Dad," Paul finally said, in an effort to rescue them all. "Remember that case I told you about last summer?"

"Which one?"

"The guy who broke into his neighbor's house and the neighbor shot him?"

Luke picked up his fork and tuned out the discussion of the legal case. Somehow there'd been a shift in the balance of power between him and his father. Was it because of Devonny? Because in his father's eyes, her history was even more damning than Luke's? He hated to think so, because Devonny was, he hoped, going to be a permanent part of his life. Which meant his father would have to accept her or cut all ties with him.

Luke was done hiding. He could feel himself getting closer to bringing every bit of his history out into the open. It was the only way, he could see that now, to banish the shadows of his past once and for all.

***

Once they were in the kitchen, Julia said, "Luke, I'm so sorry. It just slipped out."

"Wine tends to loosen her tongue. Right, sweetheart?" Paul said.

"It's okay, Julia," Luke said. "You're forgiven."

"Just for the record, I told her not to say anything unless you did," Paul assured him. He tapped Julia on the nose. "No more wine for you."

"Good," Julia said. "I can't keep up with your dad, anyway."

Luke and Paul cleaned up while Julia made coffee and sliced the pies. Russell had settled into his recliner to watch the game.

"Why'd you have to tell him the other stuff about your girlfriend?" Paul asked.

Luke could feel his defiance building. "Why shouldn't I?"

"It seemed like you did it to piss him off, is all."

Luke was aware of Julia listening but he didn't care. He continued to scrape leftover potatoes and gravy into plastic containers. "Why should he be pissed off?" Luke asked reasonably.

Paul was silent as he rinsed dishes and loaded the dishwasher.

"You know, that's actually a good question," Julia said.

Paul glanced her way and Luke welcomed what seemed like a surprising show of support. He waited, silently encouraging her to continue.

"Your father isn't dating her. It shouldn't make any difference to him who you choose to be with, should it?" She looked at Luke. "From what Paul says, you two aren't especially close and you hardly ever see him anyway."

"She has a point," Luke said to Paul.

"I'm sure she's a lovely person," Julia said.

"She is." Luke was rapidly revising his opinion of Julia and decided to quit adding "the Snob" to her name. "So are you."

Julia's cheeks turned pink. "Thank you. Not everyone gets that about me." She giggled.

"I'm pretty sure Paul does." Luke elbowed his brother on the way to the refrigerator. Luke felt better about his family than he had in a long time.

Chapter Fourteen

Devonny slept in and decided she now understood why students moaned and groaned about going back to school. She planned to thoroughly enjoy the Thanksgiving weekend. She'd shop and bake. Spend more time with Luke when he returned home tomorrow. Thinking about him made her smile. She liked him so much. Maybe more than liked. But she was afraid to put that word to what she felt.

Luke was an observer. He'd admitted that to her. How he'd always been fascinated by human nature. Which made him perfect for his job as guidance counselor to teenagers, she supposed. If she'd learned anything in the few months she'd been working at the high school it was that most of those kids wanted someone to listen to them. To hear them. To validate what they were feeling. And teenagers, she'd also noticed, felt a lot.

She'd missed all that. The drama, the ups and downs of high school life, the fights and the making up. The fickleness and the loyalties, as emotions and hormones vied for top spot.

Luke had left for Des Moines this morning but foolishly, or so Devonny told herself, she missed him. Loretta had a bad cold and everyone else Devonny knew was busy with their own families or holiday travels. She was alone and trying not to mind it at all.

She had a chicken roasting in the oven along with some new potatoes. She planned to sauté her favorite vegetables later and enjoy a delicious meal all by herself.

Then someone knocked on the front door. She couldn't imagine who it could be. Certainly not Loretta who Devonny hoped knew better than to be out in this weather. Especially since Devonny had also reminded her she was only a phone call away. A glance out the front window showed a car she didn't recognize in her driveway. She looked through the peephole and quickly drew back. She put the chain across, opened the door, and peered through the narrow opening. The very last person she expected to see stood on her stoop.

"Are you going to let me in?" her mother demanded. "Or leave me out here to freeze to death?"

Devonny closed the door, debating how to answer that question. Joy Harmon would not freeze to death. She'd get back in that car, which had to be a rental, and drive herself back to the airport, or wherever she'd come from. Devonny didn't care what she did. But she didn't want her mother in her house. Not here in this place she'd created all on her own, the one place she got a say in who entered.

"Devonny, for God's sake. Open the door."

You can open the door. That doesn't mean you have to let her in. Literally or figuratively.

Jack?

She's still your mother. But you're no longer a child. Don't let her push you around.

Reluctantly Devonny opened the door. A blast of cold air threatened to suck all the warmth out of the living room, but Devonny held her ground.

"What do you want?"

"I should think that would be obvious. I want to see my daughter."

"You've seen me." Devonny knew she was behaving childishly when she started to close the door.

Joy put her gloved hand on the door and pushed it back toward Devonny. "For God's sake, Devonny. I'm coming in."

She sidled in through the partially opened door. Devonny closed it behind her. Her mother looked the same as she remembered. Chin-length ash blond hair. A figure that benefited from regular visits to the gym. The same determined set to her jaw, the same hard look in her ice-blue eyes.

Her mother was assessing her as well. "You look like you're putting on weight," she said, narrowing her eyes to take in Devonny's oversized baggy blue sweater and leggings, the fuzzy socks on her feet. "Probably too much meat and potatoes." She sniffed the air. "You're cooking? It smells delicious. What is it?"

"Chicken. And potatoes."

Joy began to unbutton her coat. Devonny put out a warning hand. "I didn't invite you to stay."

"I'm your mother. I don't need an invitation." She shrugged out of the coat and when Devonny didn't offer to take it, she tossed it over the back of the nearest chair.

Devonny couldn't decide how she felt about her mother's sudden appearance. Resentful certainly came to mind. She couldn't get out of her head the way her mother had behaved, not just at Jack's memorial service, but ever since Devonny had defied Joy and dated Jack.

She didn't need her mother. And certainly not this overbearing, bull-in-a-china-shop one who'd run roughshod over Devonny since the moment of her birth.

Maybe that's the only way she knows how to be.

Shut up, Jack. Besides, how can you be on her side?

I'm not. But you'd be surprised what you learn once you're on this side.

Joy took a seat on the sofa like she belonged there. Like Devonny had invited her to make herself comfortable. "Aren't you going to sit down?"

"What do you want, Mother?"

"I told you. I want to see my daughter."

"How did you find me?"

Joy gave a snort. "It's not that hard. I have your social security number, and your driver's license number. A simple search of public records and there you were. Though I have to admit, Iowa came as a bit of a surprise. However did you end up here?"

"You can't stay," Devonny said.

"I don't plan to," Joy assured her.

"I don't know why you came. There's no reason I can think of why you'd want to see me."

"I had to do something. You wouldn't answer my calls. Or my texts. Or my emails."

"That's because I didn't want to talk to you. I have nothing to say to you." Devonny had deleted her mother's texts without reading them and ignored the emails. She'd deleted the voice mail messages without listening to them and had stopped just shy of blocking her mother's number altogether.

"Oh, come now, Devonny. I know you think of yourself as an actress, but there's no need to be so dramatic."

"I'll be dramatic if I want to be," Devonny declared, advancing on her mother, all the while realizing she was acting like one of the junior girls at school. "You said cruel things to me. You were horrible to Jack. You were wretched to me at the memorial service when I was, I was—"

"Devastated," Joy said in a soft, matter-of-fact way.

Devonny blinked at Joy's change of tone. "Yes."

Joy's gaze narrowed, her researcher's eagle eyes picking up every detail of Devonny's appearance. "You're pregnant," she said, staring at Devonny's baby bulge.

Only her mother could make her feel this way, Devonny realized, and she didn't like the defensiveness she felt. Like she had to explain and justify her behavior and circumstances. She didn't, of course. She was an adult. Twenty-six years old. She'd been making her own decisions since she'd escaped Joy's rule at eighteen. Joy hadn't liked it then and she probably wouldn't like it now. But it didn't matter. This wasn't Joy's life.

You go girl, Jack whispered in her ear.

"Yes," she replied to both of them.

"You weren't going to tell me?" Joy managed to sound hurt.

"It's Jack's baby," she informed her mother so there'd be no misunderstanding. "You hated Jack, remember? I can't imagine you'd feel any differently toward a child of his. So no, I wasn't going to tell you. In fact, I planned never to speak to or see you again."

"You can't mean that."

"I do," Devonny assured her.

Right now, in this moment, Devonny meant every word she said. But would she feel the same way six months or a year from now? Her anger and resentment and hurt had reached the boiling point and telling her mother how she felt released some of the pressure. She could see she'd succeeded in shocking Joy.

But when tears surged into her mother's eyes, Devonny had her own moment of shock. Devonny tried to recall the last time she'd seen her mother cry and couldn't. The woman was a rock, strong-willed, hard-headed and hard-hearted. She was a bully and Devonny had learned early on the only way to deal with bullies was to stand up to them.

"You were all I had," Joy finally managed. She rummaged in her purse for a tissue and dabbed at her eyes. "Please sit down. Please talk to me."

"I don't want to." But Devonny took a seat anyway.

"I know it's my fault you want nothing to do with me," Joy began, a tremor in her voice. "I was angry. I know that drove you away. But is this the life you want? Barefoot and pregnant in some anonymous town in Iowa? You could have been so much more, Devonny. Done so much more with your life. You had a full ride to Stanford, for God's sake."

Devonny's hackles rose. "What's so terrible about living in a small town? Or being pregnant? I'm still me. I haven't changed. I'm still the same person you raised. The one you used to take to the movies and buy ice cream sundaes for. I have a degree. So what if it isn't from Stanford. So what if I'm not using it right now? What did I do that was so terrible except love someone? The only thing that changed was I decided to live my own life instead of the one you had mapped out for me."

"I know. I know I had to let you go, but it was so hard to watch you throw away everything we'd worked for." She put up a placating hand. "Jack was exactly the kind of man I didn't want for you. I was sure he'd break your heart. Sure you'd never recover." Joy paused. "Terrified you'd end up like me."

Devonny wasn't sure she'd heard right. "What are you talking about?"

Joy gave a sad laugh. "Your father." She shook her head as if she could shake off the memory. "He was a charmer, like Jack. Good-looking. Charismatic. Rode a motorcycle. A small-town bad boy. My parents hated him. Forbade me to have anything to do with him."

This was the first time Devonny'd heard any details about her father. All Joy had ever said was that he'd died before she was born and she didn't want to talk about it.

"I was crazy about him. We took off for LA and told each other we'd never look back. Got married and next thing we knew I was pregnant."

Joy sniffed and shook her head. "That damn bike. He loved that thing. That's what killed him. No helmet. Taking a turn too fast. A drunk driver."

Devonny felt a twinge of sympathy for her mother. She had no idea. Had assumed her father was as straight laced as her mother. She'd never guessed at the heartache she must have felt, the grief she hid so effectively behind efficiency and discipline.

"After Mike died, my parents told me exactly the same thing I told you after Jack's service. I hated them for that...and I can't believe I said it to you." More tears surged into her eyes. "It took me awhile to realize what I had become, and by then..."

By then I'd stopped talking to her.

Devonny didn't want to soften her heart toward her mother. The woman had turned her back on her, had wanted to punish her for making her own choices with her own life. She still resented it. A few tears and sob stories weren't going to change that overnight. But at least she could understand her mother a little better.

"Thank you for telling me... I need to check on the chicken."

Devonny went into the kitchen. She basted the chicken and got the prepared vegetables from the refrigerator. Her stomach growled. "Settle down there. I'm going to feed you," she told the baby in an undertone.

Joy appeared. "Can I help?" She looked around the kitchen while Devonny set a skillet on the stove. "This house is darling." She crossed to the window and looked out at the backyard. "However did you end up here?"

Devonny couldn't explain to her mother that Jack had somehow guided her to Red Bud, Iowa. That he'd shown her this house and their daughter before she'd seen either with her own eyes. "Luck, I guess."

She poured olive oil into the skillet and added some butter, swirling the pan as the butter melted. Joy leaned on the counter to watch her. "When's the baby due?"

"The middle of February."

"You're tiny. Plus, that sweater could hide a multitude of sins. I didn't mean it that way," Joy hastened to add when Devonny flashed her a look. "But it camouflages well. Otherwise I'd have known right away."

Devonny slid the sliced onions into the hot pan, stirring them while they sizzled. Next came the broccoli. The zucchini. And finally the mushrooms. She seasoned them as they softened and then took the chicken and potatoes out of the oven. Her stomach growled again. She smiled. She always thought her stomach growling was the baby's way of talking to her, telling her she was hungry.

"I should go. Let you enjoy your dinner," Joy said, though she made no move away from the counter. Clearly she expected an invitation.

It's the holidays. Do you want to be like your mother? Bitterness can't be good for the baby.

As always, Devonny wasn't certain whether those thoughts were hers or Jack's, but she heard herself saying, "You're welcome to stay and eat. There's plenty." That was because she had plans to make at least two more meals from the leftovers, and take some over to Loretta later.

"I'd love to. Thank you. What can I do?"

Her mother set the table while Devonny sliced the chicken, snitching bites here and there. The baby seemed to approve.

Joy picked up her fork but set it down again when Devonny folded her hands, bowed her head and said grace over the meal.

Joy stared at her dumbfounded. "When did you pick that up?"

"I've had a lot more reason to believe since Jack died. I also take my neighbor to church and help out in the nursery. And sometimes I go to a Bible study on Wednesday evenings."

"Must be genetic," Joy muttered.

"I want you to tell me the whole story," Devonny said once they'd started to eat. "About your family. About my father. You never would talk about it before."

"I didn't talk about it because it wasn't my finest hour. And I certainly didn't want you following in my footsteps. The vegetables are delicious, by the way. What did you use to season them?"

"Salt. Pepper. Some fresh thyme." Devonny was used to her mother's evasive tactics. "You said my father was a bad boy. Was he a bad person?"

"No. Oh, no. Not at all. Although I'm not sure what kind of father he'd have made. He didn't have much of an example on how to be a parent. His father had gone to prison for armed robbery. And his mother, well, she wasn't much of a mother."

"What about your parents? You never talked about them except to say they lived in Ohio."

"They were pillars of the community. A Methodist minister and his wife. And I was their rebellious daughter." Joy looked down at her plate. "I called them after Mike died. I was pregnant and alone in a strange city and the rent was due. That's when my father said…" She gestured with her fork.

"They knew you were pregnant—"

"No. They didn't. My father didn't let me get that far. He hung up on me. That's why I never set foot inside a church again. This supposedly Christian man couldn't soften his heart for his own daughter, couldn't forgive her for the mistakes she'd made." Joy pushed the food around on her plate. "And then I do the same damn thing."

"For the record," Devonny said, "I don't consider anything I've done a mistake. If I had it to do over, I'd make the same choices."

"Even the—your film career?"

"I know you think Jack pressured me into doing them, but he didn't. He even had second thoughts once we'd committed. But Chemistry Films was trying something different, and it was something I could believe in. There's more to them than just sex. I mean, you wouldn't accuse a beautifully written romance novel of being smut just because it has sex scenes in it, would you? It's all about context. There are always going to be people who consider our films nothing other than pornographic, but I can't do anything about that."

"You never were a pushover," Joy said. She smiled. "It was one of the things I admired about you. And the thing that made me worry the most. Once you made up your mind about something there was no stopping you." She turned her water glass round and round before she glanced up. "Were you really not going to tell me about the baby?"

"Do your parents know about me?"

"Touché."

"It's not too late, you know. You could try making contact with them again."

"You're right. I could." She picked up her plate and her glass and set them in the sink. "Thank you for dinner. I should be going now."

"I would invite you to stay. But I only have one bed."

Joy shrugged into her coat. "It's all right. I found a lovely B and B nearby."

"Twelve Forks."

"Why yes."

"Tell Pat I said hi."

"Would you… Are you busy tomorrow? Perhaps we could meet for an early lunch. My flight back is at five."

"I'd like that," Devonny said, surprised to find it was true. Devonny discovered she wasn't ready to sever their ties. Her daughter deserved the grandmother Devonny had never had. She didn't have to forgive or forget. She could simply accept her mother for who and what she was, and hope her mother would be able to do the same with her.

"Eleven? I passed a diner out on the highway."

"Perfect. I'll meet you there."

Joy leaned in and kissed Devonny's cheek, then cupped it with one hand while looking into her eyes. "Thank you."

***

Luke had decided to crash on Paul's couch rather than drive home. He could have stayed in his old room, he supposed, but that meant a greater chance of a blowup with his father. He'd like for once to leave a holiday gathering on a pleasant note. Pleasant-ish.

It was late when he finally settled down but he texted Devonny anyway.

R u still up?

Yes.

Can I call u?

Yes.

"Can't sleep?" he asked when the call connected.

"I've had a lot to think about."

"Want to share?"

"My mother showed up today."

Time to tread carefully. Devonny had only told him her mother disapproved of her marriage to Jack. He wondered now why he'd never asked about her family. Probably because he wasn't ready to share details about his own. "How did that go?"

"Not good...at first."

Luke waited.

"But we cleared the air a little. She stayed for dinner."

"I'd give anything to have dinner with my mother."

"I can understand that," Devonny said. "The longer she was here, the more I began to realize she's my baby's grandmother. Do I want to hold a grudge and deprive them of a relationship? It seems, I don't know, so unfair to both of them."

"Families can be tough," Luke said.

"We had an interesting talk. I found out a few things. I'll tell you about it sometime."

"Okay."

"How was your day?"

"It was...also interesting. I'll tell you about it sometime."

He could hear the smile in her voice. "I'd like that."

"Dev?"

"Yes?"

"I miss you."

"You know what's weird?"

"What?"

"I miss you, too."

***

"I think you should reach out to your parents," Devonny said, once she and Joy had ordered lunch at the diner the following day. Or in Devonny's case, half the breakfast menu.

Joy turned her water glass in circles, watching the wet ring widen beneath it.

"They're still alive, aren't they?" Devonny said.

Joy nodded without looking up. "As far as I know."

"You've kept track of them, haven't you? I know you. You must have." The same way you kept track of me. Because you love them. You love them but you're afraid of, what? Rejection? Devonny felt she understood her mother much better now. What it must have taken for Joy to show up on her doorstep yesterday, risking her daughter's reaction. How much harder would it be for her to bridge twenty-five years of silence? To learn that her parents still wanted nothing to do with her?

Joy looked up, and for the second time in two days, Devonny saw a chink in her emotional armor. "As best I could," she admitted. She toyed with the silverware, lining up each utensil evenly. "They never moved."

"Why don't you just show up? Don't call. Ring their doorbell like you did mine."

Joy looked out the window before her gaze came back to Devonny's. "It's foolish isn't it? I'm a grown woman. I've raised a child and been on my own all this time. But I'm still afraid of facing them."

"I never thought you were afraid of anything," Devonny admitted. "You never showed it."

Joy gave a harsh laugh. "That was a front. I had to be tough. I had to be strong. I had no one to protect me. Or you. If I showed any bit of weakness..." Her gaze pled for understanding.

"But now you don't have to. It isn't weak to want a connection with your family. Or to say, 'I'm sorry.'"

"If they turn me away..." Joy blinked.

Devonny reached for her mother's hand. "If they turn you away, you'll know. You'll know what kind of people they are and that they don't deserve you. You've been without them for all these years so nothing will change. Except you can stop wondering what would have happened if you gave them a second chance."

"What about you?"

"What about me?"

Joy gestured in Devonny's direction. "They might not be so accepting of...your situation."

"Almost the same situation you were in, you mean?"

The food arrived. Devonny's mouth watered as the server set down numerous plates. Pancakes and eggs, biscuits and gravy, and oatmeal. Her mother looked at the chef's salad she'd ordered as if she wasn't quite sure where to begin.

"Mom, look, here's what I learned from being with Jack. It's my life. My choices. That goes for everyone. Your parents included. What's so horrible about anything you did? You loved a man. You married him. You had a child. Why should you be judged or condemned for that? Those weren't the choices your parents would have made for you, but they got to make their own choices about their own lives."

"Everything you're saying is absolutely true." Joy smiled and speared a chunk of hard-boiled egg.

Devonny cut into her pancakes. "I don't need their approval and neither do you."

"You don't need mine, either," Joy pointed out.

"You don't have to agree with my choices. You just need to respect the fact that I have a right to make them."

They ate in silence for a bit before Joy sat back. She eyed the plates in front of Devonny. "You're not going to eat all of those pancakes, are you?"

"Probably not." Devonny grinned. Her disciplined mother rarely indulged in such a treat. "Want one?"

"I shouldn't. But yes."

Devonny pushed the plate toward her. "Go ahead, Mom. Do something that scares you. You need the practice."

Chapter Fifteen

Devonny had almost gotten used to having Luke spooning her. He had a way of curving his body around hers and curling his arm over her expanding tummy without crowding her.

Each night he stayed over she became more aware of him as a man and of her own needs. She missed sex. A lot. With Jack there'd been a steady supply before he became ill.

That explained why, she supposed, she'd been so eager the first time Luke kissed her. It triggered those old desires in her. Those reflexes. She'd wanted to do more. Her body had nudged her insistently to do more. But to make love to one man while pregnant with another man's child? She couldn't ignore the voices in her head, whether they were hers or Jack's, especially the one that asked, What would Jack think?

But Jack's voice had been quiet lately. She didn't feel that he'd left her exactly. More that he had confidence in her ability to make the choices that were right for her and for his child without his guidance. Maybe it was time to put into practice what she wholeheartedly believed. What Jack had believed. She had a right to make her own choices and decisions. Jack, more than anyone, would respect her right to make them. He approved of Luke. So what was she waiting for?

With Luke cupped against her, she wiggled her backside against him. She knew he wasn't asleep. He responded by rubbing the front of his flannel pajama pants against her. The hand that had been lying on her tummy slid to her hip and then further back to caress her bottom through the soft cotton of her nightgown.

Every one of her muscles tensed while she held her breath to see what he would do next, but he didn't do much of anything. After all, hadn't she told him from the beginning that sex was off the menu? But she was the chef in charge of this particular kitchen and she could change the menu at any time she chose. Couldn't she?

She wanted more, but she wasn't sure how to ask for it. Or, given her current condition, if Luke would want it. She wasn't at her most physically attractive, not with this soccer ball filled with a baby poking out in front. And it might be just plain bizarre to make love to Luke for the first time now. She could imagine him screaming in horror from the room if she even suggested it. But he'd kissed her for the first time while she was pregnant. Not this obviously pregnant, though.

The hand caressing her bottom paused to rearrange a few things under the covers, tugging the hem of her nightgown up over her hips to allow that wandering hand access to her panties.

Luke scooted even closer, if that was possible, and the concern that he wasn't interested in making love to her flew out the window. He was definitely interested in something more, if the bulge pressing against her was any indication.

His hand slid beneath the waistband of her panties and Devonny's breath caught on a wave of lust. His fingers brushed along the crevice of her bottom, bringing every single nerve ending alive. She drew up one knee to allow him greater access in the direction she wanted him to go. He went there.

Devonny groaned as he sunk his fingers against the wet heat of her core. His breath was hot against her ear as he maneuvered some more, giving himself better reach. He came up on one elbow and drew her hair over her shoulder to give his lips and tongue free access to her neck and shoulder and the oh-so-sensitive place below and slightly behind her ear.

"Dev." He whispered the word so softly she wasn't sure he'd said it aloud.

She felt herself swollen and aching against his exploring fingers, wet heat seeping against them.

"Luke." She reached behind and wrapped her hand around him through his pajamas. He moaned in pleasure. Not good enough. She released him, went in through the waistband. Much better. She molded her hand around him, absorbing the shape and feel of that suede over steel part of him.

"Dev…I thought…"

Enough! She moved faster than she realized she could, given the limitations she was operating under, but she shoved the covers back, pulled off her panties, pulled Luke's pants off and sank down on top of him. She had him exactly where she wanted him. She yanked her nightgown over her head and tossed it aside.

Luke's hands landed on her thighs as she rocked against him. There was just enough light for them to see each other, or at least the outline of each other.

Luke yanked his shirt off and spread his hands across the roundness of the baby. "Is this okay?"

Devonny moved above him. "It's better than okay."

He cupped her breasts, rubbing the erect peaks with his thumbs. Devonny felt that touch all through her and she clenched even more tightly around him.

Encouraged, he half sat up so he could suckle one sensitive peak, then the other. Devonny held him close to her, her fingers buried in his hair. His hands dropped back to her thighs, each caress moving higher until his fingertips found that delicate nub now wide open for his touch. He lay back against the pillows, letting her find her rhythm, not trying to hurry her along, while he stroked her again and again.

It was a delicious kind of torture she didn't want to end. She aimed each movement toward Luke's stroking fingers, while his other hand drove her mad, caressing wherever it could reach. Her breasts, her belly, her bottom, her thigh.

Her initial burst of energy began to fade and she feared what she had wanted most out of this wasn't going to happen. Maybe she was on some sort of sensory overload. Disappointment began to seep around what seemed like such a good idea when she'd started it.

Luke, however, refused to give up. He sat up again, wedged those fingers even tighter between them, and applied pressure where she needed it. He kissed her, opening his mouth against hers, their tongues mimicking what was happening between them. His fingernail rasped against her nipple again and again and she felt the ripple effect from that touch and the one from his other hand everywhere.

Her orgasm exploded, surprising her with its power. She yanked her mouth away from his so she could cry out as the sensation seemed to go on forever, while Luke surged and thrust and found his own release shortly afterward. She stayed where she was, too stunned to move, shaking and shuddering in the aftershock.

Luke stroked her shoulders, arms, thighs. "You all right?" His voice didn't sound quite steady. She nodded, or thought she did. All she could hear was the sound of their breathing as it slowly returned to normal…

Until she farted.

It wasn't a subtle fart and certainly wouldn't go unnoticed, especially with the quiet that had descended between them.

She could see Luke's eyes widen in surprise, and the white of his teeth when he smiled. Devonny began to giggle, and once she got started she couldn't stop. Luke began to laugh too, his body shaking beneath hers before she tumbled off him and began to moan between her laughter.

"Oh, damn. It hurts. It hurts." She chuckled again. "Damn it." She tried to find a comfortable position.

"What is it?" Luke sat up, his laughter under control now. "The baby?"

"No. Leg cramp. Shit. Shit. Shit!"

"What can I do?"

"Just…" More giggles erupted. "Shove my toes back toward me."

"Like this?"

"Yes, but harder."

Luke did as she asked and in seconds the seized muscles in her calf eased.

She lay back against the pillow. Luke caressed her calf for a moment before he pulled the covers back up as they settled under them.

"I hope that wasn't too weird for you," she said.

"What? The fart? Or the leg cramp?"

"The sex."

"Are you kidding? That was…cosmic."

Devonny lifted a brow and turned to look at him. "Cosmic? What grade are you in?"

He gently poked her in the ribs. "Don't make fun of me. I'm serious."

She caught the finger he'd poked her with and kissed the tip.

"Making love with you made me feel like I was part of something bigger."

"Bigger, huh?" she said dryly and decided he needed a good poke so she gave him one.

He grabbed her hand and held on. "Not in the physical sense. Bigger as in — as in universally bigger."

Devonny's brow furrowed.

"You are strong and nurturing and, and fearless."

"No, I'm not —"

"Hush." He placed a gentle finger against her lips. "And when I'm with you, you make me feel like I can be those things too."

Devonny wasn't sure she understood, but Luke's words touched something deep inside her. She moved closer so she could kiss him. Where Jack had been all action and movement and energy, Luke's quiet presence had a calming effect. He patiently observed before he acted. He was...still. Steady. Devonny snuggled next to Luke, her arm flung across his chest.

***

Devonny came awake quickly, not sure what had woken her. The bedroom was still relatively dark in the pre-dawn, but there was an eerie circling glow of red. She blinked at the clock. Four-twenty a.m. Luke slept on. She got up to peer out of the window.

The circles of red were from the ambulance parked in front of Loretta's house.

"Oh, God!"

She whirled, searching the bed, pawing through the covers for her nightgown.

Luke sat up like someone had fired a gun. "What is it?"

"Loretta. There's an ambulance."

She struggled into her nightgown, not caring that she'd put it on backwards, grabbed her fuzzy bathrobe from the hook on the back of the door and trundled down the hall. She had to pee badly, but it could wait.

"Wait." She heard Luke bumbling behind her, struggling to locate and put on his clothes. "Devonny, for God's sake, put some shoes on. It's freezing out there."

Devonny already had the door open. She shoved her feet into a pair of low-heeled boots, and didn't bother to zip them up. She skidded down the icy steps. The iron railing was freezing beneath her hands.

"Would you wait?" Luke growled from behind her. "You're going to kill yourself."

The EMTs were carrying a gurney down Loretta's porch steps.

"Loretta!"

The old lady had an oxygen mask over her face. Her skin looked pasty white in the glow of the porchlight. Her eyes were closed.

"Need to get her to the hospital, ma'am," one of the EMTs said. Devonny tried to keep pace with them through the icy snow. Luke appeared and grasped her elbow to steady her.

"Is she going to be all right?" Devonny asked as they collapsed the wheels and pushed the gurney into the back of the ambulance.

"We'll know more once we get her to the ER." It wasn't an unkind response but it didn't tell Devonny anything.

"Shenandoah Medical?" Luke asked.

"Yep."

"We'll be right behind you."

The ambulance door snapped shut and the vehicle took off, lights spinning. There was no need for a siren at this time of the morning because there was virtually no traffic in Red Bud.

"Let's get dressed," Luke said, steering Devonny back to the steps.

"You don't have to go with me," Devonny said. "There's school today."

"You work at the school, too, or did you forget?" Luke was already dressed and sat on the end of the bed to tie his boots while Devonny tugged a sweater over her head. He admired the bulge of her tummy before the bulk of the sweater dropped and covered it up.

"They won't miss the aide."

"Of course they will. But they can do without both of us for a few hours, at least until we know what's what."

"I should have gone over and checked on her last night," Devonny fretted. "Why didn't she call me?" She donned her favorite pair of maternity jeans, then sat next to Luke and pulled on a pair of socks.

"Give me your keys and I'll go warm up your car."

"They're on the counter. I'll be out in a minute."

Luke opened the garage door and started the car. He marveled at what had occurred between him and

Devonny earlier. He didn't know how to explain to her how it had affected him. He could hardly explain it to himself. It had something to do with her being pregnant, but what was it? That elemental life force women possessed to create a new human being? He'd never quite grasped the kind of strength and power it took to grow a baby.

He'd felt like, for a moment anyway, that he was somehow absorbed into that process. Like, as he'd tried to tell her earlier, she'd shared all those traits necessary to procreate with him. That sheltering, nurturing strength she possessed.

Devonny stepped out into the freezing garage and over to the passenger's side. Luke shook off his thoughts and smiled to himself.

"I left my phone in my purse in the kitchen," Devonny said. "Loretta did try to call, but I didn't hear it." She clutched the phone in her hand. Luke could hear the anxiety in her voice.

"So she called 9-1-1. Which is probably what you'd have done, right?"

"I guess."

Once Devonny fastened her seatbelt, Luke backed out and started down the street. As he turned the corner, the tires slid a bit across the wet road.

He righted the vehicle and continued on. "You have snow tires, right?"

"Snow tires?"

"On your car. For the winter?"

"N-no. Is that important?"

"They predict an especially harsh winter this year, so yes, it could be important." He turned left at the next corner.

"Where are we going? This isn't the way to Shenandoah."

"We're going to get my Jeep."

"The roads aren't that bad," Devonny sulked.

"Not right now, they aren't. But I don't particularly like driving and I especially don't like driving in bad weather. Stay here," he said as they stopped in front of his bungalow.

Devonny wanted to be on the road and at the hospital shortly after Loretta arrived. Someone needed to be there for the old lady, to help her when she couldn't help herself. But she'd given the keys to her car to Luke and now it seemed she'd given up any choice she had in how quickly they got there.

She watched Luke start the Jeep and brush the accumulated snow off the windows. Why did he have such a nice car if he hardly ever drove it? Luke walked almost everywhere. To school. To the store. To her house. And, she supposed, anywhere else he needed to go. She wondered why he didn't like driving.

He came toward her and opened her door. Devonny turned off the engine and let him help her through the snow to the Jeep.

Once they were on the road, she noticed Luke's death grip on the steering wheel. All of his attention was focused on the dark, wet road. The sun was trying to creep through a layer of dusty gray clouds. Devonny felt like they were the only two people in the universe.

She stared out at the acres and acres of fields covered in white. Luke hadn't turned on the radio. He was so intense he was scaring her. Maybe she should have offered to drive.

"I could drive if you want," she finally offered.

"It's okay." He continued to stare straight ahead. The wipers were on a long delay mode to whisk away any moisture that might accumulate on the windshield.

"So...why don't you like to drive?" Devonny finally asked.

"I was in a bad accident back in college."

"Oh."

After a few minutes her curiosity got the better of her. It seemed Luke could answer questions and concentrate on his driving well enough. There was hardly any traffic on the road anyway. "Is that how you hurt your knee?"

Beads of sweat popped out on Luke's forehead and above his lip. His knuckles were white. "Yes. Do you mind if we don't talk about it until we get to the hospital?"

"Okay." Devonny would have liked to talk. It would have alleviated her anxiety about Loretta. She didn't like the way her thoughts tumbled over themselves with no outlet. But based on Luke's body language, there was a very good reason to stay silent.

She closed her eyes and to her surprise she must have nodded off, waking only as Luke slowed for a stoplight. He looked marginally calmer and no longer had a death grip on the wheel.

She stayed silent even after he'd parked and they'd gotten out to make their way to the ER. "Our grandmother was just brought in by ambulance," she informed the nurse behind the admitting counter. "Loretta Herman." Devonny knew a relative had a much better chance of getting information, and maybe even being allowed to see Loretta.

"I'll let the doctor know you're here. Just have a seat."

"Our grandmother?" Luke said once they were seated. He waggled his eyebrows at her.

"They'll be more forthcoming if they think we're family. I promise to come clean before they make you sign an affidavit."

***

Less than an hour later, they were called back. After their hands were sanitized and they'd donned gowns and masks, the ER doctor told him he wanted to admit Loretta with what he suspected was bronchial pneumonia. Devonny took one of Loretta's hands in hers and peered at her anxiously. Loretta's eyes were closed, but she squeezed Devonny's fingers.

"She's very weak," he said. "We'll need to do a few tests to confirm the pneumonia. Then I'd like to monitor her for a day or two to see how she tolerates the antibiotics, but if she improves we won't keep her longer than that. You can sit with her if you want until we're ready to transfer her to a room. I suggest you call and check on her later today and come back this evening or tomorrow. "Any questions?"

"Not right now," Devonny said.

The doctor left and Luke pulled up a chair for Devonny. Loretta briefly opened one eye. She was receiving oxygen through a cannula. "They told me my grandchildren were here." Her voice was raspy, her breathing labored.

"I know. I lied. I was afraid they wouldn't tell me anything or let me see you unless they thought we were related."

"You didn't need to drive all this way."

"Of course, I did. I didn't hear my phone when you called. I'm so sorry. Besides, Luke drove."

Loretta looked at Luke briefly before closing her eyes again. "I'm thinking you were otherwise engaged." Her lips twitched.

A nurse and an orderly bustled in. "All right, Mrs. Herman. Tell your visitors goodbye. You're going upstairs."

"Maybe I should stay." Devonny didn't want to release Loretta's hand.

"Go," Loretta said. "I'll be all right."

Luke said. "There's no point in us staying and you especially should not be in a hospital."

The nurse overheard them. "He's right. We'll take good care of her. Go home. We've got your contact information. We'll call you if there's any change or if she asks to see you."

Devonny pressed her lips to Loretta's forehead. "I love you."

***

Luke seemed a bit more relaxed on the drive back to Red Bud, although his concentration on the road was just as intense. She decided to chance a conversation. "Luke, I need to ask you something and it really can't wait."

Luke kept his eyes on the road. "Okay."

"Where do you stand on adult entertainment?"

Luke shot her a sideways glance. "Can you be more specific?"

"Adult films."

"Porn."

"Okay. Porn."

"Where's this coming from?"

"Let's just say I have my reasons for asking."

"Are you asking if I'm a fan?"

"I just want to know how you feel about it. In general."

"I've watched it on occasion, usually at a stag party, or some in college. I'm not what you'd call an adult entertainment film enthusiast. I save my enthusiasm for real life encounters." He shot her a smirk. "Or couldn't you tell?"

Devonny smiled at his playfulness, in spite of the reason behind her questions.

"Why are we having this conversation?"

"I'll explain. I promise. Just not right now, okay?"

"Okay."

***

Luke dropped Devonny off and promised to pick her up in half an hour and drive her to school. Once she finished dressing she pulled out the metal lockbox from the back of her closet and removed one of the discs. She kept copies of all of the films she'd done with Jack, as well as the ones she'd done with Cherry. They looked like blank DVDs with only a hand-lettered number to identify them. She chose one and tucked it into her purse.

When they arrived at the school parking lot, Devonny put her hand on Luke's arm to stop him from getting out of the car. She'd tried to rehearse what she would say, but her mind was mush. She knew only that she had to give the disc to him now, before things went any further between them. She realized she should have done this before, because last night had taken their relationship to a whole new level.

"I have to give you this," she said, handing him the case.

He looked at it. "What is it?"

"It's a…DVD. Watch it, okay, when you're alone. Not at school, certainly."

He grinned. "Why? Is it X-rated?"

In spite of herself, Devonny blushed. She looked away for a moment. "Just promise me you'll watch it and then we'll talk."

"Does this have something to do with our earlier conversation?"

"Yes."

"Okay. I'll watch it. Then you'll tell me what this is all about?"

"If you want to hear it."

"Dev, look. There's something I should probably tell you—"

"Let's talk later."

***

If anyone on the school staff noticed that he and Devonny were both dragging ass today, or that they'd arrived together in Luke's Jeep, they refrained from comment. Janet was on the phone but her eyebrows shot up when they entered the office together two hours after school started.

Somehow they survived, although last night and this morning had taken more of a toll on Devonny than him. Then again, she was carrying another human being around inside her, Luke reminded himself. Their paths crossed a few times during the day and when he asked how she was, she didn't complain.

"Let me give you a ride home after school, okay?" The weather was cold, gray and windy. She didn't argue.

Once they were in the car she said, "I called the hospital during my lunch break. Loretta's stable but still not up for visitors."

"Maybe by tomorrow she will be," Luke said. "Want me to come in?" he asked when they arrived at her house.

"No. I am probably just going to eat something, take a bath and go to bed."

"I'll see you tomorrow." Luke wanted to kiss her before she got out of the car, but neither of them wanted to give the prying eyes of the local gossips any ammunition. She squeezed his hand.

***

Luke showered back at his place, which worked to perk him up marginally, and then scrounged around for something to eat. He yawned while he waited for some leftover chicken and rice to heat in the microwave. He was going to make an early night of it as well.

The top of the DVD case Devonny had given him peeked out of the pocket of his backpack. He pulled it out just as the oven beeped. Based on her demeanor when she'd given it to him, he was pretty sure he knew exactly what it was. She hadn't known how to tell him about the films she'd done. He shouldn't have teased her, but he'd been charmed when she blushed at the suggestion.

The DVD wasn't labeled, except for a hand-written number. He took his plate to the table and set up his laptop. He wondered if she'd given him the same film he'd already seen.

He started to eat after the opening credits and the FBI warning about piracy. It wasn't the same film. This time, Devonny played a powerful business woman and Jack was her rival. Apparently, they disagreed on everything except what they liked in bed. He watched, fascinated, as they seduced each other, neither willing to relinquish power or control until they both seemed to decide, "What the hell" and physically devoured each other.

He'd stopped eating and his food had gone cold by the time the film ended. He hadn't been able to look away. Then he picked at the meal while he watched it a second time. He looked for nuances he hadn't picked up before. Devonny's character certainly seemed more sure of herself in this one. She didn't need to be rescued. Luke liked the way the short film portrayed the players as equals.

He checked the release dates. This had been shot two years after the one he'd bought. He wondered in what ways acting in these films had contributed to the evolution of Devonny as she'd become the woman she was now.

She'd been young when she'd met Jack, still a teenager when she'd married him, apparently. But the difference between her on-screen persona from that first film to this one was astonishing.

She's fascinating. At least to him. In a way other women he'd known were not. That wasn't to take anything away from them, but he hadn't been intrigued by any of them the way he was with Devonny. He wanted to uncover her, learn about her, layer by layer. And if it took a lifetime that would be okay, he realized, because he was pretty sure she could hold his interest for that long and longer.

His fascination wasn't solely because of the films she'd made. They were only one aspect of what made her who she was, and he had to admit he was curious about why she'd done them. But he'd been interested in her from the moment she'd run into him at the diner.

But was she as interested in him? He extracted the DVD and put his laptop to bed and his dishes in the sink. He padded back to the bathroom, brushed his teeth and crawled into bed. The truth was he didn't know how Devonny felt about him. She liked him, obviously, or she wouldn't have slept with him. But she was also a woman alone, in a new town, with a baby on the way. Was he simply convenient? Maybe she needed him right now. But did she want him?

If she didn't, could he make her want him? The same way he wanted her? He yawned and got comfortable under the covers, deciding he could. Even if right now he had no idea how to go about it.

***

Devonny texted him the next morning.
Did you watch it?

Yes.

Want to come for dinner tonight?

Yes.

See you then.

Luke didn't think he imagined the questions in her eyes when they passed each other at school that day. They weren't exactly sneaking around, but they were definitely trying to keep their relationship, or whatever it was, on the DL. Luke knew how small towns worked. He'd heard smatters of gossip amongst the teachers, and sometimes elsewhere, about Devonny's now obvious pregnancy. If Devonny had also acquired a boyfriend who happened to be the high school coach, that would give them even more to talk about. Luke didn't exactly relish having questions about him and Devonny thrown in his direction, either.

Mostly, he supposed, because he wouldn't have an answer if someone said, "What's going on with you and Devonny?" He'd have to say something stupidly honest like, "I don't know."

***

Luke did his best to focus on his job. Miles Winston slouched in the chair across from his desk.

"You understand," Luke said, "that a college is going to look at more than your stats and highlight reel, right? Your grades are not a problem, but take the SAT in the spring for sure. And you need to get some community service under your belt."

"Fine. Whatever." Luke raised an eyebrow at Miles's surly tone, but let it pass without a lecture. Miles would succeed or fail in a college interview on his own merit.

Luke knew Miles had been taught manners. He used them whenever he tried to curry favor from teachers or girls. But far too often this arrogant attitude took over. Luke was certain it was to cover a deep-seated insecurity and lack of genuine confidence. All too common in kids his age.

Luke opened a drawer in the credenza behind his desk and walked his fingers through the folders until he found the one he wanted. "I've got a list of places around town that will take you on as a volunteer. The county animal shelter, the library, parks and recreation. Ah, here we go."

Luke opened the file to find only a single page inside. "Shoot. This is my last copy. Let me go make a few more. I'll be right back."

***

As soon as Luke stepped into the outer office, Miles stood and began to pace. It was an open secret that Coach Bradshaw had something going with the teacher's aide. Miles wondered if the coach was getting any, since Devonny Campbell was obviously pregnant.

Probably, Miles decided.

He noticed Luke's backpack on the floor, tucked between the desk and the credenza. He'd often seen Coach trudging to and from school with it slung over his shoulder. He wondered what was in it. Miles glanced at the door, listening. He could hear murmurs of conversation in the outer office and the hum of the copy machine.

Miles didn't have time to rummage through the main section of the back pack, but he poked through the outside pockets. In the first one, he found a DVD case. Blank, except for a number written neatly in one corner. Miles slid the case into the front waistband of his jeans and scooted back to his seat.

He smiled to himself when Coach came back to his desk. There probably wasn't anything interesting on it. Just an instructional video, or raw footage for some boring guidance presentation. Miles didn't care. It was the thrill of getting away with it, like stealing a candy bar from Lane's supermarket or a pack of Trojans from the drugstore. But that sense of triumph at not getting caught never seemed to last for long.

☐

Chapter Sixteen

It was cold and clear and blessedly dark on Luke's walk to Devonny's house. He huddled inside his coat and shoved his gloved hands in his pockets. He'd added a few things to his backpack, basic toiletries and clean underwear, to name a few, hoping he'd be invited to spend the night. He probably wasn't fooling anyone, he decided, by going in the back door of Devonny's place and leaving before dawn to return to his own. But he did.

Luke tapped the door to warn her of his arrival as he let in a rush of cold air. Devonny looked up from the steaming pot she was stirring on the stove as he closed the door behind him. He paused to take in the scene, wanting to hold on to it forever. Devonny, her hair scraped up in a loose knot and curling around her temples and ears from the steam, attending to something that filled the air with such a delicious scent Luke's stomach growled in response. She wore soft pink sweats, the top of which stretched over her belly and hugged her curves everywhere else. Her cheeks were flushed, her eyes bright.

He yanked off his gloves and dropped his backpack, as he took the spoon out of her hand and framed her face in both of his. He kissed her, and it was everything he wanted it to be. He slid his fingers back into her hair, letting them warm while he teased her tongue with his. "I want you," he said, brushing his lips next to her ear.

She shivered and he straightened. He read the uncertainty in her eyes. She must have thought it had to do with the video she'd given him.

"Not like that," he corrected.

She frowned.

"Okay, yes like that, but that's not what I meant."

"Have you been drinking?"

"No. God no. I haven't had a drink in six years." Oops.

One of her eyebrows went up in question. "Why don't you take off your coat, get warmed up and set the table? This is almost ready." She turned back to the stove.

Luke did as she asked. She'd made a rich tomato-based sauce filled with chopped vegetables, spooned over whole wheat spaghetti noodles. Healthy, filling and as tasty as its aroma promised.

The house was quiet as they ate. The silence felt tense, as if suddenly they didn't know what to say to each other. He didn't like it but he didn't know how to break it either. He was afraid of saying too much or not saying enough. So, he ate and decided he'd let Devonny take the lead when she was ready.

She pushed her empty plate away at almost the same time he did. Their eyes met and she looked away first and blew out a breath. Luke reached for her hand and squeezed, rubbing his thumb along the top. "Hey, Dev. This is me, remember? Tell me what's on your mind because this silence—" he gestured between them, "is making me crazy."

She looked at his hand holding hers before she looked up again. "I should have told you about the films before now, before we—before the other night." Luke waited, sensing there was more. A note of defiance flashed in her eyes. "I'm not ashamed of them or anything." Her eyes filled with moisture and emotion thickened her voice. "And I'm sure you realized that was Jack."

Luke nodded.

"I want the DVD back, by the way."

"Sure. I've got it with me." Luke picked up his backpack from where he'd dropped it inside the door. He frowned as he zipped and unzipped the outside pockets. "I was sure I put it in here," he said. After he searched through every pocket, he sighed. "I could have sworn I brought it with me. I'll find it later."

Devonny waved a hand as if it wasn't that important. "Anyway, they're out there. You deserve to know what you're getting into. That is, if you're looking to get into anything. With me. If you do, you'll have to accept my history. It's part of who I am."

He took her hand and tugged to get her to look at him again. "Dev, I already knew about them."

Her mouth dropped open in surprise.

"After the Winston's party, you told me about Jack, remember? I'm not going to apologize for being curious. I did some digging online and I came across thc films and I...ordered one."

"You knew?" She pulled her hand away from his and stood. "And here I've been angsting over when to tell you, how to tell you. Why didn't you say something?"

Luke couldn't tell if she was angry or surprised, but he sensed dangerous waters ahead and decided to tread carefully. "I guess like you, I didn't know how. I hoped at some point you'd trust me enough to tell me yourself."

She stared at him like she couldn't believe he was for real. Then everything about her seemed to soften. "I guess I reached that point, didn't I? About two days ago."

He came to her and cupped her face in his hands again so he could look into her eyes. "It doesn't make a difference to me, if that's what you were wondering. I think those films are beautiful. They're part of your history, like you said, and they're part of what made you the woman you are now. The woman I've been falling for since you ran into me outside that diner."

"Luke…"

He kissed her and kept on kissing her because, oh God, because it was so good, and it built that slow ripple of excitement inside them both when she responded. Her fingers clutched his shirt and she started walking backwards toward the bedroom.

He got her top off over her head and unclasped her bra, holding her breasts in his hands, rubbing his thumbs over the soft peaks.

"I can't believe you want to do this," she said. "I mean, look at me."

There was little light in the bedroom except what seeped from the living room down the hall. Mostly he could see the outline of her. He let his hand drop to caress the firm mound of baby bump. "There is nothing you can do to make me not want you."

She moaned and he kissed her again, taking everything she had to offer into himself. Her past. Her present. And, he hoped, her future.

They were slower and more careful in their lovemaking, but it was just as glorious as before. She sank onto him and he gasped at the sensation of being inside her, of feeling her move against him. He lost all track of time as he caressed every part of her: hips, thighs, breasts, belly, and finally the slick swollen bud that sent her over the edge. She cried out and clenched around him, and he held her as close as he could while he surged inside her with his own release.

She tumbled to the pillow beside him, turning her back to him. He heard her sniffle. He spooned her, curving an arm around her, trying to see her in the dark. "Are you crying?"

"No… Yes."

With his fingers, he combed her hair away from her face and kissed her shoulder. He pressed as close to her as he could get, wanting to comfort her, wondering why lovemaking would make her sad.

"I feel like…" she said, her voice shaking and shuddering. "…like I'm losing Jack. B-being with you."

Luke froze. He'd known he'd have to compete with Jack's ghost, but the admission hit him hard. Was this her way of breaking up with him? Or telling him he couldn't compete?

She sniffed and reached for a tissue from the box on the nightstand. "I can feel him moving farther away, the closer I get to you."

Luke feathered his fingers along her arm, trying to understand what she was saying without putting his own spin on it.

"He's been rooting for you from the start, you know," she said with a watery laugh. Luke's fingers stilled. "So now I think, maybe…he's receding because he knows he doesn't have to watch over me anymore."

Luke resumed stroking her arm, the softness of her skin soothing his troubled mind, and he hoped, soothing her sadness as well. "Jack's part of you, Dev. He's part of what made you who you are now. I think he'll always be with you," he said. He let his hand glide over her stomach. "And her. He'll always be watching over both of you."

She rolled over so she could face him. There was enough light he could see the glint of her eyes. "When Jack started working with Chemistry, he was so excited. Claire—she's the owner—had this crazy idea to market upscale erotic films to women. She was sure there was a market out there. She was frustrated trying to break into the mainstream industry as a filmmaker so she found some backing and created Chemistry Films.

"Claire's motto was, 'For women, it isn't about the sex; it's about the story.'"

Luke saw Devonny smile in the dark. "Like the romance novels my mom used to read," he said.

Her smile broadened. "Exactly. There's nothing wrong with sex for the sake of sex, but for a lot of women, maybe even most women, the story, the relationship, gives them more satisfaction. Sexual and otherwise."

"It's about love," Luke said. "Or at least the possibility of love."

"You really do understand this."

"I watched two of your films, Dev. I don't watch a lot of porn, but I'm not sure what Chemistry is doing could even be classified that way."

"Oh, you'd be surprised," Devonny assured him.

"It's an art form. The films are short, but the writing is so tight, the scene set-up so clear, and the actual love scenes or whatever you want to call them—"

"Are you blushing?" Devonny grinned in the dark.

"Maybe. They're so…erotic without being graphic the way a lot of the porn I've seen is. It isn't just screwing caught on tape."

"I'm glad you see the difference. Anyway, Claire asked Jack if he was interested in acting in them, and he told her he was married. Claire, being Claire, asked if I'd be interested.

"I could see it was something Jack wanted to do, but there was no way I was going to be okay with some other woman having sex with my husband, even if it would help his career. But the fact was I was curious, too.

"We had a meeting with Claire and she answered all my questions, and, to be honest, I wanted to try it. I was starving for more new experiences after being so closely guarded by my mother. She wasn't speaking to me anyway at that point because she'd never forgiven me for marrying Jack. So I said yes. I never regretted it."

"But if it hadn't been for Jack, this isn't something you would have pursued, right?"

Devonny chuckled. "If not for Jack, I'd have gone along with my mother's plan. I'd probably be teaching math at a college somewhere.

"After a couple of years, he started getting more offers for other work and I took over as Claire's assistant. The films we did found a cult following and they were in high demand. The money helped us afford the house we bought before—before Jack got sick.

"And you should know this, too. With Jack's blessing, I did a couple of films with Cherry. Because Jack couldn't work, we needed the money. I wouldn't have done it with anyone else."

Luke hoped she wasn't crying again. He reached out to stroke her hair. "He'd be proud of you, Dev. Of the way you've started a new life here. He knew you could do it."

She didn't reply. Luke eased closer to peek at her, listened to the easy rhythm of her breathing. She'd fallen asleep. When he settled next to her, the baby gave a soft kick against his hand.

***

When Devonny stepped into Loretta's hospital room the following afternoon, she was relieved to find her sitting up in bed, flipping through the television channels as if she were being timed. She looked a hundred and ten percent better, compared to when the ambulance had whisked her away.

"Thank God," Loretta said when she saw Devonny. She hit the remote's power button and the TV went blank. "There's nothing but rubbish on television this time of day. I was about to go crazy with boredom."

Devonny bent and gave Loretta a gentle hug. "I'm so glad you're feeling better. What does your doctor say?"

Loretta leaned back against the pillow she'd stuffed behind her back. She was still receiving oxygen through a cannula. "The antibiotics worked. They say I can go home tomorrow, or the day after at the latest."

"And you have to take it easy? Get lots of rest?"

"Bah. I can rest when I'm dead," Loretta grumbled. "By the way, would you call my son for me and tell him I don't need him to come? Tell him I'm fine. Tell him you'll be looking in on me and he can call you for a full report, if you don't mind."

"Of course. You can count on that. If you let me know when you're being released, I'll come pick you up and get you settled back at home."

"That's so much trouble. And you in your condition."

"Stop it. Luke can come with me. I know he'll be happy to help."

Loretta raised an eyebrow. "Oh? And how do you know that?"

"Because we're…" How should she explain what she and Luke were? Friends? Sleeping together? In love? "I just know he'd be happy to help."

"Mmhmm."

**

Luke frowned as he surveyed the inside of his house. He'd looked everywhere for the missing DVD, becoming even more certain he hadn't lost it. He specifically remembered watching it while sitting at the kitchen table. Afterward he'd returned it to its case and zipped it into the outside pocket of his backpack so he could return it to Devonny the following day.

It couldn't have fallen out of his backpack because he'd closed the zipper of that pocket. The only possibility left was that someone had unzipped the pocket and taken the DVD.

He slumped in a chair and mentally reviewed yesterday. He couldn't imagine any of his coworkers doing such a thing. What about the kids who'd been in his office? Two freshman boys had gotten into a scuffle in the locker room and had been sent to the office. A couple of kids stopped by to pick up one form or another, or to ask for help with college essays or applications. But none of them had been alone in his office.

No, wait… what about Miles Winston?

He wouldn't put it past Miles to go snooping around the minute Luke stepped outside to make a few copies. Miles was one of those kids who could turn on the charm whenever he wanted to, but he could also be sneaky as hell. Luke had seen him in the drugstore once with something in his hand, while he furtively looked around. At the time Luke had wondered if Miles shoplifted. But a parent of one of the students had distracted Luke, and when their conversation concluded Miles was gone.

But if Miles had taken the DVD, Luke couldn't accuse him without proof. He got a bad feeling in his gut. Not only about what Miles might do with that DVD, but also because he'd have to tell Devonny it had gone missing.

Chapter Seventeen

"You shouldn't be out in this weather," Devonny scolded Loretta as she escorted the old lady to the car. "It's miserable. And you've only been out of the hospital for a week."

"Oh, for goodness sake, stop complaining. A little cold air and wind and snow isn't going to hurt me. I've survived worse weather than this over the years."

Devonny clamped her mouth shut. There was no reason to badger Loretta, but Devonny had begun to rethink her relocation to Iowa. She needed to stop checking the weather in LA. Sixty-three degrees and sunny made her feel even worse about the cold and clouds in Red Bud today.

At least she'd left the car running to keep it warm. She settled Loretta in the passenger seat, and wondered again about Pat's invitation to lunch. "Just a few ladies from church," she'd told them. "Melody will be there. Danielle from the diner. A few of the others you've met." Before Devonny could say anything, Loretta had accepted for both of them. Devonny reminded herself of her resolve to become more involved in the community. She'd already been spending Sunday morning services in the nursery, helping Pat's niece, Melody with the little ones. Melody also ran a local daycare center.

But today, Devonny would rather curl up in bed with a bowl of soup or a mug of tea and a good book. She hadn't slept well last night and didn't feel like socializing. But Loretta wouldn't hear of canceling.

Devonny got behind the wheel, steeling herself not to complain. Not when Loretta was clearly looking forward to the lunch. Devonny drove slowly and carefully over the thin layer of snow covering the streets. Once at Twelve Forks she helped Loretta out of the car, keeping a firm grip on her arm as they negotiated their way to the porch.

Pat had decorated the inn for the holidays with wreaths on the door and old-fashioned colored bulbs twining along the railing and the eaves. Devonny pushed open the door to the scent of old wood and furniture polish mixed with cinnamon. "Hello," she called. "Pat?" She and Loretta took off their coats and hung them on the coat tree near the door. "Maybe she's in the kitchen," Devonny said as they started toward the dining room.

As they entered, the women gathered around the beautifully decorated table yelled, "Surprise!" and began to clap and cheer.

Devonny gaped at the decorated cake in the middle of the table and the pile of gifts wrapped in pinks and blues and yellows. It took her a moment to process what was happening. A banner overhead read: "Welcome Baby." She blinked at the assembled faces. Janet and Lauren from the school office were there. So was Petty Winston. Pat and Melody and a few other women she'd met at church. And Cherry.

Devonny surprised everyone, including herself, by bursting into tears. She covered her face with her hands. Cherry came forward and wrapped her arms around her. "What's the matter, baby?"

"I don't know," Devonny croaked. "I think I'm in shock. I can't believe you flew in for this. I'm so happy to see you!"

"Hope she keeps it together when the mystery guest arrives," said Pat.

Devonny was about to ask what Pat meant, when she noted the look on Loretta's face and pointed an accusing finger at her over Cherry's shoulder. "You knew!"

Everyone laughed. Someone offered her a tissue and she got herself under control. "Sorry about that." She teared up a bit more. "I'm very emotional these days, I guess."

"It's all right," Pat assured her. "Come in and sit down and have something to drink."

Her friends clustered around her as if they were hens and she an injured chick. A plate of delicious-looking finger foods appeared in front of her and soon Devonny was relaxed and talking with all of them. The warmth of community enveloped her. "Everything's so simple here," she said to Cherry, who'd claimed the chair next to her.

"Maybe it just seems that way," Cherry said cryptically. Devonny looked at her, but Cherry's gaze was on Petty. Devonny wondered if she was the only one aware of the vibes between the two of them.

Devonny was about to say something else, but a pair of hands, fingers icy cool, covered her eyes. "Guess who?"

"Mom?"

Her mother dropped her hands and hugged her from behind. "You don't think I'd miss my daughter's baby shower, do you? I got here just as you were coming inside."

"But, but how…who?" She looked at the assembled faces around her, including Pat and Cherry. Of course, Pat could have reached her mother since her mother had stayed at the Twelve Forks Inn and would still have her contact info. Cherry certainly knew how to reach her. "You guys." She tugged her mother's hand so she'd take the seat next to her and could hug her properly. "I'm glad you're here," she whispered.

"Me too," Joy whispered back.

"Okay!" Pat clapped her hands. "Now that our mystery guest has arrived, let's get her something to eat and something to drink so we can open presents!"

The pending arrival of Devonny's baby seemed more real to her than ever as she opened the gifts. They were not extravagant, but everything was practical and thoughtful: tiny sleepers in neutral colors; crib sheets, a bath set, teething rings and burping cloths, and bibs. Cherry, being Cherry, gave her a silver spoon from Tiffany's. "I want to know at least one person who was born with a silver spoon in her mouth," she joked. Melody had crocheted a baby blanket, and Pat gave her a handmade quilt.

Joy gave her books. Complete sets of Little Golden Books and Beatrix Potter and the Dr. Seuss classics Devonny had grown up with.

***

"Can we have lunch tomorrow?" Joy asked, once all the gifts had been loaded into Devonny's car and she, Loretta and Cherry were preparing to leave.

"I'll be at work," Devonny reminded her.

"Why not dinner tonight?" Cherry piped up.

"I thought you were staying over with me," Devonny said. "Or do you have other plans?" Petty was fussing with details of cleaning up even though Pat had already told her she didn't need help. Obviously she was waiting for Cherry.

"Excuse us for a minute," Cherry said to Joy. She dragged Devonny to a quiet corner. "Why don't the four of us get together?"

"What!" Devonny eyed her mother, then Petty. "You've never gotten along with my mother."

Cherry grinned. "Neither did you, but something's changed, Dev. I can feel it. Ever since you left LA, ever since…" She gestured at the room and the space beyond. "Iowa. Somehow, it's affected all of us. You. Me. Petty. Your mother. You made changes in your life and it started a chain reaction. The four of us together? That kind of concentrated energy? Who knows what will happen?"

This kind of wild enthusiasm for the unknown wasn't unlike Cherry. She was a big believer in seeing a glimmer of possibility and charging headlong into it with all the gusto she could muster.

"An explosion, most likely." But Devonny thought of her mother thrown into the mix of Cherry and Petty's tenuous relationship. Not to mention Devonny's peculiar set of circumstances.

"Let's invite them to your place. Open some wine, see what happens."

Cherry's eagerness was contagious, as always. Devonny suspected part of Cherry's motivation was tied to her fascination with psychological experiments. But this time, Devonny found herself completely onboard with the idea.

She glanced over to where Loretta was chatting with Janet and Lauren. "We should invite Loretta, too."

"Of course."

"Okay. Let's do it."

***

By the time the group gathered around the dining table to a light meal of pasta salad and soup, crackers and cheese, Devonny began to think Cherry was on to something

Whatever reservations Joy once had about Cherry seemed to have disappeared and, much to her surprise, Joy and Loretta had hit it off. Petty was already acquainted with everyone except Joy. The four of them chatted their way through a bottle of wine while they clustered around the kitchen under the guise of helping Devonny prepare the food. She refilled her glass with sparkling water and joined them.

"I have an announcement to make," Joy said, once they'd filled their plates. Her gaze held Devonny's. "After I leave here, I'm going to Ohio."

Loretta caught the look that passed between mother and daughter. "Ohio? What's in Ohio?"

"My family," Joy said. "I haven't spoken to them in twenty-five years."

"Well," Loretta proclaimed. "I guess maybe you're overdue then."

"Mom, are you sure?"

"I'm sure." She smiled. "I thought a lot about it after my last visit. I can't explain what changed, except seeing you here made me realize it's possible to change, to try something new, something different. To start over."

Cherry grinned at Devonny. "Told you."

"I don't know what will happen, but I'm going to find out. I'm looking forward to finding out."

"I wasn't going to say anything," Cherry said. "But I'm going to make a big change in my life, too." All eyes turned in her direction. "I'm moving to Shenandoah."

Devonny set her fork down. "Shenandoah?" That was only a half hour away.

"Yes! I looked at a few places to rent online and I'm going to see them tomorrow. I'm done with LA and I want to be closer to my BFF and my Godchild."

Devonny bounced up and down in her chair. She leaned over to hug Cherry. "I can't believe this! This is amazing!"

"I'm done with LA. Here I can focus on finishing my book. I might even teach at the college. The hard part will be adjusting to the winters."

Loretta rolled her eyes and snorted. "California girls are soft."

Petty's fork clattered to her plate. "I… I guess I've got an announcement, too." She waited a few seconds and Devonny began to wonder if she planned to say anything else. "I'm leaving Doug."

Loretta narrowed her eyes at the younger woman. "You sure you want to do that?"

Petty didn't look a hundred percent confident, but she said, "Yes. It's been coming for a while now." She glanced down at her plate before facing them again. "I was afraid. Actually, I still am afraid, but being with all of you, seeing how strong you are, made me realize I'm strong too.

"Devonny, Cherry told me about your husband, and I admire the way you struck out on your own, without even knowing where you were headed or — or how you'd get there, or what would happen when you arrived. You're a survivor.

"And Joy? I know I just met you and I can only imagine what it would feel like not to have contact with your family for such a long time, and then try to heal those relationships. I mean, my family's always been right here in Red Bud. They've never abandoned me, although they might in the future..." Her gaze fixed on Loretta next.

"Loretta, I know it can't be easy, losing your husband, and your son hundreds of miles away, but you keep going."

"Easy to do when there's not much choice."

"But you don't give up. I just hope I'm as strong as you. And Cherry," her voice softened as did her expression when she looked at Cherry, "You told me what you've been through, and you rose above it to make a life for yourself. You're smart and funny and loving. And I'm so glad I met you because you make me feel like I can do anything. You made me realize I can choose to change my life and that I'm strong enough to do it."

Petty focused on her plate. Cherry put an arm around her and squeezed, and kissed her cheek. "You're tougher than you think you are. We all are. And if your family doesn't stick by you, your friends will. Right ladies?"

"I propose a toast," Loretta said. They all held their glasses aloft. "To girl power." She giggled. "No. To woman power."

"To woman power," everyone chimed.

Chapter Eighteen

Miles could not believe his luck. The DVD he'd stolen had one of Devonny Campbell's films on it and it was hot! Hotter than some of the others for sure. He'd waited until his parents had gone to bed to check it out.

His dad was all fired up about Ms. Campbell now, like she was the absolute worst person in Red Bud. "I'm going to be mayor, and Devonny Campbell is going to help me get elected," his dad declared over dinner the other night.

As usual, his dad was blowing hot air, but Miles pretended to be interested. He even pretended to agree with his father. "She's poisoning young minds," Doug ranted. "Even my own son's."

Doug hadn't noticed when his wife rolled her eyes, but Miles saw everything. Since no one was interested in his opinion, he spent most of his time observing. Lately, his mother was barely able to conceal her contempt for his father. It made Miles feel funny in his stomach. He knew a bunch of kids whose parents got divorced. God knew his parents seemed to have more than enough reasons to be done with each other.

Maybe if his dad got to be mayor, he'd be happier. He'd be focused on more important things and stop being so critical and well, mean to him. Maybe, if his dad was mayor, his mother would be happier, too.

That was probably where his idea came from. A way to do Devonny Campbell in for good. She'd be in such big trouble, she'd probably have to leave town, which was what his dad wanted. It's what all the people who were going to vote for him would want too. And Miles had figured out a surefire way to make it happen.

His plan would require some sacrifice on his part, and it hinged on gaining the cooperation of someone who might not be so willing to help. But Miles had decided he had to give it a shot anyway.

***

Miles covertly watched Brandi Valentine all through fifth period. Brandi Valentine. Now there was a porn star name for you. But Brandi was about as far from being a porn star as you could get, and Brandi Valentine was her real name.

Brandi was what Miles and his friends termed "unfortunate looking." He didn't know where they got that term. From some movie probably. But the description fit Brandi. Miles had teased her unmercifully in elementary school and tortured her every chance he got in junior high. But once they'd started high school, he basically ignored her. Now, however, he needed her for his plan to work.

He'd been thinking about his approach. What he'd say. How she'd respond. Brandi was the smartest girl in school, but that was book smarts, not people smarts. She was involved in lots of activities, but she had few close friends. Mostly she hung out with the other brainy nerds. As far as Miles knew, she'd never had a date. In a school the size of Red Bud High, Brandi having a date would be big news.

The bell rang and Miles purposely took his time gathering his books so he could be right behind Brandi as she left the classroom. He fell into step next to her in the crowded hallway. "Hey, Brandi."

She glanced up at him through the thick lenses of her glasses. Her bushy eyebrows shot up. "The great Miles Winston acknowledges my existence. Alert the media. Hell's frozen over."

"Aww, come on, Brandi, don't be like that. I thought we were friends."

She actually snorted. "Since when?"

"Hey, Miles." One of the cheerleaders waggled her fingers at him and flipped her hair over her shoulder as they passed each other.

"Hey, Macy," Miles replied, but kept on walking with Brandi.

"Go. Go, boy," Brandi said as if she were talking to a dog. "I'm pretty sure Macy just gave you the heel signal."

"I'd rather hang out with you," Miles said. He sent his best smile in Brandi's direction.

"Since when?"

"Since now."

Brandi stopped in front of her locker and fiddled with the combination. Miles leaned against the wall and watched her. She turned her body so the combination was blocked from his view. He saw a hint of pink rising in her cheeks. Brandi actually had a decent complexion, he noted. Clear, finely pored skin with zero makeup. She had the thickest, curliest hair he'd ever seen and bright blue eyes behind the glasses with their harsh hornrims. Maybe if Brandi had a fashion stylist, if she lost a few pounds, got some contacts, trimmed those eyebrows, and made a few other changes, she might not be half bad to look at.

"Want to go to the Shake Shack with me?"

Brandi's mouth dropped open as she turned to face him. "Are you for real?"

"Of course. What's the big deal?" Miles wondered if she'd fall for his innocent act.

"Guys like you don't ask girls like me to go to the Shake Shack and you know it. So what gives? Did you lose a bet? Going to invite me to the prom and drop pig's blood on me?"

"Man, Brandi. With that kind of attitude, it's no wonder guys don't ask you out."

"Whatever, Miles." She sorted through the books and notebooks in her locker, rearranged them and stuffed the ones she wanted into her backpack.

"So…that's a yes?" He did his hopeful, pleading, look-how-cute-I am face. He'd practiced it in the mirror again this morning.

She closed her locker, but she didn't walk away.

"Hey, Miles. You coming?" His buddy Connor called to him from across the hall where a bunch of the guys had gathered.

"In a minute," he said, waving them off.

"I'll buy you a shake," Miles wheedled. "And fries."

Brandi watched his friends retreat before she turned back to Miles. "Seriously. Did you lose a bet or something?"

That was such a good twist Miles wished he had come up with it. Even though he hadn't, there was no reason he couldn't use it. "Yeah. How'd you know?" He sent her another of his coaxing smiles. "You were voted least likely to go anywhere with me because I've been such a jerk to you since—"

"Forever." Brandi finished for him.

"You're right."

"And inviting me out for a milkshake is supposed to make up for years of torment?"

"Fries, too, don't forget."

Brandi was not amused. "What happens if I don't go?"

Miles hadn't thought that far ahead. The consequences would have to be believable, the stakes high. There wasn't much of importance on the horizon, except for… "I have to skip prom."

Brandi's eyes widened. "You agreed to that?"

Miles weighed the importance of his plan against attending the biggest event of his junior year. He had to commit. "I did."

He could almost see the wheels turning in Brandi's head. She had come to a decision. He could tell by the way her posture changed. She smiled at him. Not that he'd given her any reason to, but he wasn't sure he'd ever seen her smile before. Maybe because she'd had those God-awful braces since sixth grade. The braces were gone now, and when she smiled her whole face lit up. "I know you're up to something, Miles. I know there's more to this, but okay."

The Shake Shack dated back to the fifties and spending Friday afternoons after school there was a time-honored Red Bud tradition. Kids clustered in groups around tables and the counter and the jukebox. Miles's group shoved in closer in the corner booth to make room.

A couple of the guys gave Miles "What gives?" looks, but he ignored them. Brandi seemed reluctant to get too close to Connor, or to Miles for that matter and Miles found himself perching on the very edge of the seat. Brandi hugged her purse to her ample chest and kept her eyes on the table. Miles wondered if she'd ever been in the Shack on a Friday afternoon. He couldn't recall ever seeing her there. If he was going to get what he wanted from her, she was going to have to feel comfortable enough with him to give it up.

He leaned forward to get into her line of vision and grinned. "So what's it going to be? Chocolate? Vanilla? Strawberry?" He bumped her shoulder with his. "Or are you going to make me guess?"

She looked at him as if she expected any milkshake he brought her would be poisoned. "Vanilla." She lowered her voice. "And I swear to God, Miles, if you do anything to make me look stupid, I'll find a way to get even with you."

"Ah," he said dramatically. "You wound me." He nudged her shoulder again and got up to place their order.

He could sense Brandi watching his every move as if she truly suspected he had a vial of arsenic in his pocket and planned to spike her milkshake with it. Sometimes Miles didn't like himself very much. When he was little he'd wanted attention so badly that when he didn't get it, he tended to act out against anyone he perceived to be powerless against him.

Sound familiar?

That thought came as a bit of a shock. Yet Miles was a sucker, always trying to win his father's approval. Miles glanced back at Brandi. Her gaze was still focused on him. She'd tuned out the other kids who were laughing and cutting up next to her. Miles didn't send one of his fake smiles her way this time. Is that how Brandi felt about all the teasing and torment he'd sent her way since kindergarten? While all she'd wanted was friendship? Approval?

He turned back to the counter. Less than thirty minutes with her and Brandi had made him think about a whole bunch of stuff he'd rather not think about. Focus, you idiot. Besides, he wasn't going to be mean to Brandi anymore. He was going to be sweet as pie to her. Because that's the only way he could get what he wanted.

***

Miles drove Brandi home and parked in front of her house. She'd thawed out a little after the milkshakes and fries, but she was still pretty uptight. It was almost dark now and cold outside. No lights were on at her house. Miles put the car in park but kept the engine running. "I'll walk you to the door."

Brandi put her hand on his arm to keep him from getting out of the car. "Miles, wait." He'd never noticed how full her lips were. How wide her mouth was, but not in a bad way. He had a sudden image of her mouth on his, of her taking him in her mouth. He had to tamp down the fantasy before he got a boner and embarrassed himself. He could imagine her telling the whole school how he got hard, when she hadn't done anything but put her hand on his arm.

"I know you want something. You can tell me now. Or not. But it's going to cost you, just so you know. I'm not an idiot. A guy like you doesn't ask someone like me to the Shake Shack without an ulterior motive. And I'm not buying your story about that bet."

Miles decided to go for broke. "Okay. You put together the morning announcements at school, right?"

"Yes."

"Film them, edit the video, upload it?"

"Yes."

"Do you think you could teach me how it's done?"

Brandi narrowed her eyes. "Why?"

Miles hadn't come up with a good reason that wasn't the truth, so he made one up on the fly. "I'll probably need to know how in college. I'm pretty good with making game video and I can upload it alright. But I want to know how to edit and add music. And how the program you use works."

"That's it?"

"That's it."

Brandi still looked suspicious, but he sensed her weakening once again. "Hmm. I do most of it after school or during lunch."

"Not a problem."

"I can show you how to edit and how the program the school uses works. But I want something in return."

"Name it."

"I want to be your girlfriend."

"Wait, what?"

"Until after prom."

Miles nearly choked. "Prom?" That was three months from now. Maybe four.

"After that I'll break up with you."

"You? Will break up with me?"

"Yes. I'll have decided you're not mature enough for me."

That got a surprised laugh out of him.

"You don't have to do anything. Except pretend I'm your girlfriend and take me to the prom."

"Pretend?"

"Yeah. You know. Walk with me between classes. Hold my hand. Wait by my locker. No one else has to know it isn't for real, but you can't flirt with other girls. That will make everyone believe we're a couple."

"Why?"

"Why do you think? I'm sick of being ignored, more than I was sick of being picked on before high school."

"Can I think about it?"

"Nope. Yes or no. Right now."

Miles blew out a breath, but he didn't have any other options. "Okay. Yes."

He heard her let out the breath she must have been holding. "Man, you must really want to know how I put together morning announcements."

"You have no idea."

He walked her to the door, sliding his hand next to hers as they mounted the porch steps. "Okay, look, if I'm going to pretend to be your boyfriend, then I should at least be able to sell it. Can I kiss you? For…practice."

She smiled. All those years she'd worn braces had worked a minor miracle. Behind her glasses her eyes sparkled. Brandi Valentine almost looked pretty. He pressed his lips to hers. Briefly. "Do that again," she said. "Please."

He did. Only this time he lingered longer and she kissed him back. She shocked the hell out of him by parting her lips. The tip of her tongue darted out. The next thing he knew, she was sucking on his tongue and that boner he'd worried about earlier made a surprise appearance. He knew she felt it because by that time there was no space between them.

She ended the kiss and he eased his hold on her. "Where'd you learn to kiss like that?"

She grinned, and he couldn't help but notice her lips were wet and swollen. He got even more turned on. "I might never have had a date, but I've had several book boyfriends."

"Book boyfriends?"

"I read a lot, Miles. Goodnight."

She unlocked the door and disappeared into the house.

"Book boyfriends?" Miles muttered on his way back to his car. "What the hell are they?"

Chapter Nineteen

"I have to tell you something," Luke said after they got on the road.

He kept his hands on the wheel and his eyes on the road while he tried to make himself look more comfortable than he felt. It was Christmas morning and they were on their way to Des Moines. Luke knew he didn't deserve to be comfortable. Not after what he'd done.

"What's that?"

He sent Devonny a quick glance. She looked adorable in a long fuzzy sweater in a soft shade of pink over light gray leggings. Evidently it was true. Pregnant women glowed.

"I told my family about you at Thanksgiving."

"Oh?"

"Actually, I told Paul before. And he told his girlfriend, Julia. Julia had a little too much wine before dinner, and blurted the news to my dad."

"What was the news? That you date? Or that you're dating me?"

Luke choked on a laugh. "That I'm dating you."

"We don't exactly date, though. We haven't even been out for a cup of coffee, have we?"

"You're right. We'll have to do that sometime. Want to go to prom with me?"

"Why do I get the feeling there's more you want to tell me?"

"Because you're highly intuitive and I'm kind of a jerk?"

"You are?" Devonny feigned shock. "This is the first I'm hearing of it."

"All Julia did was mention your former career in films. But once she did, I told him everything else about you. I feel like I used you."

"You do?"

"I'm not proud of it."

"I should hope not." Devonny seemed amused. "In what way do you think you were using me?"

Luke sighed. He'd only seen this aspect of his behavior in retrospect, but what he'd done was unfair to Devonny. He shouldn't have given his father any more ammunition with which to prejudge her.

"I used what I knew about you to test my father. Things have never been great between us and the last ten years or so they've been even more strained. At Thanksgiving, I guess I decided I'd had my fill. So I kind of threw you to the wolves. Well, your past, anyway. I thought if he doesn't treat my pregnant, former adult film actress girlfriend, who's the best person I've ever met, better than he treats me, I could be done with him. I could walk away and think he doesn't deserve a relationship with me. Or with you."

"Luke—"

"But it wasn't fair to you. I should have let him meet you first and form his own opinion. He didn't ever need to know about your previous career. It's too late now. I apologize."

Devonny turned to gaze out the window at the empty fields.

"Dev? I'm sorry. It was a rotten thing to do."

"Was it?"

"Yes."

"Are you sure about that?"

"Pretty sure."

"I didn't even mention you to my mother when she showed up over Thanksgiving. I still haven't."

"Oh." Luke knew what that meant. He had a lot more invested in this relationship than Devonny did. He thought for a moment about how dismal his future would be without her in it. While he'd been picturing that future—her, him and the baby—she'd been anticipating...what? Letting him down gently at some point?

Devonny gave a chuckle which held no humor. "The weird thing is, I think it's for the same reasons you told your father about me."

"How's that?"

"You wanted your father to judge me and find me unsuitable so you could be done with him. I figured my mother, after being so disapproving about Jack, would be appalled to learn I'd moved on to another man so quickly. I didn't tell her because if she doesn't know, she can't condemn me. Or you."

Luke ruminated, trying to make sense of Devonny's logic, before he said, "I guess no matter what, there's always a part of us yearning for parental approval. Sometimes it makes us do stupid things."

"It's not her approval I need. It's her acceptance of my right to make my own decisions. I never knew my grandparents. I want her to have a relationship with my child, but it won't happen if she criticizes every choice I make."

"True."

"Can't we just be? You and me? Do we have to buy into what everyone else thinks about who we are or why we're together?"

"No," Luke said. "We don't have to buy into it."

"This is working, isn't it? You and me?"

"It is." Maybe she wasn't thinking about dumping him after all.

"I don't care if your father disapproves. I don't know him and I don't have to know him. After today, he can choose never to see me again."

"If he does, he'll never see me again either," Luke said.

"As for my mother—"

"I'll meet her when you think the time is right."

***

Devonny lapsed into silence. She sensed Jack's presence. It had been awhile, but it was definitely there. But his voice was silent. Maybe he'd eavesdropped on her conversation with Luke. She could imagine him ready to step in if Luke's father said one wrong word to her. You don't have to, she told him in her head. Because Luke will.

She looked at Luke. It was cold and cloudy out but the roads were clear. His concentration rarely wavered except for the couple of times he glanced her way. He kept both hands on the wheel and the speedometer hovered near the speed limit.

He was so very different from Jack, but she could admit now that she'd been attracted to him from the very first. He had a different kind of strength. A different personality. But there were similarities too. Intelligence. Warmth. Humor. Loyalty.

I'm falling for him. This didn't scare Devonny the way she thought it might. Maybe because Jack seemed to have given his stamp of approval. Maybe because there was room in her heart for both of them.

Luke looked at her and she smiled at him before he turned his focus back to the road. "I'm looking forward to meeting your family," she said.

***

"Hi, Dad," Luke said when his father opened the door. "This is Devonny."

"Merry Christmas, Mr. Bradshaw," Devonny said.

Russell gave her an assessing look up and down as Luke took her coat. "Good to meet you," he said, his tone even. They followed him to the kitchen.

Paul and Julia were already there. Both were wearing aprons over their clothes. More introductions followed.

"How can I help?" Devonny asked.

"What's your stance on peeling potatoes?" Paul asked.

Devonny grinned. "I'd consider it an honor."

Paul looked at Julia. "Sorry, babe. You've been replaced."

"Thank God." Julia untied her apron and handed it to Devonny. "Luke can help me set the table."

"What about me?" Russell asked. "Got no use for an old man?"

Except for Devonny, who was tying on Julia's apron, everyone froze, eyes fixed on Russell. Luke and Paul exchanged looks. "Paul's the chef and chief delegator,"

Luke said before he escaped to the dining room with Julia.

"Want to cut these Brussels sprouts in half for me, Dad?" He set out a knife and cutting board and the bag of vegetables. "Just put them in this pan."

The limited counter space in the kitchen put Russell right next to Devonny. He started on his task. "So, Luke says you work with him at the high school."

"I'm a teacher's aide."

"Do you like it?"

"It's okay. I'd rather be teaching though."

"Teaching what?" His tone was genuinely curious, but with a hint of suspicion.

"I'd like to put my degree in math to use."

"You went to college?"

"Mmhmm. I've been giving some of the kids extra help during lunch a few times a week. Between you and me, I'm not very impressed with their algebra teacher."

"Education in this country's gone to hell in a handbasket," Russell said. "Kids haven't got a clue about anything useful except how to send them text messages or play some computer game."

Devonny drew Russell out, asking him to share his thoughts on the subject, and occasionally Paul joined in with a comment of his own. Soon the potatoes and Brussels sprouts were ready and Paul took over. Luke and Julia returned.

"Let's have a snack and something to drink to tide us over until dinner," Julia suggested. She brought out a cheese tray from the fridge and opened a bottle of wine.

"No wine for me," Devonny said.

"Of course," Julia said without missing a beat. "What would you like instead? A soda? Mineral water? I brought both."

"Water would be fine."

"Two waters, please." Luke crowded in next to her and helped himself to cheese and crackers.

"I'll have a beer, thanks for asking," Russell grumbled. He helped himself to one from the fridge. Julia patted his arm. "I was getting to that. You know I wouldn't leave you out."

"'S okay. I been serving myself for some time." He popped the top and took a drink.

This was not the scene Devonny had pictured, based on Luke's description of his relationship with his family. Everyone seemed relaxed. His father had been nothing but polite. "You have a lovely family, Mr. Bradshaw. Thank you for including me."

Russell regarded her for a moment before he said, "Glad to have you."

Paul took a break along with everyone else and had some wine and snacked from the cheese tray. Devonny noticed his gaze and Luke's colliding more than once.

She made small talk with Julia, asking about her work, which Julia was only too pleased to talk about. Russell and Luke went to check out the football games. Devonny helped Paul with the rest of the meal and before long they were seated around the dining table.

The only thing missing, although no one openly acknowledged it, was Luke's mother.

Chapter Twenty

Devonny picked her way carefully across Loretta's driveway and through the snow back to her house. She'd made sure Loretta was settled for the night and had everything she needed, including a telephone close at hand. Ever since her return from the hospital, the older woman didn't seem to mind as much having someone fuss over her.

Luke would arrive shortly. They planned to make hot chocolate, turn on the fireplace and exchange token gifts. Luke had promised a surprise for her and she smiled realizing how much she looked forward to that. But she wasn't entirely sure she was ready to start any new traditions with Luke. Not yet. Although she'd enjoyed spending yesterday with Luke's family, in some ways, the holiday had been a bit of a bummer. She and Jack had always exchanged gifts, even when times were lean. They'd cook something special or join friends for a meal. And when they got home they'd don costumes and pretend to be a naughty version of Santa and Mrs. Claus.

Devonny's head came up when she heard footsteps crunching through the snow behind her. She was almost at her steps and turned to see who it was. A man marched across the frozen ground.

"I want to talk to you," Doug Winston said as he approached.

"We have nothing to talk about."

"Oh, yes we do. Let's go inside." He grabbed her elbow. She jerked it out of his grasp but refused to take a step back, to be cowed by him.

"Keep your hands off me," she hissed. "You can't just grab me like that!"

"Can't I? Listen, bitch." He leaned toward her, his face red with rage. The sour stench of alcohol on his breath triggered her gag reflex. "Nobody wants a whore like you in this town. You think you can come in here and mess with my life? Turn my son in to the cops? Sic your lesbo girlfriend on my wife? Petty's moving out. She's filing for divorce." Doug poked her hard in the chest.

"If you so much as touch me again—"

"Oh, get off your high horse. I'm sure you're used to getting pushed around. Just like you've spread your legs for more than—"

Devonny slapped him so hard her hand hurt. She could feel the jarring impact all the way up her arm. His fingers locked around her wrist in a bruising grip and she cried out. Doug's eyes were hard and glittering with rage. "You want to do this out here?" he growled, "So everyone can watch? But that's nothing new to you, is it? You're used to having an audience—"

Something moved in her peripheral vision and the next moment, Doug released her so abruptly Devonny lost her balance and landed butt first in the snow. A fist connected with Doug's jaw, whipping his head around. He staggered back a few steps, but then he came at Luke like a raging bull. Luke sidestepped him before Doug could connect and throw him off balance. Surprisingly agile, Doug pivoted and came at Luke again.

This time Luke was ready. They circled each other, each looking for an opening.

Devonny got on all fours and pushed herself up to stand, backing away to a safe distance.

"I told you to leave her alone," Luke said.

"You've got no say in this. Why don't you leave her alone? Or are you here looking for the same thing I am."

"I sincerely doubt it." Luke feinted and when Doug fell for it smacked him hard on the side of the head.

"What the fuck sissy kind of move was that?" Doug said, shaking his head.

"Worked, didn't it?"

"You're afraid to get too close and fight like a man. All you know how to do is run."

"I'm not running now," Luke countered.

"Good. Stick around so I can beat the crap out of you."

"Bring it on."

Doug launched himself at Luke and knocked him to the ground. Devonny swore she could hear the breath escape Luke's lungs when Doug tackled him. She edged backward up the steps and ran into the house to grab her cell phone in case she needed it. When she got back outside, the two of them were rolling in the snow, pummeling each other as best they could in such close quarters.

Doug was heavier, but Luke was in far better shape. She could hear Doug rasping for breath while he tried to throw Luke off. But Luke was having none of it. He held Doug down and pressed an arm across his windpipe. He spoke to Doug in a low tone. Devonny couldn't hear what was said but she saw Doug reluctantly nod. Luke applied pressure to Doug's throat one more time before he rolled to a stand. He reached to help Doug up, but the other man glared at him and hauled himself to his feet, wheezing heavily.

"You'll pay for this," he said to Luke as he backed toward his car parked on the street. His gaze flickered to Devonny. "This isn't over."

Luke waited until Doug started the engine and sped off on the snowy street until the taillights disappeared around the corner.

Luke herded her inside and pulled off his coat. He eyed her up and down. "Are you okay?"

She nodded shakily.

"What the hell's going on, Dev? What was that about?"

"I'm not sure exactly," she said.

"He threatened you?"

"He didn't quite get that far. How much did you hear?"

"Hardly anything. But I could tell by your body language."

"He's angry," she said. "A-about Cherry and—and Petty. And about Miles's locker being searched."

"Which had nothing to do with you."

"He thinks it did."

"Doug's an idiot."

"No argument there." She tried for a smile. Luke stepped close enough to take her in his arms and hold her. She pressed herself as close as she could get to him and laid her head on his chest. His chin brushed her hair. "Petty's moving forward with the divorce. She's making plans to move in with Cherry. Maybe she told him tonight. That could be what set him off. Why he was drinking."

"We should call the cops. You can press charges."

Devonny stepped back. "He didn't do anything to me."

"He threatened you. He put his hands on you. That's assault."

"You're the one who should press charges." She inspected his knuckles. The right one was lightly scraped and slightly swollen.

"If I do, he'll say I attacked him first. Doug's planning to run for mayor so I can guarantee he's not going to the cops. But I don't want him coming around here again like he did tonight."

"Petty warned me. I guess I should have listened."

"What?" Luke's gaze sharpened. "When was this?"

"A couple of weeks ago. He knew about the films, and he'd been talking about how he could use my background to bolster his campaign. She wanted to give me a heads up."

"Why didn't you tell me?"

"I didn't take it seriously. I thought it was just Doug blathering."

"I'd say it's gone way beyond that."

"I know. Look, if he shows up again, I'll call the cops, but for now let's not involve them and make a bigger deal out of it than it is."

"I'm okay with that. But I'm afraid Doug's going to make a big deal out of it all on his own."

Devonny pushed back the emotion that tried to surface and attempted some sense of normalcy. If the going got tough and Luke couldn't handle the pressure, she reminded herself, she was better off without him in her life. If she was going to be involved with a man, he'd have to accept her, her baby, and her past. It had become so easy to picture Luke being that man. But this was a small town with a small town mindset and small town values. She was worried someone like Doug could turn them all against her.

"Still want hot chocolate?" She looked up at him.

"Yes. And I want my present, too."

"What are you? Five?"

"I was once."

From his pocket he withdrew a wrapped package.

She reached for it. "Gimme."

"Now who's five?" He held it away. "Let's light the fireplace and get our hot chocolate. Then we can open our presents."

Once they were settled, Luke offered Devonny the wrapped package. She tore the wrapping away to find a silver picture frame Christmas tree ornament. In it was a photo of the two of them, one Julia snapped on Christmas Day. Devonny fingered the edge of the frame and stared at the image. Would she hang this on her Christmas tree next year? Was this the beginning of the next chapter in her life? Was she ready to say goodbye to Jack?

She bowed her head over the tiny frame and willed the tears filling her eyes not to fall, but they did.

"Too soon?" Luke asked.

She tilted her head back, doing her best to blink the tears away. Was what she felt for Luke edging the feelings she still had for Jack aside? Despite everything she knew about Jack wanting her to move on, it still seemed a betrayal of him, of what they'd once had. She'd always have the memories they'd made together. And, hadn't she already moved forward?

"No," she reassured Luke. "I'm just being emotional. A year ago…"

"Jack was still alive."

Her eyes watered again. They'd known Jack was sick last Christmas. That it would be their last one together. So they'd made it extra special, gathering all their close friends and family for the holidays. Taking lots of pictures. And now she had a new picture. She'd somehow managed to reframe her life, but it had happened so quickly, and she wasn't sure she'd adjusted to it yet.

Then she remembered what was in the gaily wrapped box she planned to give Luke. It had seemed right when she'd decided to do it. And…it still did. She'd have to get used to these skirmishes her brain had with her heart, that was all.

She smiled, dabbing at her eyes with her knuckles. "Sometimes I feel like there's a fight going on inside me. I think it's the present trying to knock out the past. It confuses me."

Luke put an arm on Devonny's shoulder and pressed his forehead to hers. "I don't want to push you. But you're the best thing that's ever happened to me. Sorry if that sounds corny. But I'm not going anywhere unless you tell me to."

Devonny bit her lip. "Um, you might want to open this." She handed him his present.

He tore the tiny bow off and pushed the wrapping aside. He opened the box and lifted out a silver keyring engraved with his initials. A single key dangled from it. Luke's eyes locked with hers.

"It's the key you gave me. The day I bought your house."

"You're giving it back to me? Are you — are you leaving?"

Devonny laughed. "No, Luke, I'm not leaving. I made a copy. That key's for you."

"But that's like… That's kind of a big deal. Are you sure? I mean — "

"I'm sure."

Luke allowed the moment to sink in, and slowly smiled. "Well, in that case, thank you. I love it." He leaned forward for a kiss.

She wrapped her arms around his neck. "Merry Christmas."

Chapter Twenty-One

Maybe New Year's Eve was lousy timing, but Luke decided push had come to shove. They'd spent the past week together. Devonny wanted to shop the after Christmas sales for decorations she could use next year. Cherry arrived for a brief stay, and she and Petty had given them the grand tour of the house they'd rented in Shenandoah. Then the four of them had gone to dinner. Luke had shown Devonny the farmhouse outside of town he'd put an offer in on. It needed a lot of work but it had good bones. She agreed it would be the perfect summer project.

It was now or never and never was not an option. If he wanted to keep moving forward in his relationship with her, he had to come clean with Devonny. Tell her everything.

He waited until she was ready for bed, wrapped up in her fuzzy bathrobe, her face scrubbed clean. She looked radiant. Whether she felt that way or not, that's how she always looked to him. He didn't want to think about losing her, but he knew he had to tell her about the lowest point of his life and the depth of his addiction.

"What's wrong?" Devonny plopped onto the sofa, sitting cross-legged to face him.

"Nothing. Why?"

"You look so serious. Like you got some bad news."

"Actually, I was about to give you some bad news."

Her brow crinkled. "About what?"

"About me."

"Luke, this isn't funny. Are you sick?"

"No. No. Nothing like that." He sighed and looked around the room at flames flickering in the fireplace, the knickknacks on the mantel, the touches Devonny had added here and there that made the room so inviting.

"Luke!"

He turned back to her. "I told you I go to AA, but I didn't tell you how bad things got before that. I told you I was in a car accident back in college, but I didn't tell you the whole story about that, either."

Devonny waited patiently. Had she sensed how difficult this was for him?

He sighed again and ran his fingers through his hair. "God!" he said in exasperation. "I hate this."

She reached for his hand. "What happened?"

He looked down at their clasped hands. He knew what he wanted. Devonny. Whatever else he did, where he went, how he lived, it wouldn't matter if she wasn't there with him.

"I was nineteen," he began. "My girlfriend and I hadn't been getting along. We were at a party over the winter break. I'd had a couple of beers. She was talking to her ex and I didn't like it.

"I made her leave with me even though she didn't want to. We were both angry at that point. I don't even know why we were still together to tell you the truth. Why I didn't just let her go.

"The weather was bad. I wasn't drunk, and by that I mean, I wasn't over the legal limit. But I was angry. We were arguing. She was pissed off and had a good reason to be. I'd behaved like a jackass at the party.

"I took a curve in the road too fast. The car hydroplaned. We slid off like the road was made of fresh ice. I couldn't get any traction, couldn't correct out of the spin. The car slammed into a tree and that's the last thing I remember before I woke up in the hospital."

Luke couldn't tear his gaze away from Devonny. It was the only thing keeping him going. Her thumb rubbed the back of his hand over and over in a silent effort to soothe him. "They told me April died instantly. I killed her." Tears surged into his eyes and hers misted in sympathy. He swiped at his with the back of his hand. "I found out later she was pregnant. First trimester. I didn't know about it."

Tears slid over Devonny's eyelids and dripped to her cheek.

"I was pretty banged up. My knee was never going to be the same. I'd killed my girlfriend, my child. I could kiss my football career goodbye, along with my scholarship. Hell, I'd be lucky to walk normally again. Six months later my mom died."

The damn tears built up again and he wiped them away. "She'd been sick for a while, but my dad said the stress of the accident and everything that happened afterward made what she'd been going through that much worse. I couldn't be charged with DUI, but April's parents sued mine because I was insured under my parents' policy. They'd all been friends before this happened but I was responsible for killing their daughter and grandchild.

"I got out of the hospital after the second surgery in time to attend my mother's funeral. I couldn't even be a pall bearer. My dad had always considered me a screw-up, and this only made things worse. Not like Paul, who was the golden boy from the moment he was born. We laugh about it now, and to give him credit, Paul never liked the way Dad treated me, but...

"I was in no shape to go back to school. I had to have a couple more surgeries and a whole lot of physical therapy. A lot of pain medication, too, which works even better if you chase it with a shot or two of Jack Daniels.

"To say I was depressed would be an understatement." Luke looked at her hard, trying to drive his point home. "I was suicidal."

She nodded.

"The doctor started reducing the pain meds, so I started drinking more to compensate. It helped to drown out my father telling me what a disappointment I was or how April's parents were going to take him for everything he had. When I couldn't get more pills and JD wasn't doing it for me, I tried weed. I found other ways to get pills, but they were expensive. Then I found heroin."

Devonny caught her breath.

Luke went on, relentless now. She had to hear it all, know it all. He was afraid he might find himself right back there where he'd been ten years ago, but there was no going back. "I was very clever about it. No obvious needle marks. Going between the toes, for example. Usually addicts don't start there, but I did. Because I didn't want anyone to know, of course. I couldn't leave any telltale signs. It made the pain go away, at least for a while."

Luke remembered how pathetic he'd been. At nineteen he hadn't been man enough to accept the consequences of his actions. He'd wanted to hide from them, wallow in his pain. And he'd still be doing it, if it wasn't for Paul.

"My dad must have suspected something. He barely spoke to me during that time and when he did, it was to let loose with another dose of disappointment and frustration. He was grieving too, I can see that now. But at the time all I could feel was my own pain. Anyway, Paul showed up out of the blue one day. He was in his first year of law school and the last thing he needed was to take care of his messed up brother.

"He sat down with me and we started doing shots. That's the last thing I remember until I woke up in rehab. If it wasn't for my brother I'd be dead. Or a junkie out on the street. But most likely dead."

"I'm glad you aren't dead," Devonny said.

He gave her a lopsided smile. "Me too. Most days."

"Is there more?"

"No, not really. I was lucky to be in a good program. Ninety days inpatient. I moved in with Paul for a while after that, got a sponsor, got a job and went to meetings every day for a year. Eventually I went back to school, graduated, and got a job at the high school."

"You went through an awful lot all at once."

"Yeah. Most people like to space their tragedies out over a lifetime. Not me."

"Thank you for telling me."

He looked at her expectantly. "That's it?"

"What do you want me to say?"

"I don't know. But I've told other people — women — even less than I told you and it was enough to make them run away."

"I'm too pregnant to run anywhere."

"Devonny."

She gave his hand a tug. "It's part of your history, Luke. Part of what makes you the man you are now, isn't it?"

"I guess so."

"You expect to be condemned for something that wasn't your fault. You had an accident and someone died. A lot of other stuff happened. You were a kid and you couldn't handle the guilt you felt. But that was then. You really need to cut yourself some slack."

"Maybe I don't deserve to."

Devonny's eyes flashed. "Don't deserve to what?"

"To—to—I can't explain it."

"Try."

"I don't deserve…forgiveness. Acceptance." He looked her square in the eye. "I don't deserve someone like you."

"Why?"

"Because I'm still responsible, even if I'm not to blame. Even if I wasn't legally drunk, a few beers slowed my reflexes just enough to make a difference. And afterward I wasn't strong enough to avoid a path of self-destruction, nor could I pull myself out of it. Maybe it will happen again and I'll drag the people I love down with me."

"I can see why you feel that way. I know you must think it's everyone else who can't forgive or accept, but maybe it's you. Maybe you need to forgive yourself. Accept yourself for who you became. Who you are now instead of hanging on to this story you tell yourself about why you don't deserve to be happy."

"I didn't deserve that."

"Luke—"

"Those words of wisdom. But I definitely needed to hear them."

"They're from Jack."

"Jack? Is he talking to you? Right now?"

Devonny giggled, which lightened the somber tone in the room. "No, but he hated when people passed judgment on someone for something they'd done. We all have a journey. That's what I learned from him. And everyone has mountains and valleys and stumbling blocks. But there's a purpose in everything. It isn't always good versus bad. Everything isn't white and black. Jack always looked for some deeper meaning. I try to do that too." She cocked her head as if something had occurred to her. "That's why you don't live here. I wondered why you'd sell your grandmother's house. You told me you didn't deserve a place this nice. That's why you sold it."

Luke looked down.

"Oh, Luke." She leaned forward to hug him and landed awkwardly on top of him. Her belly got in the way of everything these days.

"Maybe," she said, as he cuddled her and kissed the top of her head, "you should tell your story every chance you get. Not just at meetings. Find a way to use it in a way that would help others. Put it out there and it will lose its power."

"I want to. But I've been afraid of what it will cost me."

"In terms of?"

"My job, for one thing. Some of my relationships."

"You can always find another job," she said.

"That's probably true. Maybe. Would you want your teenager exposed to a recovering addict on a daily basis?"

"I would if that recovering addict was you. Don't you think what you've been through makes you more empathetic toward the kids? That's a valuable trait in a guidance counselor. And a coach. You listen. And you're the most patient person I've ever met."

"I was afraid to tell you."

"I'm glad you did."

***

There was a tap at Miles' door. He glanced up from his laptop when his mother stuck her head in. "Can I talk to you for a minute?"

When he didn't object she came in and closed the door behind her. This was so unlike her, Miles didn't know what to make of it. They'd never been close. She wasn't one of those touchy-feely moms who hugged all the time and made a big fuss over you. She made sure there was food in the house and his clothes were clean. Beyond that, he couldn't recall his mother making much of an effort to connect. There'd been no bedtime stories or late night chats that he could remember.

Apprehension gnawed at his gut. He closed the laptop and crossed his arms. And waited.

She took a seat on the edge of his bed like a cat who couldn't decide if that's where it wanted to be. Miles almost expected her to turn around and leave without saying a word.

She tried to smile at him, but she didn't quite make it. She was having trouble making eye contact. When he couldn't stand the suspense any longer, he said. "What's wrong?"

There was a split second of hesitation before she said, "Everything."

She rubbed at the crease in her slacks, staring at the black fabric. She exhaled on a sigh that carried the weight of the world with it. "I'm sorry, Miles. I'm so bad at this. So bad at so many things where you're concerned."

Miles couldn't argue that. It was nice to hear her admit it, but it didn't dispel the anxiety churning in his stomach.

"There's no easy way to say this, so I'm just going to say it." Again, she hesitated before she came out with it. "I'm going to divorce your father." She searched his face for a reaction. Miles wasn't surprised, but sadness swamped him. He looked away, trying to suck it up, not to let her see how he felt.

She reached a hand toward him, but when he stiffened, she pulled back without touching him. If she touched him, tried to comfort him, however awkward it was, he knew he'd lose it.

"I owe you an apology—"

"Why? Are you divorcing me too?"

He'd hurt her, he could see by the way her eyes flared, but dammit…

"No. I'm not divorcing you, Miles. I'm apologizing for being a lousy mother. You deserved someone better than me. You're a good kid, and I'm sorry I couldn't be there for you in the way you must have needed me to be." She lifted her hands and let them fall back into her lap. "The truth is I shouldn't have married your father. I made a mistake. I was young and I didn't know who I was or what I wanted. I caved in to the pressure from my family instead of standing up for myself. And once we were married…" She gave him a beseeching look. "I was afraid, I guess."

"Afraid of what?" His mother had always seemed so independent, so sure of herself and her own strength.

She gave a sad laugh. "Oh, you name it and I was afraid of it. Afraid of your dad's reaction if I said I wanted out. Of his anger. Of what my family would say, or other people in town. Afraid of admitting things to myself."

"So what changed?" Miles had a pretty good idea, but he wanted to hear it from her.

"I did. I met someone who made me examine the life I was leading, and my relationship with your father. What I've been doing isn't right for me. It isn't healthy."

Miles frowned. "So…who's going to get stuck with me?"

His mom's eyes went wide open. "Oh, Miles. Please don't think like that. I don't think of myself as stuck with you. Motherhood may not come naturally to me, but I do love you. And I'll always want what's best for you."

Miles wasn't entirely sure he believed her, but he wasn't willing to share that particular thought aloud, either.

"Nothing's going to change. At least, not right away," she went on. "Your dad and I have some things to work out before we move forward. But when the time comes, I hope we can all sit down together and decide what will work best for you, okay?"

She gave him a brave smile that practically begged for his reassurance. And she was his mom, no matter what. The only one he had, so he said, "Okay."

She patted his knee and stood. At the door she turned back and took a couple of steps toward him. "If there's anything you want to know or want to ask me..."

Are you gay? Have you got something going with that actress from the party? Do you know the shit I'll have to take if you turn into a complete dyke? What's with the porn hidden in your closet? Why did you always let Dad smack me around and never say anything?

"I'll let you know," he said and reached for his laptop.

"Okay." She left and closed the door behind her.

Miles shoved the laptop away and crossed his arms. "Shit."

Chapter Twenty-Two

Devonny hadn't paid much attention to the rumblings of the townspeople until Nick approached her and asked her to step into his office. He closed the door, something which aroused Devonny's curiosity.

Nick folded his hands on his desk and got straight to it. "I know when you took the job here you told me you weren't planning to continue work once your baby arrives." He cleared his throat. "Have you decided on an exact date?"

"Why do you ask?"

Nick cleared his throat again. "We…seem to have a bit of a sticky situation here, Devonny."

"We do?"

"You are aware that Doug Winston is head of the school board."

"Yes."

"And that he's running for mayor."

"Yes."

"Do I need to spell it out for you?"

Devonny frowned. "Evidently you do."

Nick looked grim. "Apparently you performed in some, uh, adult films for that film company you were employed by."

"True."

"A fact you neglected to mention during our interview."

"I told you about my past employers, and gave you their contact information," Devonny reminded him.

"You didn't ask for details about my previous job because it wasn't relevant to the position I was applying for. Has that changed?"

"Devonny, you have to understand…"

"Do you have an issue with my job performance?"

"No, of course not."

"Have I done anything inappropriate since I've been here? Broken any rules? Are there any complaints against me from students or teachers? Or parents, aside from Doug?"

"No."

"Exactly. What is the problem?"

Nick sighed. "The optics are bad, as they say in politics. Certain members of the school board have suggested it would be in the school's best interests if I asked for your resignation. And since you planned to leave before the end of the school year anyway, perhaps it would be best in order to avoid any…so that…what I mean to say is—"

Devonny refused to help Nick out. He could ask for her resignation or he could fire her, but she'd be damned if she'd quit before she was ready, and certainly not to give in to a bully like Doug Winston. If he wanted a fight, he'd get one, because Devonny had already decided she wasn't going anywhere. She'd leave this job on her own terms, but she wasn't leaving Red Bud, and if the good citizens of the town didn't like it that was too bad.

"I'm embarrassed for you," Devonny said.

"For me?"

"You've put yourself in an awkward position."

"Put myself—?"

"You could have stood up for me. You could have explained to Doug and the other board members that they have no reason to terminate my employment without cause, a fact of which I'm certain they are already aware. You could have told them my past employment has nothing to do with my current job performance. You could have reminded them I cleared their own background check without a problem."

"I—"

"You could have mentioned I spend my lunch breaks tutoring kids who are struggling in algebra because Bob Sylvester doesn't teach them jacksh—what they need to know to pass the tests he gives them."

"Devon—"

"But instead you decided to take the path of least resistance. You call me in here and try to get me to resign because you think that will solve the problem." Devonny stood. "But I am not the problem. Doug Winston is. And so is anyone who backed him on the school board. If he's going to pull something like this, what kind of mayor is he going to be? One who uses threats and intimidation to further his agenda? It's not good enough that I'll be leaving this job soon. You and the board believe it will look better for you if you force me out now. So here's what you can do: You can go back to them and you can tell them no way am I quitting before I'm good and ready. And if Doug wants to make my former film career an issue in his campaign, game on. I'll bury him."

"Devonny—"

"Try not to get caught in the crossfire." Head high, Devonny slammed Nick's office door behind her as she left. She was shaking from nerves and rage and a tiny bit of fear that perhaps she'd gone too far. From the hallway she marched through the glass doors to the outside.

You go girl.

That had to be Jack. She could picture him applauding her.

She had no coat and the freezing cold hit her before the door had closed. She couldn't stay out here long, she knew, but she kept walking, to the end of the administrative and visitors' parking lot and back, working off the unsettled feelings.

She hadn't planned far enough ahead. She knew she'd been naïve to think no one in Red Bud, Iowa would find out about her films. Use her past against her. She should have realized that no matter how provincial, traditional or quaint the town appeared on the outside, like everything else, it had an unsavory underbelly. There was good and bad in everything and everyone.

She'd never thought too much about what she and Jack would tell their future children about the films they'd done together. Parenthood had seemed a far-off time and Devonny had never questioned the future too much. She was too busy trying to live in the moment with the man she'd expected would be with her forever. Together they'd figure out the answers.

She recalled a long-ago conversation she'd had with Cherry, who was finishing up her master's degree in psychology at the time. "Honey, no one wants to think their parents ever did it. And the last thing any kid wants is video confirmation. Would you want to watch your mom and dad go at it?"

"Yuck! No!" Devonny had agreed. "Except, well, if it meant I could see my dad who I never met. Maybe I would want to. I wouldn't have to watch it all."

"Okay. Right. But you're not typical. Most kids don't want to know about their parents' sex lives. Trust me on this. There are a lot of actors who've performed in mainstream films where they had to do love scenes. What do you think they tell their kids?"

"I don't know. It's their job."

"Exactly," Cherry agreed. "Hey, kid. It's my job. It's what puts food on the table and Nikes on your feet. You got a problem with it?" Cherry laughed. "That's what will keep me in business when I start my own practice. Kids with issues."

"I don't want my kids to have issues."

Cherry wrapped her arm around Devonny's shoulders and squeezed. "You and Jack will be great parents. You'll figure it out."

"I hope so."

But Jack wasn't here now and Devonny wasn't sure how well she'd do figuring things out without him.

As if reminding her that she wasn't alone, the baby started to kick and she cradled the mound of belly through her sweater. "It's okay," she told the baby as well as herself. "We've been doing all right so far, haven't we?"

Taking a deep breath, she went back inside, and after a stop in the ladies' room, back to her desk. Janet and Lauren looked up but she managed to smile at them and say nothing. "You okay?" Janet asked.

"Fine. Just brushing up on The Art of War."

She knew the other two were exchanging looks behind her back, but she didn't care. She was too busy formulating a plan, something Doug Winston wouldn't see coming.

***

Luke watched Devonny chop and sauté and stir with surprising aggression as she explained what had happened in Nick's office. She was glorious in her outrage, her ire and the heat from the stove caused her cheeks to flush, which accentuated the fire in her eyes.

When he smiled at her she glowered. "This isn't funny."

He tried for a serious tone. "No, it isn't."

"Then why do you look so pleased?"

"Because I'm here with you. I've never seen you take up a cause before. You're magnificent."

Her lips curved and she stopped stirring for a moment. "I am?"

"Definitely."

"I'm going to check with HR first thing Monday, but I'm pretty sure they can't fire me without cause."

"Of course not. Not officially. But they can let you go whenever they want by pleading budget constraints or something. You don't have a contract. And if they discover something their own background check missed, they can use that as grounds for termination. They might fire you first and worry about any possible repercussions later. Whether or not they do depends on what kind of sway Doug really has. I consider Nick a friend, but I can't say I'm pleased with the way he's handling this."

"I know he has a job to do. But I'm not a bad influence on the kids…am I?"

"Don't be ridiculous. You know those kids adore you. Nobody would skip lunch in the cafeteria with their friends two or three times a week if you weren't actually helping them."

"It's just…I was going to quit soon anyway, but now I feel like I can't go without a fight, or until I decide I'm ready. The Doug Winstons of the world get their way too often because no one stands up to them. The things Cherry's told me about how he treats Petty…ugh, it makes me sick. I feel like I have to stand up to Doug, not only for myself, but for everyone people like him push around."

"You're fighting for all the people who aren't strong enough to fight for themselves. How can I not admire the hell out of someone like that?"

Devonny stared at him, her eyes bright. "Luke?"

"What?"

"I love you."

"You do?"

"Uh huh."

"Well, how about that?"

She stepped closer to his stool at the end of the counter. "You get me. I don't know how I got so lucky to have found you."

I do.

Jack sounded a little smug for once. It made Devonny smile. She leaned forward and kissed Luke. He buried his fingers in her hair and lengthened the kiss before he looked in her eyes. "For the record, I'm crazy in love with you. Not like you didn't already know."

She grinned. "Now that I think about it there were a couple of signs."

***

Mid-morning the next day Luke pushed the door to Winston Properties open and strode past the receptionist to what he assumed was Doug's office.

"Excuse me, sir. Excuse me!" The receptionist screeched. "Do you have an appointment?"

He heard the wheels of her chair roll but didn't look back and didn't knock. Doug looked up but didn't bother to feign surprise. He and Luke stared at each other before Doug's gaze shifted. "It's okay, Margaret." He waited a beat until she retreated. Luke closed the door and crossed his arms as he regarded the other man. Doug took a sip from a steaming mug as if Luke barging into his office happened daily. "What do you want?"

"I want you to leave Devonny alone."

"You're not in a position to tell me what to do."

"I'm in a position to kick your ass if you come after her again."

Doug eased back in his chair and drummed his fingers on his desk. He didn't look worried. "And I'm in a position to see that she loses her job. I'm in a position to expose her for what she really is—"

Luke took two steps forward. "Don't you dare—"

Doug leaned back in his chair. "And I can see to it that you lose your job, too."

Luke waited. He'd been pretty sure what kind of cards Doug held, but he wanted to see them laid out on the table so he'd know what he was up against.

"You think I don't remember you? I'll admit it took me awhile. I knew I'd seen you before, but couldn't recall where. And then it hit me. Those family sessions when my brother was in rehab. Your brother came for those meetings too. Successful attorney in Des Moines now, isn't he? And you? You gave up being a junkie and ended up here."

Junkie. Luke flinched and looked away for a split second.

"I didn't object when you were hired. God knows old Carl Franklin wasn't doing our team any good and I had a talented kid heading into high school, so I figured what the hell. I'd let you take your shot.

"But Devonny Campbell? She's been nothing but trouble since she got here and I mean to see her go. You come in here and threaten me again, and I'll make sure you're run out of town right along with her."

"What did she ever do to you?"

"She called the cops on Miles, for one thing."

"That's bullshit and you know it. She had nothing to do with it."

"Miles told me she saw him in the hallway—"

"When he was supposed to be in class? News flash, Doug. Miles is not the most trustworthy kid."

The ruddiness in Doug's complexion deepened. "Are you calling my son a liar?"

"I'm saying if Devonny saw him, other people might have as well. And I'm telling you she had nothing to do with the search that day. Nothing."

"Of course you'd say that. She's a professional who's not making you pay for it."

"Watch it," he warned. Luke refused to let Doug's crudeness goad him into a step he wasn't ready to take.

"There's something called moral turpitude, Bradshaw. The school board takes it very seriously. We can't have our young people, our children with their impressionable minds, influenced by those with questionable histories. It's not to be tolerated. So I suggest you watch your step."

"She's done nothing but good in this community since she got here. She looks out for her neighbors and volunteers at the church. She's done nothing but help those kids you're so bent on protecting. So back off."

Doug leaned forward as if he wanted to burn Luke with the strength of his stare. "A background in the porn industry is unacceptable for a school environment. Do you know what it will do to this town when word gets out? And trust me, it will get out. The school board will get nailed for hiring her, for allowing her to work with and influence children." He sat back. "She's out of here. It's up to you whether you go with her or not."

Luke leaned on the desk, bracing himself so he could get in Doug's face. "We're not going anywhere. You want a fight? You got one."

"Please. Calling it a fight suggests the possibility you'll win. I'll make sure you never work in any school in this country again. Is she really worth losing your career over? She must be one sweet piece of ass if you—"

Luke leapt over the desk and shoved Doug. His chair crashed into the credenza behind him. Luke had never felt such rage. It wasn't just the threats, it was how Doug refused to see Devonny as anything but a sex object, regardless of what she'd accomplished. His fingers were reaching for Doug's throat. He pictured himself squeezing, seeing Doug's eyes bulge out, the breath leaving his body.

The door behind them flew open. "Oh, my God!" Margaret screeched. She had a phone in her hand. "I'm calling the cops."

Luke froze. He wouldn't be able to protect Devonny from behind bars. He was afraid he'd done more harm than good by coming here today. He settled for grabbing Doug by his jacket and shoving him one more time. "Call her off."

"Margaret," Doug yelled. "Hang up the phone. We don't need the sheriff here."

"Are you sure?" her worried gaze went from Doug to Luke and back.

"Yes, dammit. It's a simple misunderstanding. Nothing more."

Chastened, Margaret nodded and returned to her desk.

"There's no misunderstanding," Luke said, softly enough so Margaret couldn't hear. "I think we understand each other perfectly." Luke let him go and turned to leave.

"You're going to regret this, *Coach*. All of it."

Luke turned back. "Oh yeah? Maybe I won't. Not after I have a chat with a certain massage therapist about how often you've required her…services."

☐

Chapter Twenty-Three

Emmaline crossed her arms and listened to Doug rant as he paced at the foot of the bed. She hadn't expected to see him tonight. She'd taken a lavender-scented bath earlier and was already in bed with one of her favorite magazines when he'd shown up.

Her heart had lifted at the sight of him, but he'd barely acknowledged her. Now it seemed, his only interest was recruiting her for his cause, and she was growing more irritated with him by the minute.

"I've got it all planned," he said. "Even though the election isn't for months. 'Keep Red Bud Clean' is a catchy slogan. *The Record* will do an interview. God knows that paper could use some actual news. I'll drop a few choice words into a few influential ears at the diner. Give a speech at the Rotary Club. The townspeople deserve to know they've been hoodwinked by a newcomer. It's brilliant, right?"

Emmaline understood the gist of Doug's plan. He'd had a bug up his ass about Devonny Campbell ever since the night of his big party. Emmaline had heard all about it, about Devonny's LA friend, Cherry, cozying up to his wife. Emmaline had actually found that encouraging. Petula was fooling no one, except perhaps Doug.

He was also sure Devonny Campbell sicced the drug-sniffing dog on his son's locker earlier in the year. And ever since he'd discovered her former career in the porn industry, he was determined to destroy her. But what bothered Emmaline was that he seemed to be doing it more for his career than any sense of genuine moral outrage. "What has the woman done that's so terrible?"

Doug stared at her mouth agape. "How can you ask me that? Have you heard one word I've said?"

Emmaline tossed her magazine aside. "Oh, yes, I heard it all." Her *lover* was rapidly ruining her peaceful evening. "That doesn't mean I agree with it."

"What are you saying?"

"I'm saying I've heard only complimentary things about her from everyone but you. Katrina Clark told me how Devonny helped her daughter with algebra. Set up a lunchtime study group in the library. Her daughter was flunking and now she's making A's. Melody Callahan over at the day care says Devonny helps out at the church nursery every Sunday. She drives her neighbor to church and to her doctor's appointments. Visits her in the hospital. Devonny Campbell does not sound like the horrible person you're making her out to be. In fact, she sounds like the kind of person you'd want more of in this town."

Doug sneered. "A person who takes her clothes off for a living?"

"That's something she *did*, Doug. Not who she is."

"I guess you're an expert."

"Do you know who you sound like? Your father. Congratulations, Doug. It took you forty years, but you turned out exactly like him."

"I did not!"

"Oh really? You're acting as judgmental about Devonny Campbell as your father was about me. He had no idea who I was. He only knew my last name, the color of my skin and where my family came from. And he decided that wasn't good enough for him or his son. Admit it. You have no idea who Devonny Campbell really is and you don't want to know. You see what you want to see, and use that to get what you want, just like your father used you to get what he wanted."

"Leave him out of it."

"I will not!" Emmaline was sick inside. She'd convinced herself she had the chance she'd always wanted with Doug. His wife was ready to leave him. But it seemed the boy he'd once been, the one she'd loved so desperately, had turned into an even worse version of his father. Sadness swamped her. "He made your life miserable, forcing you to marry Petty so her father would agree to sell him that land. He didn't care who got hurt, and right now you don't either. All you can see is your own ambition."

"That's not fair. This is nothing like that. This is about the public trust. How can you trust a porn star around your kids?"

"Listen to yourself! What the hell do you think she's going to do? Show them her movies instead of *Sesame Street*?"

"What about working at a high school full of boys with raging hormones? Word gets out about her and it's going to disrupt the whole school. She's already got Luke Bradshaw under her spell. And he's old enough to know better."

Emmaline shook her head and sighed. "I think you should leave."

"Emma—"

Emmaline froze him with her stare. "And, if you go through with this manufactured vendetta you've got against Devonny Campbell, don't ever come back."

He took a step toward her. "Emmaline. You don't mean this."

She pointed at the door. "I mean it, Doug. Go."

Rather than backing down, her ultimatum seemed to only stiffen his resolve. "Fine. If that's the way you want it."

She heard the door slam and his car engine growl as it drove away, spitting gravel as he sped out of the driveway onto the pavement.

She'd lost all interest in her magazine. The tranquility of her night alone was shattered, and with it, she feared, her heart. When would she ever learn her lesson? Doug Winston had more of his father in him than she'd realized. Doug Winston was always going to let her down.

***

"Are you ever actually going to let me *do* anything with these programs? Or am I permanently sidelined?" Miles had been following Brandi around at school since the winter break ended. He made sure if she was working on the morning announcements, he was right by her side.

Brandi had patiently explained every step of the process and answered Miles's questions, but he'd yet to touch the keyboard while in her presence.

She gave him a sideways glance before she returned to concentrating on what appeared on the screen. The Key Club announcement about the pancake breakfast on Saturday.

"You said you wanted to learn the program."

"I did. I do. I have. I was hoping to get some hands-on experience, though. If you know what I mean." Miles slid his hand beneath Brandi's hair and brushed his fingers across the back of her neck. A flush crept up her throat. Her fingers stilled on the keyboard and she stared at the screen. "Come on. Watching isn't the same thing as doing."

He slid his fingers behind her earlobe. Brandi closed her eyes. He continued to stroke her. He'd been *stroking* her for weeks hoping she'd give in and give him what he wanted. Every Friday they had a date at the Shake Shack, although after the first week, she'd ordered a diet soda and refused to share his French fries.

At her door they kissed. It was weird. He liked kissing her. She seemed to enjoy it too. But every time he started thinking about taking it to the next level, she told him goodbye. She never invited him in and he didn't push it. Except he kind of wished she would so he wouldn't have to go home.

Miles didn't have to be good at math to put two and two together. Things had been worse than ever between his parents. His mom had the divorce talk with him, but nothing had happened. Yet.

Miles hid out in his room most days and tried not to get in his parents' way. But he couldn't avoid the weird vibes in his house. Maybe there weren't any in Brandi's house. Maybe her parents were normal. He'd never met them. That made him feel…he didn't know how he felt. There wasn't a good reason why Brandi would introduce her pretend-boyfriend to her parents. He guessed he was feeling used. Which was dumb because he was using Brandi, too. He didn't understand this jumble of feelings he had.

Usually on a Friday after he dropped Brandi off he'd hang out with the guys, go to a movie or the arcade in Shenandoah, or play pool in Connor's rec room. Sometimes, though, he didn't feel like hanging with his friends. He was tired of dodging their questions about Brandi. Tired of pretending everything was all right.

But he hadn't given up on his plan, because succeeding meant no more Devonny Campbell. She was the reason everything was screwed up, and once he helped his dad get rid of her, everything would go back to normal. Or, at least, as normal as it had ever been.

He knew from his dad's rants the past week that he'd tried to get Principal Foster to fire Devonny. When that hadn't happened, he'd set up a meeting with the human resources director. The way Miles looked at it, his plan was like extra insurance. One way or another, Devonny Campbell was going down. She'd be humiliated. Ostracized. She'd have no choice but to leave town. Then everything could go back to the way it was.

"Come on," he crooned next to Brandi's other ear. He pushed her hair aside. "You can sit right here and make sure I do it right." He nuzzled her. She made a sound in the back of her throat. Miles smiled. Girls were easy.

"O-okay," Brandi said.

Finally!

Miles pressed his lips to her cheek. "Thanks. You're the best."

They switched seats and Brandi leaned close to him, watching him work. Soon the announcements for tomorrow were complete. Miles leaned back in the chair. "So with this program, can you download clips from videos? Like from movies or YouTube or the internet?"

He tried to keep his tone casual, but this is what he *really* needed to know how to do.

"You can. But we don't. Usually because of copyright infringement. If you want to use clips, you need permission. We're only allowed to use royalty free stock footage."

"Oh. It would be cool if we could. I've seen shows on TV where they insert a line or two from a movie or music video into an interview or something. It's funny."

Brandi started to gather the few things she'd unloaded earlier and put them into her backpack. "It's just high school morning announcements, Miles. We're not that sophisticated."

"I realize that. I just wanted to know if it was possible."

"It is. We don't do it."

"Would you show me how to do it anyway?"

Brandi sighed. "Why?"

"I'd like to know, is all. It seems pretty complicated and you're good at this."

Girls liked compliments. Even girls like Brandi who pretended to be immune to them. He found a way to be sincere when he complimented her, too. It was always about how smart she was, how good she was at the things she did. He should probably compliment her on what a good kisser she was sometime, too. She'd melt like the vanilla milkshake she pretended she didn't want.

"It's not *that* complicated," she said. "Here's how you do it."

***

Miles glanced both ways before he ducked back into the computer lab. He was supposed to be in the cafeteria eating lunch, but today was Thursday and he knew he wouldn't have another opportunity. He'd studied the DVD he'd stolen from Coach Bradshaw and he'd decided on the clip he wanted to use. The part where Devonny and the guy started tearing each other's clothes off. It'd be obvious what kind of film it was and he'd freeze it before the guy got Devonny's lacy black bra completely off, while his mouth was on her boob and her head was thrown back in ecstasy. That's what everyone would see last. He smiled to himself, imagining their reaction.

He chose the computer station he and Brandi always used. He'd made a copy of Friday morning's announcements. All he had to do was splice in the addition and re-upload it to the school's system and schedule it to run on Friday. Thanks to watching Brandi, he already knew the passwords.

Chapter Twenty-Four

Devonny hit the snooze button on her alarm clock for the third time but resisted opening her eyes. She hadn't slept well. Getting comfortable was becoming increasingly difficult these days and it seemed once she found a position where she could fall asleep, the baby decided to do a few somersaults, or kick a foot or a knee or an elbow into Devonny's bladder. And each time — it had been three last night — Devonny had to start all over trying to get comfortable.

Today was the day, she decided. She was going to give Nick what he wanted. She was going to give him two weeks' notice. Working at the school wasn't enjoyable any more, anyway. Nick acted like she wasn't even there. And the frost level seemed to have affected Janet and Lauren. Either they knew more than they were saying, or they were simply confused by the weird vibes that now permeated the office.

At least she'd be leaving on her own terms and not because of Doug Winston. Luke had told her about his visit to Doug's office. He'd admitted in hindsight it had been a bad idea. She loved that he took up for her, but the last thing she wanted was for him to lose his job because of her.

Besides, Devonny wanted to enjoy the last weeks of her pregnancy. She wanted to sleep when she felt like it, put the finishing touches on the nursery, relax and indulge, and enjoy the final stage of her baby's development.

It didn't matter if she was late for once, she told herself as she sluggishly got up to dress. She made herself a cup of tea and drank it while she did her hair and put on the bare minimum of makeup. In fact, she decided, she might not even finish out the day. She might tell Nick the moment she arrived this was her last day, if that's what he wanted.

By the time she parked near the football field, she was feeling slightly guilty about her decision. The long main hallway was empty and her footsteps echoed on the linoleum. From the classrooms she passed she could hear the morning announcements playing before roll call and classes began.

She opened the office door and stepped inside as Nick strode out of his office. His gaze locked with hers and he had a look of outrage on his face she'd never seen before. Lauren and Janet didn't greet her as they normally would. Instead they simply stared at her in astonishment.

"What — ?" she began but Nick cut her off before she could even ask the question.

"In my office, Devonny. Now."

Nick waited until she walked around the counter past him before he followed and closed the door decisively.

She'd barely sunk into one of the chairs in front of his desk before he was standing behind it.

"You're fired," he said through clenched teeth. "I should have followed my instincts and insisted you leave last week. Now I'll be lucky if I don't get fired right along with you."

"Why? What's happened? Is Doug Winston on your case again? Because I already decided to—"

"Doug Winston is the least of my concerns right now. The fact that you appeared half-naked on this morning's announcements in front of some extremely impressionable teenagers is a slightly more pressing matter."

"What? *What* are you talking about?"

"See for yourself." Nick swiveled his computer screen so she could see the frozen image of herself. She stared at it horrified, recognizing it for what it was. A scene from the last film she'd done with Jack. The one she'd given Luke to watch. The one that had gone missing.

"Want to see more?" Nick said nastily before he hit the replay button. "In case you still think your termination isn't justified."

Devonny stared at the screen as the announcement segment played before it was rudely interrupted by the start of that scene. She and Jack coming together in desperate passion. Her practically tearing his shirt off, him yanking on her blouse until the buttons popped, their mouths and hands all over each other.

Uh oh, Jack said in the back of her mind.

"Oh, God." She focused on Nick. "How did this happen?"

Nick swiveled the screen back around. "I assume you mean how did one of your adult films find its way into the morning announcements? I don't know. I intend to find out. As far as you're concerned, gather your things and go. And if I find out you had anything to do with this—"

"Of course I didn't!"

"Because you've got a grudge against me—"

"Nick, for heaven's sake—"

"I'll see you're prosecuted to the full extent of the law."

"Now you're just being paranoid."

Nick stood and pointed at the door. "Just go."

Devonny went straight to her desk, aware of Janet and Lauren's questioning looks. She took the few personal items stored in her desk drawers and stuffed them in her purse.

Luke stepped out of his office and waited until she handed her keys to Janet. "I'll walk you out," he said.

"I'm really sad you're leaving," Janet said."

"Me too," said Lauren. "But Nick didn't have a choice."

"He's afraid they'll fire him over this," Janet informed her. "Otherwise he would have been nicer about it."

Their loyalty and defense of Nick struck Devonny as both comical and sad. "I understand," she told them. "I'm going to miss you both."

She saw only sympathetic looks on their faces. Not condemnation. Not contempt. Sympathy. And friendship. She tried to smile at them. "Bye."

"Bye, Devonny," the two women called.

Devonny waited until they were outside before she spoke to Luke. "The DVD I gave you—"

Luke looked grim. "I *knew* I had it with me that day. I put it in my backpack so I could return it to you."

"Someone stole it."

"And we know who. Dev, I'm so sorry."

"Me too." Their breath puffed out in front of them. "You know what's funny? I was going to quit today anyway."

"Ironic, maybe. Not funny."

"I guess."

"I'll come over after school. You'll be okay until then, right?"

That made Devonny smile for real. "I'll be fine. But I love that you worry about me."

He hooked an arm around her neck and pressed his lips against her hair. "Be careful going home. And call me if you need anything."

He watched her drive out of the parking lot. He went back inside with a fierce look of determination.

***

By the time Luke returned, Brandi Valentine was already there. Nick signaled both of them to come into his office. Luke steeled himself for what was to come next. Brandi was on track to becoming valedictorian. She had an exemplary academic record and involvement in the kinds of activities colleges like to see. She was a smart girl. Except perhaps in her choice of boyfriends.

"Brandi," Nick began. "You realize we have a problem here. I'd like you to tell me what happened."

"I don't know. I really don't know!"

Luke noticed Brandi's bottom lip was quivering. She held her hands tightly clenched in her lap. Tension radiated off her. She was holding it together but barely.

"It's my understanding from Mr. Brothers that you are in charge of the morning announcements."

"Yes."

"In fact, Mr. Brothers told me he's found you to be so trustworthy, he tends not to double check your work."

Brandi nodded.

"Am I to understand, then, that you and you alone are responsible for what we saw in the announcements this morning?"

"I told you, I didn't do it!"

"But you know who did, don't you?"

Brandi looked away but didn't reply.

Nick and Luke exchanged glances before Nick spoke again. "Brandi, you understand something like this could compromise your academic future, don't you?"

Brandi looked at her clenched hands and nodded. A tear slid down her cheek.

Nick gentled his tone. "If you know who inserted that segment, protecting them likely means that you and you alone will bear responsibility. Mr. Brothers tells me you and he, as well as Mrs. Horton, are the only people who have the passwords to the announcement program."

Brandi remained silent, head down.

Nick sighed and looked at Luke again. Luke shifted in his chair and leaned forward, elbows on his knees, hands clasped. "Brandi, neither Principal Foster nor I believe you were responsible for this. As far as I can tell, there are a couple of other possibilities. One is the program was hacked. We'll have Mr. Brothers take a look at that possibility as soon as he's free. What's more likely is that someone got hold of the passwords and added that clip when no one was in the computer room. Probably someone with a grudge against Ms. Campbell. Someone who wanted to embarrass her. Someone who wanted to make sure she lost her job."

Brandi did not look up.

"You've been spending quite a bit of time with Miles Winston lately, haven't you?"

That got Brandi's attention. "Some," she said carefully.

Luke didn't look at Nick. He kept his gaze on Brandi and waited to see if she'd say more. She didn't. "All right, Brandi. Go back to your classroom. We'll let you know if we need to talk to you again."

After Brandi left, Luke made sure the door was closed and turned to face the principal. Nick's expression was one of sadness mixed with disappointment. "That girl's just like my sister. Letting some guy screw up what could have been a promising future."

"I didn't know you had a sister. I've never heard you mention her."

"She's a dancer in Las Vegas." He looked away in embarrassment. "We don't talk about it."

That was one of the things Luke had noticed living in a small town. Even though it seemed everyone knew everyone else, they didn't really *know* each other.

"You know I had no choice but to let Devonny go after this," said Nick, getting back to business. "Not with Doug Winston and the entire school board already breathing down my neck. I'll be lucky if they don't fire me too."

"Devonny was going to tell you today she was quitting. This whole thing has turned into one big mess."

"That's an understatement."

"You know Miles Winston is responsible for the announcement snafu, don't you?"

"I figured. But I doubt we'll be able to prove it. Not unless Brandi gives him up. Even if she does, Doug's going to find a way to spin this to his advantage. And he'll remember anyone who gets in his way."

Luke pursed his lips. "Let's think about our options before we do anything. You talk to Brothers. I'll work on the Miles/Brandi angle. We'll figure it out."

"I hope so. Because this is not the kind of publicity this school needs."

***

Brandi escaped her last class early by begging for a bathroom break and was waiting for Miles in the parking lot. He'd managed to avoid her all day. First she'd been hurt. Then disappointed. But now she was fuming. He'd used her. All this time, it was all just for a stupid prank.

She saw him walking out with his buddies, all cocksure of himself until he saw her standing next to his car. Then his steps slowed and his expression changed.

She'd told herself not to believe there was anything real between her and Miles. She told herself not to fall for him, that they were only pretending. But each time he kissed her she sensed there *was* some kind of genuine feeling behind it. That maybe Miles liked her or something. She wanted to believe that. Because she liked him. She wanted that fairy tale, where the geeky girl goes to the prom with the most popular boy in school. But like all fairy tales in real life, this one wasn't going to come true. At least not for her.

"Why'd you do it?" she asked when he was close enough.

Miles glanced around. Other students were nearby, chatting in groups, some still edging past to get to their vehicles. "Not here," he said.

He unlocked the car and Brandi slid in before he could tell her not to. He backed out.

"Do you realize what you've done, Miles?" Brandi asked before they were even out of the parking lot. "Do you realize how much trouble I'm in?"

"Why would you be in trouble? You didn't do anything."

"No. I didn't do anything, except teach you everything I knew about those programs. Who do you think they're going to pin this on? Why, Miles? I don't get it. What have you got against Ms. Campbell, anyway? Is this about your dad? Why'd you have to involve me?"

"Wait. You didn't tell them I did it?" Miles said as he turned onto her street.

"No. I didn't."

"Why not?"

"Maybe I should have."

"But you didn't." He said nothing for a moment, as if trying to process that one thing. He didn't say another word until he'd parked in front of her house.

***

They got out. Brandi didn't even question he'd follow her inside. They took their coats off and Miles looked around. The living room was a little cramped and a lot boring. Everything was beige. But it also looked comfortable with a big old saggy sofa with soft cushions and a recliner parked in front of the TV.

They took up positions on opposite ends of the sofa. "I want an explanation, Miles. You owe me that much."

Miles had thought a lot about how to play this, about what approach would work best with her. He'd decided to play on her sympathies. Tell the truth, but embellish it a bit. He was confident when he was done, she'd be putty in his hands. She might, he hoped, even offer him more than a kiss.

He tried not to think about what might happen if she did, or how it felt when she pressed her voluptuous curves against him. He shifted his position on the sofa.

"Spill it, Miles, or I go in tomorrow and tell Principal Foster everything."

"My parents are splitting up." He blurted it out, not at all the way he'd planned. And the moment he did, he felt a surge of emotion he couldn't hold back. Saying it aloud to another person made it true in a way he hadn't been able to accept before. *My parents are splitting up.* "It's because of Ms. Campbell. Ms. Campbell and her friend."

"What friend?"

"Some blond bitch that does those movies, too. She came to our party and she—my mom—got to be friends with her."

"What's wrong with that?"

Miles shook his head, knowing Brandi didn't understand what he meant by "friends" in this context. "*Friends.* My dad didn't like it. They started fighting. I mean, they always fight or ignore each other. But the fighting got worse." Miles sniffed. He wondered if he let go of the emotion he was hanging onto, if he started crying for real, whether it would disgust Brandi or make her more sympathetic to him.

"He told my mom she couldn't be friends with that bitch and she told him to go to hell." Miles's voice broke and Brandi slid closer. She put a hand on his shoulder and rubbed gently, as if that would soothe his distress.

"Then my dad got this idea to run for mayor and clean up the town. Starting with Ms. Campbell, because of those movies she did. I heard him say it wasn't right how she could influence us at school."

"But everyone loves Ms. Campbell," Brandi pointed out. "She's helped a bunch of kids with algebra."

"It's the principle of the thing," Miles said, knowing he sounded like his father and hating himself for it. "My mom was mad at him, and every night I had to listen to him rant about it and my mom yelling back. I wanted to make things better. I thought if I made sure Ms. Campbell got fired, she'd leave town, dad would be mayor and he'd be happy. And they'd stop fighting and they wouldn't split up."

Miles sagged back into the sofa. He knew how childish what he'd said sounded. He was five years old again, wondering why he couldn't make his parents happy, why he could never win his father's approval. Tears filled his eyes and this time he didn't even try to hide them. He was suddenly so tired and he knew what he'd done wasn't going to change anything. Not for his parents. They'd still hate each other. They'd still split up. And he'd be even more alone than he had been before.

He ground the heels of his hands into his eyes. He was a despicable human being. Brandi was a decent girl and he'd used her. Was still using her. He'd done something mean and stupid and for what? Yes, he'd resented Ms. Campbell and blamed her for introducing that blond chick into his family. But his parents had been miserable before she'd ever showed up. Who's to say they wouldn't have split up eventually anyway?

At the very least he owed Brandi an apology. Then she'd kick him out of her nice warm living room with the comfortable saggy sofa. She'd kick him out of her life for good because that's what he deserved. But it was also the last thing he wanted.

"Why didn't you tell me all this before? About your parents, I mean."

"I didn't want to talk about it because that means it's really happening."

Brandi crossed her arms. Miles couldn't blame her for pulling back. "So instead of facing reality, you decided to throw me under the bus."

He couldn't speak around the lump in his throat. He was about ten seconds away from totally losing it. But he didn't get up. He didn't leave. It was like he was stuck here in these cushions that held him in a comfortable grip. He chanced a look at Brandi. She didn't look angry, exactly. She looked...curious. She was waiting for an answer.

Saying he was sorry wasn't going to be nearly enough. Not with a girl like Brandi. Miles didn't understand why he cared. He didn't want her to think he was a jerk, even though he was. Even though, at the moment, he felt completely worthless. And why wouldn't he? He'd been told often enough by his father he was.

"I have to start dinner."

That was the last thing Miles expected Brandi to say. She'd been sitting there watching him like a bug under a microscope, considering which leg to pull off first. He thought she'd remind him he should say "sorry." But the last thing Brandi would do was beg for an apology. Brandi, he had learned, did not beg. He had the uncomfortable feeling he might be the one doing the begging, because at that moment he knew he wanted her forgiveness and understanding. He didn't want to lose her as a friend. Or whatever what was between them might turn into.

"Dinner?"

Brandi stood. "Mmhmm. It's pasta night. You're welcome to stay." Brandi stood. "Or go."

Miles couldn't believe Brandi was inviting him to dinner. She should kick him out of her house. In fact, she never should have let him inside in the first place. He thought he had her pegged, but the truth was he didn't understand Brandi Valentine at all.

He considered going home. To the beautiful house with the carefully refinished antique furniture he wasn't allowed to sit on. To the cold kitchen where most nights everyone scrounged for their own dinner, because his mother was in her studio and couldn't be bothered to prepare a meal. To another night alone in his room.

"Okay." He followed Brandi into the kitchen which was as homey and warm as the living room. The cabinets had been painted navy blue, and at some point the countertop had been replaced with a smooth, cool, milky-white surface. Quartz maybe, or granite. The appliances looked like they'd been upgraded recently, too. There was a table near the window that looked out over the backyard. But it was growing dark and there wasn't much to see this time of year. French doors led to a deck, and he imagined in the summer, Brandi's family spent a lot of time out there.

Brandi had opened the refrigerator and was removing an armload of vegetables. She set them on the counter and went back for more.

"Can I help?" Miles asked. He had no idea where those words came from. He'd never helped prepare a meal before. He'd just get in the way. But he supposed it was his way of finding out if the offer to stay was genuine or not. Why didn't she kick him out? Tell him to go to hell? That she wanted nothing to do with him?

"Can you chop vegetables without cutting your thumb off?" Brandi was already rinsing peppers and zucchini and mushrooms at the sink.

Miles watched her from where he stood on the other side of the island. Her back was to him. "Why don't you throw me out? Don't you expect an apology?"

Brandi set the vegetables aside and turned the water off. She turned to face him, bracing her hands on the edge of the counter. "I don't want you to apologize if you're not sorry, which I don't think you are. So your apology would be insulting and meaningless. I didn't throw you out because I wanted you to explain why you did it. As for dinner..." she looked around the kitchen. "I don't know, Miles. You had your reasons for setting me up and I guess I can understand. Even if I think they were stupid reasons. I don't like what you did. But I'm also finding it really hard to be mean to you right now."

"But you don't really want me to stay?"

For the first time, Brandi looked uncertain. She looked at the floor and spoke so softly Miles barely heard her. "I'm not sure what I want."

That makes two of us. "So where are these vegetables you want me to chop?"

***

An hour later Brandi's parents arrived, bringing with them a burst of cold air from the back door, and equally surprised expressions.

"Hi Mom. Dad. This is Miles. He's staying for dinner."

To their credit, they recovered from the shock quickly. Mrs. Valentine was the first with her coat off. "Nice to meet you, Miles," she said. She was built like Brandi, all generous curves and curly hair.

"Miles?" Brandi's dad asked, studying him. "Miles Winston?"

"Yes, sir."

Mr. Valentine shook Miles's hand. "Nice to meet you. Eagles sure had a tough season, this year."

"Yes, sir, we did."

All through dinner, Brandi's dad talked football with him, happy to relive his own tenure as a tight end at Red Bud High. Miles caught Brandi's mom smiling indulgently at her husband a time or two and both complimented Brandi on the meal. Which, as it turned out, was delicious. His own mother did not enjoy cooking and the meals she occasionally produced were uncreative at best and bland at worst. And any discussion of football during the season consisted of his father explaining how Miles could have improved his performance.

When dinner was over, Miles carried his plate to the counter. Brandi opened the dishwasher. Her parents disappeared into another part of the house. He watched her rinse and arrange the dishes in the racks.

"You have to cook and do the dishes?"

"Yes, Miles. I'm my parents' slave. That's why they had me." He stared at her. She glanced up and rolled her eyes. "We take turns so we each get two nights a week of cooking and clean-up. On Saturday we go out or order pizza."

"That's so…" Miles trailed off.

Brandi raised an eyebrow. "So what?"

"I don't know. Family-ish?"

"I don't think that's even a word." She stowed the last of the dishes in the machine and closed the door. She opened a cupboard and rummaged through an array of plastic containers until she found the ones she wanted. She turned to the counter and divided the remaining pasta into two portions, then stowed them in the refrigerator. "Lunch for Mom and Dad tomorrow."

Back at the sink she scrubbed the pans and bowls she'd used and set them on the drainer. Rinsed the sink and dried her hands. She turned back to Miles. "I have homework. You should probably go."

"But, what about, you know…what happened today?" Miles's pasta-filled stomach began to tie itself in a knot.

"You mean, am I going to turn you in to save myself?"

"Yeah."

"That depends on you."

"On me?"

Brandi looked at him steadily. Not like she was judging him or like she was mad at him. Like she was expecting something from him. Only he didn't know what. "I don't know what you mean," he said, hoping for a hint.

"I guess you'll have to figure it out, won't you, Miles?"

He followed her to the door where she handed him his coat. He shrugged into it even though he didn't want to leave. She opened the door and crossed her arms, waiting for him to walk through it. She wasn't going to hug him or kiss him goodbye. Maybe—and he shied away from the thought—she was done with him. "See you," he said.

"Goodnight, Miles."

"Thanks for dinner."

"You're welcome."

The door closed firmly behind him, leaving him out in the cold.

Chapter Twenty-Five

Devonny and Luke slept in the next morning since it was Saturday. Luke had stopped hiding the fact he spent most nights with Devonny. Right now, it was the least of the things the gossips would have to talk about.

He took a cup of coffee to the living room and opened the shutters. He saw several people milling around in the street in front of Devonny's house. "What's going on out there?"

He heard her humming to herself as she prepared breakfast. He didn't want to do anything to destroy her happy mood. But when he saw the signs, he didn't have a choice.

He went into the kitchen. She took one look at him and asked, "What's wrong?"

"There are people outside. They have signs."

"What?"

She went to the window and watched the small band of protestors holding up signs made of white poster board lettered with black marker. "Keep Red Bud Clean" they chanted. She squinted to see what the signs said. *Protect Our Children. Devonny Campbell Must Go.* And, of course, *Doug Winston For Mayor.*

"Oh, for God's sake. That guy's even carrying a pitchfork."

"Yeah. But it's just to hold up his sign."

Devonny went back to the kitchen and resumed her meal preparation. "That's it?" Luke asked following her. "I expected more of a reaction."

Her eyes flashed in his direction and she smiled in a way he'd never seen before. "Doug wants a fight, I guess."

"What are you going to do?"

She tilted her head in the direction of the street. "I'm going to bury Doug Winston. And a guy like Doug? He won't even see it coming."

"We should go talk to those people out there. Get pictures and video of them protesting."

A gleam came into Devonny's eye. "Don't stop there. Call the local newspaper, TV and radio stations, if Doug hasn't already. He's not out there with them. Someone's bound to say something that will make a worthwhile sound bite."

"Good thinking. Let's get dressed. I'll come with you."

"I want to see what they're willing to say to my face."

***

While getting dressed, Devonny had an idea. Luke went outside while she was in the kitchen. When she joined the group, she had four mugs of hot chocolate on a tray. "Good morning," she called to them. "Would you like something to warm you up?"

The protestors looked at each other uncertainly. Devonny couldn't read their expressions, bundled up as they were, but she didn't sense any real hostility from them. She held the tray closer to the man nearest her. He yanked the scarf away from his mouth and said, "Oh, what the hell. Thank you." He took a mug from the tray. The others followed suit.

"You're Devonny Campbell?" the first man asked.

She sent Luke a quizzical look. "You're protesting my presence in Red Bud and you don't even know who I am?"

"This is Walt Collins," Luke said. "He's got a farm outside of town."

"I'm trying to earn some extra cash to pay off my kids' Christmas."

"Me too," a middle-aged woman piped up. "My husband got injured on the job three months ago. We need the money." She shivered and held the rapidly cooling hot chocolate closer to her reddened cheeks.

"Is Doug Winston *paying* you?"

"Eight bucks an hour. Cash. He called us all last night."

"Are you saying you don't have anything against me, personally?" Devonny looked at all four of them in turn.

"Lady," said the youngest guy, "I could care less about your skin flicks. I want to pay my mom's electric bill so I can get the heat in her trailer turned back on."

A car came to a stop across the street and a young man dressed for the weather got out and came toward them.

"Let's go back inside," Luke said to Devonny.

"You all do what you have to do," she said to the group. "If you need a bathroom or anything, knock, okay?"

Devonny and Luke retreated to the house. "I need to go talk to Loretta. She's going to wonder what's up out here."

"Want me to come with you?"

"Yes. But I'll go by myself." She kissed him and went out the back.

Loretta opened the door and the warmth and scents of her kitchen enveloped Devonny. "Cinnamon coffee cake," she said as Devonny pulled off her gloves, scarf and hat. "You want some coffee? Or some tea?" Her question set off a coughing spell. She turned away and covered her mouth with a tissue until it passed.

"No, I'm fine. Thank you." Devonny laid her hand against Loretta's cheek and then across her forehead. "That cough of yours worries me. Have you been back to the doctor?"

"Old fool," Loretta scoffed. "Claims it's bronchitis again. Gives me one prescription after another and I'm still coughing. Don't worry about me. What's going on out there?" She tilted her head in the direction of the street.

They took their usual seats at the kitchen table. "Doug Winston is targeting me in his mayoral campaign because, well, I did some adult films a few years ago."

"What's that got to do with anything?"

"You don't seem too surprised."

"Honey, you get to be my age, not much can surprise you anymore. I never did care for Doug Winston. He and my Stevie were in the same grade. Doug was a bully then and he's a bully now. Made my boy's school years a right misery. 'Course his dad was even worse. It don't surprise me one bit Doug's found someone new to pick on. Didn't necessarily expect it'd be you, though."

"He says I'm a bad influence on the kids—"

Loretta snorted. "Because you took your clothes off and paraded around in front of a camera? Not that I cotton to such behavior, mind you. But it's neither here nor there, 'specially if it's in the past. I can tell you've got a good heart. And probably not a mean bone in your body. And I'm not the only one in town who feels that way."

"Unfortunately, someone put a clip from one of my films on the high school's morning announcements. They fired me."

Loretta ruminated for a moment. "Who did it?"

Even though Luke was a hundred percent sure Miles Winston was the culprit, Devonny didn't want to accuse him without proof. "We don't know for sure."

"Someone with a grudge against you. Got any ideas who that might be?"

"Maybe," Devonny hedged. "But I don't want to be the cause of any trouble."

"But you're not, are you? Doug Winston's the one causing the trouble. He always was, even when he was a kid. If he wasn't the center of attention, he was making someone miserable so he could be. A Holstein don't change its spots."

"I'm not sure what I'm going to do."

Loretta gave Devonny a thoughtful look. "I used to tell Stevie the only way to deal with a bully was to stand up to him. But Stevie didn't have it in him to do that. I think you do, though. Give him hell."

Devonny covered Loretta's hand with hers. "Thank you for being my friend."

***

Luke had cleaned up the kitchen by the time Devonny returned. "There's a reporter from the local paper out there. Must be a slow weekend."

Devonny peeked out the front window. "You want to make your escape now? I'm going to invite him in."

"Are you sure you want to do that?"

"Why not? I've got nothing to hide and nothing to be ashamed of."

"I'll put on another pot of coffee."

***

From the front window Devonny watched the young reporter from the *Red Bud Record* take photos of the protestors with a digital camera. When he looked at the house, she opened the door and gestured for him to come. He hustled toward her as if afraid she might slam the door closed before he got there.

"Miz Campbell? I'm Hunter Bowles with the *Red Bud Record*."

"Please come in," Devonny said, anxious to shut out the cold air. She couldn't help but smile as she took his coat and hung it up. His youth and earnest air were at odds with the conservative tie she suspected he'd borrowed from his father. Dark hair flopped over his forehead and round Harry Potter-style glasses gave him a serious, studious look.

"Do you know why Mr. Winston is targeting you?" he asked, once the preliminaries were out of way.

"You'd have to ask him," Devonny said.

"But you must have some idea."

"I'd prefer not to speculate." Devonny had decided to let Doug slit his own throat. He'd started this, but she was going to end it.

"It's my understanding you acted in adult films at one time."

Devonny turned the full wattage of her smile on him. "That's true."

"Do you think that's why Mr. Winston began this protest? Because he feels you're a bad influence on the people of the town?"

"As I said, you'd have to ask him. But if we're all going to be held accountable for what we've done in the past, he should be digging into everyone's history, don't you agree?"

"I'm not allowed to have an opinion," the young man said. "How did you come to be working at the high school?"

"I answered a want ad posted in your paper and interviewed for the job."

"Didn't they do a background check?"

"I was told they did, but it might be best if you checked with the school board or human resources."

"You were in direct contact with students while working at the high school?"

"I was hired to work in the office as a teacher's aide, but yes, I had contact with some of the students as a math tutor."

An insistent knock sounded on the door. "Excuse me," Devonny said.

"You're Devonny Campbell?" the woman on her stoop asked. She was bundled up for the weather. Behind her stood a familiar girl wearing a pink knit cap.

"Hi, Kelly," Devonny said. She turned her attention back to the woman. "You must be Kelly's mother." She offered her hand and the other woman shook it. "Yes, I'm Devonny Campbell. Please come in."

"I'm Katrina Clark. Thank you." The woman eyed Hunter before she turned back to Devonny. "Look, Kelly told me about what happened at school." She glanced uncomfortably at Hunter. "Could we talk in private?"

"If it has to do with termination of my employment at the school, I believe Mr. Bowles here is already aware. Or he soon will be."

"Okay. Well, what I wanted to say, and you can quote me directly," Katrina said, fixing Hunter with a determined look, "Is I hope you can continue helping Kelly. I'm willing to pay you to tutor her as needed. Bob Sylvester taught algebra when I was in high school, and I struggled the same way Kelly did. Except there was no one there to help me the way you've helped her."

"But—what about my past? Doesn't that concern you?"

"What concerns me is giving my daughter the best shot at getting into college."

"Excuse me, Mrs. Clark?" Hunter spoke up. "Would you join us for a few minutes? I have some questions for you and your daughter, and I'd like to add your thoughts to my article."

Katrina looked at Devonny, and Devonny gestured toward the sofa.

***

LOCAL MOMS STAND UP FOR FORMER PORN STAR

Devonny cringed when she saw the headline in the *Red Bud Record* on Monday. There was the photo Hunter had taken of her with Kelly and Katrina Clark. Below it was one of Allie Perkins and her mother. Kelly had made sure to mention to Hunter they'd be just as supportive. Devonny read the article through quickly and a second time more slowly. Hunter had stuck to the facts. Doug Winston had been unavailable for comment. What a coward. Doug was hoping Devonny would be crucified by the townspeople and vilified by the press coverage and he wouldn't have to lift a finger.

But if this was the only article published about her, it would only matter to a few people who were inclined to judge her anyway. Something Katrina had said during the interview in answer to one of Hunter's questions had stuck with her, though. When he'd asked if she had any reservations about exposing her daughter to someone with Devonny's past, fearful of the influence she might have, Katrina had given him a look.

"Knowledge is a powerful thing," she'd said. "I didn't know about Ms. Campbell's past before, and I was grateful she was helping my daughter. I never thought twice about any influence she might have over Kelly, other than as a math tutor. I only heard positive things about her and I only saw positive results. You're asking me if I should change my opinion now because now I have this information about Ms. Campbell's past. The answer is no. My opinion would only change if I saw something negative happening with Kelly and I knew Ms. Campbell was the cause." She'd turned to Devonny and smiled. "Somehow, I don't think that's going to happen."

Devonny'd thought at the time, the reverse was also true. She hadn't said anything because she was ready for the interview to be over. But what if she met an ex-con? Would she make a judgment about him because she knew he'd been in prison? What if he'd been an exemplary citizen prior to his incarceration? Suppose he'd spent his life taking care of a disabled parent and working two jobs and coaching Little League? Would the rest of his life's work be eclipsed by what she knew about him? As Katrina had said, knowledge was a powerful thing. And judgments were often made with very little knowledge.

Devonny wandered into the baby's room. She loved the way it had turned out. The soft colors. The big window to which she'd added a shade and valance. She wanted the room filled with sunlight and laughter and fun. She couldn't wait to bring her baby home and start their lives together.

She thought about secrets and how damaging they could be. She'd never attempted to keep her past a secret. But she hadn't advertised it either. Even though only a few years had passed, that time in her life seemed long ago now. She was in a different place. Almost a different person. She'd begun the next chapter of her life and once she'd turned that page, she'd wanted to shed the past. But she hadn't. And maybe the people in this town, people like Doug Winston, wanted to make her pay for it.

But she refused to regret her film career, apologize for it or be shamed by it. She wondered what secrets lurked in Doug Winston's past. Or any of the other townspeople who might decide to judge her. She wondered how *they'd* like it if every deed they'd done was exposed and examined and offered up for public scrutiny. How would they react?

Everyone had things they'd rather others didn't know. Everyone feared being judged, being ridiculed, being shunned. If this town wanted to rally behind Doug and make her their target, they'd get what they deserved. Devonny would see to it.

But surely it would never come to that.

Still, she called Chemistry to warn Claire, just in case.

***

"Honey, I'm afraid this thing is already starting to snowball. I've already had phone calls from some of your local press," Claire said once she and Devonny connected.

"Besides the newspaper?"

"I think so. Hold a minute. My latest assistant can't hold a candle to you, by the way. I'm still not sure I've forgiven you for abandoning me. Here it is. A producer from KIOW. That must be a television station."

"I think it's the one in Shenandoah."

"And the *Des Moines Register*. Assistant editor for features."

"Great. I'd hoped the *Red Bud Record* would be the only paper interested."

"I can handle the press. You know that. I've got my public relations people working on it. I miss you, by the way. Sorry I couldn't make the shower."

"I would have loved to see you. Thanks again for the rocking baby cushion."

"They said it's the latest thing. I hope it works."

Devonny laughed. "Me too."

"Seriously, Dev, what can I do?"

"I'm not sure I need you to do anything. I just wanted to give you a heads up. I'm not trying to hide anything. Not that I can. Those films are out there. My acting credits are public, even if it's a stage name. I'm going to let the shit hit the fan and by next week I hope it will be old news."

"Do you want me to have my people contact these reporters?"

"It's up to you, Claire. A local guy running for mayor is making me a target for his campaign. That's where it started. But one way or another I'm going to end it. I'm going to end him."

"That's the spirit!" Claire was quiet a moment. "Dev, hold on, I've got a couple of ideas. A few things I can put out there from my end that might help both of us. Let me work on it. You take care of yourself and that baby, okay? Love you."

"Love you too, Claire." Devonny hung up, wondering if she'd put something in motion she might not be able to stop.

Someone knocked on her door. She saw a news van parked at the curb.

***

"Where do you go from here?" The redhead from the ABC affiliate asked.

"I'm not going anywhere. I'm going to have my baby in a few weeks and focus on being the best mother I can be. Then we'll see. But I'm not leaving Red Bud. This is my home now."

"You mentioned your interest in teaching. Do you think any of the local schools would hire you, now that your history is public?" The reporter was earnest and serious.

"I don't know. I imagine, given the attention span of the average American, this will be old news before long."

"Not if Mr. Winston decides to keep it in the forefront," put in the reporter. "The election isn't until May."

Devonny grinned. "In that case, maybe I'll have to run for mayor."

***

"What do you think?" Devonny asked Luke after they had watched the interview on the five o'clock news.

"I think *you* were brilliant." He smoothed her hair back and kissed her. "Now it's up to every other reporter to do a fair story."

"You think they won't?"

"I think they're reporters and Doug's got a lot of sway around here."

Chapter Twenty-Six

Devonny had no idea how Claire managed it, but within a week she had both of them booked for an interview on the *Samantha Powers* syndicated talk show. They'd be doing their interviews remotely, but Samantha Powers was huge on both television and radio. She was known to ask hard-hitting questions of her controversial guests.

Devonny had driven to the television studio in Shenandoah over Luke's objections. Mostly, it seemed, his objection was her going alone. "I'll be fine. The baby isn't due for a couple more weeks. And if I suddenly go into labor, the hospital's in Shenandoah, you know." She'd tried to tease him out of his concern, but it wasn't working.

"The stress of all this publicity isn't good for you. I don't know what your friend Claire was thinking. This could have waited until after you have the baby."

"No, it couldn't. This is news now. And it's the only way to beat Doug at his own game. If I don't go out there now, the public will think I'm afraid or ashamed. I can't afford to let him win."

Luke tried to smile. "I understand. But I think you're doing too much. I worry about you."

Devonny moved into his embrace. It was wonderful to have someone fuss over her. Luke was like Jack in that way. She loved Luke's arms around her. He made her feel safe and protected. *Loved.*

Thank you, Jack. She was convinced it was Jack who had led her to Red Bud, to this house. To Luke. Somehow he'd been a part of orchestrating a scenario where his wife and his child would be safe and loved, once he couldn't be there for them.

Perhaps it was wrong to give Jack, or his ghost, so much credit. It might all be in her head. But Devonny didn't believe that, and had no other explanation. And it made her feel good to think Jack hadn't stopped looking out for her, hadn't stopped caring for her even after he died.

"I will text you when I'm leaving and I'll text you when I get there. I'll text you once the interview is over and I'll text you when I'm on my way back. If I stop texting you, you'll know to start worrying, okay? Otherwise, assume I'm fine and I'll be back as soon as I can."

Luke moved back so he could look into her eyes. "I don't know how it happened, okay? But you are precious to me now. If I'm overly protective, it's because being without you, *anything* happening to you, terrifies me."

"Noted," she said with a slight smile. "I promise I'll be careful and I'll stay in touch. And if anything bad happens, I solemnly vow you will be allowed to never let me forget it."

Finally, that brought a smile to Luke's face.

She and Claire had discussed strategy for days. Calling and texting each other with ideas and ways to get their message across. They knew Samantha would do everything in her power to get under their skin and make them foolishly lose their tempers. It was her style. She often used insulting tactics to force her subjects onto the defensive. Claire and Devonny were hoping they could outwit her.

The opportunity came toward the end of the interview. Samantha seemed frustrated she hadn't been able to get either Claire or Devonny to admit to doing anything wrong or immoral. Claire had equated her films with steamy romance novels, because essentially that's what they were.

"But Devonny, aren't you ashamed about your part in those films? How do you think your daughter will feel when she's old enough to realize her mother's erotic films are available online? That perhaps a boy she's dating might have seen her mother naked, and more?"

"Before I answer that question, Samantha, could I ask you one and I hope you'll answer honestly."

"You can ask. I don't promise to reply."

"Did you by chance see any of the *Shades of Grey* movies, or read the books?"

Samantha didn't hesitate. "Yes. Yes I did."

"Both the books and the films are rather graphic, aren't they? Do you feel ashamed for having watched or read them?"

"That's hardly the same thing."

"So you don't feel ashamed. You find that kind of content in literature or film perfectly acceptable."

"I didn't act in the films," Samantha pointed out. "I didn't write the books."

"No. But what you're implying is, not only should I feel ashamed for having acted in a few erotic films, but so should Dakota Johnson and Jamie Dornan. And, you're implying that every consumer should be ashamed for watching or reading a film or a book with erotic content. Or ones with graphic love scenes such as

Outlander or *Game of Thrones*. Should we shame every actor and actress and writer connected to them? Or the publishers and film companies and publicity departments."

"That's not what I meant —"

But Samantha had given Devonny a soapbox on which to stand and she wasn't ready to get down just yet. "But it is what you're implying. I acted in a few films with my husband, who is also the father of my child, and therefore I should be ashamed of what I've done. Of what he did. And by association, my child should be ashamed of us for doing it. Even though we did nothing illegal or criminal.

"The fact is, we're all trying to figure it out. Love. Sex. Relationships. We're all looking for understanding and knowledge and what works and what doesn't work. We all make mistakes and sometimes we triumph. But the search for those things is what makes us human. It's what we share, that seeking heart.

There was a pause before Samantha said, "I see we're out of time. Thanks to my guests, Devonny Campbell and Claire Reddington of Chemistry Films. We'll be right back."

The studio guy started forward to disconnect Devonny's mike when Samantha's voice stopped him. "Devonny? Are you still there?"

"I'm here."

"I just wanted to say you were great. I love it when a guest knows how to push back. I can't wait for the call-in segment. The Twitterverse is going to go crazy."

Devonny could only imagine how lively that segment would be. She was glad she'd closed her social media accounts when she'd left LA. She didn't want to know what the Twitter trolls would have to say about her. "Thanks, Samantha."

The minute she was free of the microphone, Devonny called Claire. "How do you think it went?"

"Honey, you were brilliant. We both were, if I do say so myself," Claire crowed. "This is going to boost Chemistry Film's exposure ten times over. We're going to celebrate in person as soon as we can. Champagne's on me."

"Claire, thank you. For everything." Emotion suddenly clogged Devonny's throat.

Claire must have sensed it and wisely ended the call with, "I'll be in touch, sweetie."

Devonny stopped in the restroom before she got in her car. As promised, she texted Luke. *On my way home.* She hesitated only a moment before adding, *Love you.*

Chapter Twenty-Seven

Two weeks later, Luke ushered Devonny out of the hospital. Darkness had fallen an hour ago and several inches of the snow he'd hoped to avoid had accumulated on the pavement and cars.

He made sure Devonny was settled and comfortably buckled in before he started the engine and wipers. He turned the heat up full blast and glanced across at her, trying not to let his irritation show. After school they'd driven straight to the affiliate TV station in Shenandoah so Devonny could be interviewed for a segment to air on Tucker Carlson's show. She'd promised Luke it would be the last one. The taping took longer than expected and afterward she'd insisted on stopping at the hospital and staying with Loretta until the old lady fell asleep. Loretta's immune system had never quite recovered after her first hospitalization. She hadn't been able to kick the bronchitis and had developed pneumonia again.

If they'd left an hour ago, they'd be home already and they'd have avoided the bad weather. Now he'd have to negotiate the highway from Shenandoah to Red Bud at night on a snowy road.

Devonny wiggled around in her seat as he backed the Jeep out of the parking space. "You okay?" he asked, although she probably wanted to ask him the same thing.

"Yes, but my back has been hurting today."

"Because you're doing too much. These interviews. The time you spend on the phone. You pretend it isn't stressful, but it has to be. Not to mention all the time you've been spending at the hospital. You're worn out."

"If I agree I've overdone it, will you lay off?" She gave a deep sigh. "I can't wait to get home and get into bed."

Luke was tired and irritable and he didn't care for Devonny's testy tone of voice. "It's going to take longer than usual," Luke warned her. He had his usual death grip on the steering wheel. "You better hope the snow plows are out already, or we're crawling home."

He headed toward the main highway. Snow flew at the windshield and the visibility grew worse as he approached the outer edge of Shenandoah.

"You know we could get a motel room for the night instead of driving back in this." He passed a chain motel. The parking lot was packed and a neon *No Vacancy* flickered under its sign. "Not there, obviously."

Another motel appeared a half mile later on the other side of the road. Another no vacancy sign was out.

"Is it that bad?"

"If the plows are out, which I assume they are, we should be okay."

"I want to go home."

Luke spared a quick glance at Devonny, surprised at the uncharacteristic desperation in her voice. He admired her dedication, but he'd fallen into lecture mode more than once about how she was wearing herself out. She'd been to the hospital daily, fussing over Loretta. That's probably why her back hurt, from being either on her feet or spending so much time in the uncomfortable chair in Loretta's room the past few days.

Although several of the local and regional media outlets had shown interest in her story, today's interview would go national, just as the Samantha Powers segment had. Devonny had been apprehensive about it, fearing the backlash from Carlson's conservative audience. What Devonny probably needed most was a good night's sleep. Maybe some hot chocolate or a cup of chamomile tea first. He'd make one or the other for her as soon as they got back to her place. "Did you even remember to eat today?"

"I nibbled off of Loretta's tray. They give her so much food and she certainly doesn't have much of an appetite. But it's weird. I wasn't too hungry today." She turned to grin at him. "Maybe the baby's *done*."

Luke tried to smile at her attempt at humor, but mostly he concentrated on the road, forcing himself to tamp down the anxiety that clawed at his insides. He'd driven this very same road too many times to count, at least once a week, sometimes more, for the past couple of years. He knew it well. It was flat and straight and the drive back to Red Bud usually took about forty-five minutes. But it would probably take twice that now, because he refused to drive at anywhere near the speed limit in these conditions.

There was already a couple of inches of snow on the road, but he had confidence in his Jeep with its snow tires and four-wheel drive. Previous snowfalls had been plowed and pushed to the side of the road, and in some places it was like a low wall along the pavement. Beyond the walls of snow were shallow drainage ditches, and beyond those nothing but empty fields.

"I know I'm not supposed to talk while you're driving, but I doubt Doug Winston will continue to use me as the poster child in his 'Clean Up Red Bud' campaign once he sees this interview."

"You thought that after the Samantha Powers show aired. You know the Fox News policy: Fair and Balanced. As soon as they interview Doug they'll air both segments."

"I'm sorry you're caught up in all this."

"Maybe we should have filed a police report after that night in your yard. At least the harassment would be documented. That would have hurt his election chances for sure."

Devonny turned to look out her window. "I know. But I didn't want any trouble. I didn't want to call attention to myself. And now look what's happened."

"Dev, it's not your fault. It's great the way you're standing up to him."

"I don't want to—" she broke off and squirmed some more.

Luke reached over and lowered the lever on the heat. "What's the matter?"

"I'm uncomfortable and my backache is getting worse."

"Are you sure it's just a backache?"

"What else could it be?"

"I don't know. Could you be in labor?"

Devonny turned to stare at him. He glanced her way for a second and saw the rising panic in her eyes.

"You think I'm in labor?"

"I don't know. God, I hope not, because if you are we'll have to turn around and drive back to the hospital."

"It eased up a bit."

"Maybe you should take your boots off and elevate your legs," Luke suggested. "Take some of the pressure off your lower back."

"Good idea." Devonny unzipped her boots and pushed them off. She hooked her heels on the edge of the seat where they promptly slid off. "Nope. That's no good."

"Can you put them on the dashboard? Or turn sideways and put them on the console? Or over here in my lap."

She gave him a devilish grin. "Ooh, kinky."

She wiggled around some more until she could stretch her legs enough to press her feet against his thigh.

"Better?" he asked without taking his eyes off the road.

"Not really."

Devonny gasped and reached around behind her, pressing a hand to her lower back.

Luke's gaze turned briefly to her. "What is it?"

"I think that made it worse."

She spun back around. She reached for the lever to adjust the seat back to recline further and tried putting her feet on the dashboard. "Anyway, now that I'm not working and there's nothing else scheduled, I'm going to ignore everything and concentrate on getting ready to bring the baby home."

"Thanks to Doug, you'll never be able to work in a public school district again, you know that right? That's assuming you ever wanted to."

"I started working at the high school because I never got to go to high school. I wanted to see what it was like.

But I've been thinking more and more about getting a teaching certification."

"You have?" Luke squinted into the darkness and the snow. Visibility had deteriorated even further. He figured they were about halfway home. He hadn't seen a snowplow yet and only two other cars had crept along in the opposite direction. It was like he and Devonny were alone in the world. "I have to be honest, Dev. I don't know what school would hire you under the circumstances."

"I could tutor, though. If nothing else, I learned there's at least one teacher who's not doing a very good job. SAT prep courses. Stuff like that. I might like it better. I could set my own rates and make my own schedule. What do you think?"

They hadn't talked about the future, he realized. Nothing past the baby coming. He had no idea what Devonny's plans were. She said she loved him, but was that because he'd become the guy who scratched an itch Devonny couldn't reach? With all the focus on her films the past couple of weeks, it was like Jack was still alive. Luke didn't want to be the guy standing in for her dead husband, competing with her memories of him. He wanted to be her new leading man. Permanently.

Panic gripped Luke's gut. What if —

A scream cut through Luke like an expertly thrown knife. He automatically hit the brake, which, he realized too late, was the absolute worst thing he could have done. The Jeep began to skid and then made a frightening three-hundred-and-sixty-degree turn, churning through the low wall of snow. Luke's instincts kicked in and he tried to steer with the spin, but it was too late. The Jeep slid into a deep ditch and thumped against something solid before it stopped and settled at a right angle with the highway. He blinked and stared at the road, which was rapidly disappearing in the snow. The wipers were still going double time and the heat still poured from the vents, but the Jeep's rear end was wedged deep.

Luke sat for a moment, stunned. His nightmare came back to him in full force. Driving in bad weather, arguing with a woman, causing her death and that of an unborn child. Slowly he turned to look at Devonny. He saw the panic in her eyes, but she was still alive, thank God. So was he. Shook up, but alive. And, he hoped, uninjured.

"You okay?"

She gave a shaky laugh. "M — my water broke."

Luke stared at her. "Your water...?"

He glanced down but he could hardly see anything in the dim glow of the dashboard lights. He flicked on the interior lights to see wetness dripping off the leather seat and seeping into the floor mats and carpet below. His gaze came back to Devonny's face.

She released her seatbelt and pressed both hands to her lower back. "Ow, ow, ow," she moaned.

"You're in labor." That would go down in the annals of history as the dumbest stating-the-obvious comment he'd ever made.

She bent forward, trying to ease the pressure on her back. "Apparently."

"But you're not hurt?"

She shook her head, her breath coming in short, shallow pants.

"Let's see if I can get us out of here so we can head back to the hospital." He forced confidence that he didn't feel into his tone. He released his seat belt. "Sit tight for a minute."

A strained laugh forced its way through her lips. "No pun intended, right?"

He squeezed her elbow. "Right."

He yanked the hood of his coat over his head and stepped out into the blowing snow. The Jeep's back hatch opened and a gust of cold air swept in. Devonny shivered. "Sorry. I need a flashlight," Luke said. She glanced back to see him unzip a duffle bag and rearrange a few items before the hatch closed.

***

Devonny got out of her wet slacks and panties while Luke was outside. She panted her way through what she now realized was a contraction. The pain slithered around from her back to her belly. After it eased up, she used her scarf to dry the seat as much as she could and pulled her coat down under her as far as it would reach. Her socks were damp and her legs were bare. Was she going to give birth in the front seat of Luke's Jeep?

Might as well. You've already ruined his car.

Not now, Jack, okay?

Luke's door opened and he slid back into the driver's seat, bringing a rush of cold air and snow with him. "How you doing?"

Devonny held up her index finger and massaged her belly, which grew hard with another contraction. She moaned and panted in misery when it stopped. "I don't think," she said between breaths, "we have time to make it to the hospital."

"I don't think I can get us out of this ditch anyway. We're dug in near a culvert. The quarter panel is crushed but the four-wheel drive might get us moving."

Devonny waved a hand at him which meant both "stop talking" and "do whatever you need to do." She could only hope he understood before another contraction robbed her of coherent thought. She surprised herself by emitting a long, painful Tarzan-like howl before she sagged back, panting.

Luke threw the Jeep into four-wheel drive and pressed on the accelerator. The Jeep drew forward slightly, then sagged into the snow. Luke reversed with the same effect. "There's nothing for the wheels to grip and it can't get over or away from that culvert, I don't think. We managed to get a lot of snow packed under us too." He tried turning the wheel first right and then left, accelerating and reversing both times, but it didn't help the vehicle's position.

Another contraction swept through Devonny. "This isn't going to work. I need more space."

"Okay. Hang on." Luke climbed into the back and folded the seats flat. "I've got a couple of stadium blankets back here," he told her. "I'll come around and get you, okay? I don't think you can crawl back here between the seats."

"Yes, I can. Give me a sec." She waited out the next contraction with an accompanying moan. "Okay, I'm coming. Get out of the way."

Luke scrambled as far back as he could. Devonny shrugged out of her coat and tossed it in his direction. He spread it out on the fairly flat surface. She heaved herself over the console, her belly swishing against the side of both the seats until she cleared them, turned herself around and lowered onto the coat Luke had spread out.

"I'm glad I already slept with you," she said absently as she adjusted her position. She was also happy she was wearing a long sweater, which was not only warm, but reached to mid-thigh.

Luke chuckled covering her lower half with one of the blankets. "Why's that?"

"Bec*aaaaaaaaaaaauuuuuuuuussss*se," she howled. She was sweating by the end of the contraction. She wiped her brow. "Maybe you won't be grossed out by all of this." She indicated her swollen belly. "And you've already seen me naked."

She knew that wasn't quite the same as being a witness to childbirth, but fortunately Luke refrained from saying so. "I'm going to call the hospital now," Luke said. "And tell them where we are so they can send an ambulance, which I hope will be following a snow plow and, God willing, there will be a tow truck right behind the ambulance."

"This is really happening, isn't it?" She cried out as another contraction began.

"Did you see *Gone With the Wind*?" Luke asked.

"A long time ago, why?"

"There's a line in it that fits this situation perfectly."

"There is?"

"'Miss Scarlett, I don't know nuthin' bout birthin' babies.'"

"Me either."

"They taught the basics when I volunteered at the fire department, but that's all. If the space between your contractions is any indication, we're both about to find out how it's done, ready or not."

Luke concentrated on his phone and soon made contact with the emergency dispatcher. He had to pause halfway through his explanation of where they were and what he needed, while Devonny yelled at the top of her lungs.

He put the phone on speaker. The dispatcher assured him she'd notified emergency services and they'd be there as soon as possible, but because of the weather it could be a while. She would stay on the line with them for as long as necessary. She outlined some supplies they'd need. Something to tie off the umbilical cord, scissors or a knife to cut it. She agreed twist ties and a pocket knife would probably be sufficient.

"Do you know if she's fully dilated?"

Luke's gaze crossed with Devonny's. She gave him a blank look. "Uh, how would we know?"

"Do you have enough light to see the cervix, sir?"

Devonny giggled at Luke's confusion before she moaned again.

"Tell me what to look for," he said.

"See if you can see the baby's head. If she's fully dilated, she'll be crowning soon, assuming she hasn't already."

"Mind if I take a look?" Luke asked Devonny.

"Be my guest."

He ducked below the blanket with the flashlight. "I feel like I'm looking into a black hole," he said.

Devonny started to laugh at Luke's description, but the laugh turned into a yelp which morphed into a long guttural scream.

"Jesus!" Luke shoved the phone aside and wedged himself into the corner to sit Indian style. He held one of Devonny's ankles in each hand. "Slide down here. He used his knees to brace her feet. She supported herself on her elbows. "How's that?"

She nodded because she couldn't talk. Because there was another contraction. Luke shoved the blanket aside. The flashlight had rolled away, but he ignored it. Devonny felt the brush of his hand on her inner thigh. He spread the palm of his other hand on her belly.

"Whenever you're ready, Dev. I'm here, okay." His gaze flickered to hers. She nodded. Somehow it seemed the rightest thing in the world that Luke should be delivering her baby. That it was just the two of them here in this cocoon of relative warmth in the middle of the cold and snow and wind outside.

She wasn't afraid, she realized. Not of this. Not of being a single mother. A widow. Of living her life alone. Not of people like Doug Winston who wanted to twist her past into something sick and ugly. Not of anything. Because she knew, right now, something she'd always known. That no matter what, there would always be people like Luke. Good, decent people who'd stand up for what was right and do what had to be done. The kind of people whose loyalty never wavered and who stood strong in the face of adversity. They were the kind of people whose example you'd want your child to follow.

***

Luke refused to panic. "It's going to be okay," he said as the baby's head crowned. He had no idea how long it took, once that happened, for a baby to be born. But he felt pretty sure, it wouldn't be long. He'd seen this somewhere, on TV probably, that he could feel

Devonny's contractions if he kept a hand on her belly. Sure enough, he felt it grow hard as the muscles contracted and she cried out in pain. The baby was making its way down the birth canal.

The dispatcher had raised her voice because he hadn't answered her in several minutes. "Can you be quiet, please?" he called in the direction of the phone. "We're trying to have a baby here."

Once again Devonny's laugh turned into a wail. "It's okay, hon." He glanced down. "I see the top of her head. She's got hair. Black I think."

"If you can see the head, she can start pushing," the dispatcher said.

"Hear that," Luke said, catching Devonny's eye. "You can start pushing."

"Yippee."

"On the next contraction," the dispatcher instructed.

Luke felt the contraction begin. "Okay, go. One, two, three, push."

Devonny sat up, supporting herself with her hands and pushed.

Luke laughed this time. "I've got half a baby."

"Couple more and you might have a whole one," the dispatcher quipped. "Check the baby's mouth and neck as soon as you can. Make sure there's no umbilical cord interference."

"Okay," Luke agreed, wondering what he was supposed to do if there was.

He reached around to locate the flashlight and set it in his lap, pointed in the baby's direction.

The moment he touched Devonny again, she had another contraction. She half sat up and pushed without

Luke telling her to, before she lay back panting with the effort.

Luke stared at what he could see of the baby. She was tiny and delicate. He could hardly believe there'd been this whole little person curled up inside Devonny the whole time. In awe of what was happening, he cradled the baby's head in one hand.

Devonny sat up again the second her next contraction started and pushed. This time, the rest of the baby slid out and Luke was barely fast enough to catch it.

"It's here!" Luke cradled the baby in his hands. "What the hell do I do now?"

"Wipe any mucus away from its nose and mouth," said the dispatcher. "Make sure it's breathing."

Luke used the hem of his shirt to wipe the baby's face. She opened her eyes and gave a startled look of affront before she began to squall in outrage.

He started to laugh and realized tears were running down his face. Devonny's daughter was about the most beautiful thing he'd ever seen. He looked up to see Devonny smiling tiredly at him.

Carefully he wrapped the baby in the other blanket and handed her to Devonny. She quieted as Devonny crooned to her and Luke followed the dispatcher's instructions on how to tie off the cord, and wait until it stopped pulsing before cutting it. She explained about the afterbirth.

"Is there supposed to be this much blood?" Luke asked the dispatcher.

If You Knew

Chapter Twenty-Eight

Luke took the phone off speaker and listened to the dispatcher's instructions. He wrapped Devonny's lower half as best he could in the blanket. She paid no attention, transfixed instead by the baby.

Luke was surprised to find that less than an hour had passed since the Jeep had come off the road. He felt somehow as if it had been several lifetimes.

Although he'd left the lights on and the engine running with the heat on max, it couldn't compete with the cold that seeped in from outside. Not to mention the rear of a Jeep was not the most comfortable place to be in any circumstances. It didn't help that his bad knee was throbbing like a son of a bitch.

"How you doing?" he asked softly, not wanting to interrupt Devonny's first interaction with her daughter.

"It's a little cramped back here, but honestly? I'm on top of the world. She's perfect, isn't she?" Devonny smiled.

"Just like her mother." Luke took a moment to think. "It's probably best if you don't move around too much. Otherwise I'd suggest putting the seats up so you could be more comfortable. I guess I can put one of them up, actually. You can sit there, with your back against the door and put your feet up on the other one. Want to try?"

"Okay."

He shrugged out of his coat and helped Devonny sit up so she could put it on. He pulled one of the rear seats upright and took the baby from her. Devonny kept the blanket wrapped around herself as she eased her way into the seat. "Your car is ruined, you know. I'll have to buy you a new one."

"I'll get it detailed. It will be fine."

"Uh huh. Bet you're wishing you'd sprung for those expensive floor liners."

He handed her the baby once she was settled. "Any better?"

"Some." She squirmed a bit so the door handle no longer dug into her back. "But my feet are like ice."

Luke untied his boots and pulled off his socks. He leaned across to tug them over Devonny's feet.

"Are you going to give me the shirt off your back, too?"

"Actually," he said, as he pulled his sweater over his head, I was thinking if you wrap the baby in my shirt, we can use that blanket to cover both of you and you'll be warmer." He pulled the shirt off and handed it to her, then put his sweater and boots back on. Once she had the baby wrapped in the soft flannel, he spread the blanket over both of them. "How's that?"

"Good." The baby whimpered. "I'm going to try to nurse her. I've never done it before, though. Um…if you don't mind, I'd prefer not to have an audience.

"Gotcha." The front seat was off limits since he couldn't get to it without stepping over Devonny, and he didn't want to take a chance of accidentally kicking her or dislodging any of the makeshift coverings.

He sat behind her seat, facing the same direction she was and studiously stared at the window. He could hear her adjusting her clothing and the fussing of the baby. She cooed to it in the most natural way, talking softly to it, telling her they were going to figure this out together. Then he heard the unmistakable sound of sucking.

"I think I did it," she said excitedly.

Luke wanted to look, to be a part of another first, but he didn't. "That's great."

"It feels weird."

"I bet."

"But a good weird."

"Does it hurt?"

"A little at first, but no. Not really. You can look now if you want to."

Cautiously, Luke peered over the seat. Devonny cradled the baby close against the curve of her breast. He couldn't see much in the shadowy light, but there was something natural and elemental about the way the two of them were connected. A lump formed in Luke's throat as he thought of Jack. He wondered if he was here, the way Devonny believed he was, if could see his wife and his baby. But Luke felt honored that he'd been the one here in the flesh.

Luke and Devonny were quiet for a while. The snow muffled everything except the sound of the engine and the sweet suckling noises the baby made.

"Luke?"

"Yeah?"

"Thank you."

"You did all the work. I just supervised."

"Please don't joke. I couldn't have done it without you."

"Okay."

"I'm tired."

He could hear it in her voice.

"They should be here soon," he said, hoping it was true.

"Luke?"

"Yes?"

"If anything happens to me, take care of her, okay?"

Now he was worried. "Nothing's going to happen."

When she didn't respond, Luke spared a glance her way. Her head had fallen onto her shoulder. The baby was still cradled close to her body, but she was quiet now. "Dev?"

He looked more closely at her and the baby. He touched Devonny's throat, felt for a pulse. She'd either fallen asleep or passed out from blood loss. Luke hoped it was the former. He got the flashlight and shone it on them. The baby appeared to be asleep as well. Luke covered Devonny up as best he could, tugging her top back down, his fingers brushing against the softness of her skin.

He glanced out the window and saw faint light in the distance. The cavalry! It drew slowly closer. Headlights from the snow plow, surely, and the red and yellow lights of an ambulance behind it. In minutes both vehicles parked.

Luke reached over and opened the door near Devonny's feet. "She's here, he called. The baby, too." While one of EMTs prepped the gurney, the other reached for Devonny's wrist.

Luke held the baby while they worked to get Devonny out of the Jeep and into the ambulance.

"You'll have to ride with us," one of the EMTs informed him. "There's no tow trucks available. The baby's okay, right?"

"Seems to be. She was nursing before she fell asleep."

"They'll check her over in the ER." He handed Luke a blanket. "Okay, let's go."

Luke turned off the Jeep's engine and the lights, grabbed Devonny's purse, and held the baby close to his chest until he got to the ambulance's cab, which was blessedly warm.

The baby seemed nearly weightless, curled there, wrapped in his flannel shirt and covered by the blanket. He wondered how much she weighed. Six pounds? Seven? Tiny, yet self-contained. Substantial. He could feel the heat from her body against his chest. He feathered his fingers across her head, feeling the wispy strands of dark hair.

The driver got back in and gestured toward the baby. "Let me check her over real quick." Luke turned her and the medic pressed a stethoscope to her tiny chest and moved it around while she squirmed, but did not cry out. "Lungs and heart sound okay," he said. He peered closely at the baby in the interior lights, cradling her head, checking her mouth and eyes. He wrapped her back up and returned her to Luke. "Looks like a healthy specimen."

The snow plow performed a three-point turn and the ambulance did the same, snuggling up behind it for the trip back.

The snow continued to fall in wet heavy flakes. Luke expected his Jeep would likely be buried by morning, though that was the least of his worries. The baby seemed fine, but Devonny? He began to pray to a God he hadn't been sure he believed in that she would recover.

***

Three hours later, Luke was hunched over in the uncomfortable ER waiting room chair. They'd taken the baby away from him, given him a set of scrubs to change into, and told him absolutely nothing.

He hadn't bothered to fudge on the truth, figuring they'd have Devonny's marital status in her medical records already anyway. He could have said he was her husband. Her fiancé. Boyfriend. He wasn't sure what his status was.

He was always surprised how long it took to get information in a hospital. Especially in an emergency situation. Especially if you weren't a member of the immediate family.

He was emotionally drained and anxious. He scrubbed his hands over his face. He'd had one cup of the hospital's vending machine coffee in an effort to stay alert, but after a few sips of the bitter brew, he'd tossed it.

The ER was deserted except for him and a skeleton staff because of the storm. He hoped to God there was an actual doctor somewhere on duty.

He was about to get up and demand some information from someone when a door opened and a man in scrubs similar to his, but with a stethoscope around his neck and an official hospital ID tag, came out.

"Mr. Bradshaw?"

"Yes?" Luke got to his feet.

"I'm Doctor Baker."

"How's Devonny?"

"We've decided to admit both her and the baby," Doctor Baker said. "It's best under the circumstances, although the baby didn't require any medical attention. You did a good job with the delivery."

"But Devonny?" *Did I fuck that part up?*

"She did experience some excessive bleeding. It sometimes happens, for a variety of reasons, during childbirth. We're giving her a transfusion and then she'll be moved to a room. We'll need to monitor her closely for the next day or two. The nurse will let you know when you can see her."

Luke sank back into his chair in relief. "Thank you, Doctor."

"You're welcome. Take care now."

Luke rubbed his eyes as the doctor left, not surprised when they came away slightly damp. Devonny was going to be fine. As soon as she was up to it, they were going to get a few things straight between them. The non-defined status of their relationship was going to change. He wasn't sure how quickly he could move from there to husband and step-father but he was damned well going to find out.

***

When Devonny woke up for the third or fourth time she wondered how anyone ever slept in a hospital. Each time she drifted off, a nurse seemed to show up to check her vitals, knead her abdomen, or hand her the baby to nurse.

That part, Devonny didn't mind at all. She was already in love with this little girl she and Jack had created. Watching her nurse was entrancing.

This time, though, there was no nurse nudging Devonny awake or making so much noise she woke up anyway. This time it came naturally. She saw Luke in the padded vinyl chair across from her, a hospital blanket clumsily thrown over him. His hair was tousled and his arm dangled over one side. Devonny smiled. She was all too aware of the feelings surging through her. He'd appeared the moment she'd decided to start on this new life of hers. She hadn't expected a man to be a part of it, but after she'd run into him outside the diner that first day it seemed they'd been running toward each other ever since.

Luke was like a rock beneath the surface of a rushing river. If you were being swept downstream by life and everything felt out of control, he'd be the thing you didn't know was there but you could hang onto just the same.

She wanted to hang onto him, she realized. Forever. She still couldn't believe how they'd ended up here. From that first kiss, to the nights they'd spent together, to him delivering this munchkin of hers last night.

"What do you think?" she whispered to the baby, who had fallen asleep at her breast. "Luke would be a good daddy, wouldn't he?"

Startled, Luke sat straight up. "Huh? What?" He blinked and saw Devonny in the grayish light seeping in through the curtained window.

She made a few wardrobe adjustments.

"Are you okay? How are you feeling?"

"I'm fine. I'm tired. I can't wait to go home so maybe I can get some real sleep."

He stepped across to the window to look out at the blanket of white. It had stopped snowing at least. "As soon as we score some wheels and they get the road cleared. How's this one?" He brushed a gentle finger across the top of the baby's head.

"She's perfect. And that's from an impartial source." Devonny grinned.

"Like mother, like daughter." Luke didn't smile when he said it. Their eyes locked while something neither was ready to put into words passed between them.

"Want to hold her?"

She passed the baby to Luke. "Wow." His gaze flickered to Devonny. "I can't get over how little she is. And that she fit—" he inclined his head. "in there."

Devonny giggled. "I know. But I've got to be honest with you. I'm glad she's not in there anymore."

"So am I." Luke chuckled.

Devonny squeezed his arm. "Thank you."

"You already thanked me."

"I know, but I've been thinking about how you've always been there from the minute I set foot in Red Bud. I thought I was going to be alone with her. But I'm glad I'm not. I'm glad it's you here with me."

"Me too."

A nurse bustled in to check on Devonny. Luke turned his back and walked to the window with the baby until she was done. "You can take a shower later if you feel up to it," the nurse said. "There's a clean gown in the cupboard there."

"I packed my hospital bag carefully because I didn't want to forget anything," Devonny told Luke after the nurse left. "It's sitting next to my front door."

"What do you need?"

"Stuff like clean underwear, shampoo, deodorant. Which I doubt they sell in the hospital gift shop."

"Probably not. But there's a drug store in the next block. I can head over there as soon as it's open and get whatever you need. Make me a list. I'll be happy to babysit while you shower."

"What would I do without you?"

***

At the drugstore Luke got a cart and carefully chose what he put into it, per Devonny's list. He liked her fat, curly handwriting.

He picked out some socks for her and some for himself as well, because he wasn't quite sure what happened to the ones he'd put on Devonny's feet last night. But he didn't care for the way his bare feet stuck to the inside of his boots.

She'd written "granny panties, size six." He wasn't exactly sure what those were. None of the packages were labeled as granny panties. He got a three-pack of white women's briefs in the correct size. Devonny would have to make do.

He'd never bought feminine hygiene products before. He'd never realized how many choices there were, but he found the brand in the correct box color Devonny had requested, thinking this is what it meant to be a man. Or at least a man in love. There was nothing he wouldn't do for Devonny. Up to and including buying maxi pads for her.

Shampoo. Deodorant. Moisturizer. Body lotion. Toothbrush. Toothpaste. That part was easy.

In the baby aisle, he was again confounded by the array of products created for infants. Devonny had asked for tee shirts, a baby blanket, and a romper, just in case she needed them. The baby clothes she'd planned to bring were in the same hospital bag she didn't have. And she didn't like not being prepared.

Luke found himself drawn to a soft pink romper. It had delicate white stripes running through the pale pastel. He put it in the cart before he saw a yellow one with kittens wearing bows around their necks. He put one of those in the cart as well. Then there was a headband with rose appliqués. He got one of those, too. And booties. Pink booties with white bows. She'd need booties, wouldn't she? Of course she would. Definitely she'd need that stuffed pink teddy bear. And the fluffy white cat with the red ribbon next to it…

He'd have liked to bring Devonny flowers, but there weren't any to be had. He settled on a couple of chocolate bars instead. He'd seen the food on her hospital tray.

The snow plows had been working all night and the main streets at least were partially cleared. He'd call to see about a tow truck for the Jeep once he got back to the hospital.

Chapter Twenty-Nine

By the next day, Devonny was feeling much better. She'd had her fill of the hospital and was ready to go home, but her doctor refused to release her until the following morning.

"We don't take chances in a case like yours. I don't expect further complications, but it's best to wait 48 hours to be sure."

Reluctantly, Devonny agreed to stay, but she wasn't happy about it. The only bearable part was having the baby, whom she'd named Lucy Joy Campbell, with her.

Yesterday afternoon Luke's Jeep had been towed to the local dealership and they'd offered him a loaner. He'd returned to Red Bud last night but promised to be back after school today. But that was hours away and the hospital hours dragged by.

The baby napped in her basinet. Devonny gazed out the window, although there wasn't much to see since her room overlooked the roof of the lower level and the parking lot beyond. She'd flipped through the television channels earlier, but like Loretta, found nothing of interest.

As if she'd conjured her by thinking of her, the door opened and Loretta appeared fully dressed, being pushed in a wheelchair by a smartly attired man who looked to be in his forties. Right behind him came another man, who looked like he'd stepped out of a Calvin Klein ad.

"Loretta!" Devonny cried, ridiculously glad to see her friend looking so well. "Did you get my message?"

"I did. But you and this young 'un of yours were already the talk of the hospital. Quite the dramatic entrance she made."

"You're telling me." Devonny glanced at the two men.

"This is my son, Stevie," Loretta said, indicating the man who'd been pushing the wheelchair. "And his husband, Marcus."

"It's *Steve*," he said, as if the emphasis would change a lifetime of Loretta referring to him by his nickname. "It's nice to finally meet you in person, Devonny," Steve said. "Thanks again for taking such good care of my mother."

"You're welcome, but I didn't do much. She wouldn't let me."

"Oh, we know," Marcus put in. "She's been fussing at us for coming since we got here. Haven't you, Retta?" He gave her shoulder an affectionate squeeze.

"You boys worry too much. You didn't need to come all this way."

Although Devonny had spoken to Steve on the phone a couple of times, Loretta had never talked much about her son and she'd never mentioned that he was married. Yet she seemed to have a good relationship with both men.

But maybe others weren't quite as understanding of Steve's sexual orientation and life choices. Unlike LA, where it seemed everyone was inclined to overshare, in Red Bud Devonny'd noticed personal information was closely held. In fact, she hadn't known until recently that Lauren had three children or that Janet was going through a difficult divorce. And Devonny had worked with both women for months.

"I'm not contagious, but the nurse told me I should wear a mask if I hold the baby," Loretta said, holding one up. "If it's okay with you."

"Of course."

"Okay, if I pick her up?" Steve asked.

"Sure."

Devonny watched as he carefully lifted Lucy from the basinet and placed her in his mother's arms. The three of them looked down at the baby, enthralled. "She's so tiny," Marcus murmured.

Steve slipped his arm around his husband's waist and kissed his cheek. "Pretty soon, we're going to have one of these."

If this was news to Loretta, she didn't acknowledge it. "She's sure got a lot of hair," she commented. "And a sweet face." She glanced up at Devonny. "You do know you've got a babysitter living right next door to you, don't you?"

"Babysitter? I thought I had a fairy godmother living next door to me."

Loretta looked pleased. She rubbed her chin across the top of Lucy's head before handing her back to Steve. Loretta lowered her mask and wheeled her chair closer to Devonny. "I'm sure glad everything went all right and you're okay."

"Me too. They won't let me go home until tomorrow, though."

Loretta reached up and laid her hand on Devonny's. "That's fine. You take it easy and get your strength back. The boys are taking me home and I've got strict orders to get lots of rest. Those two won't let me do anything else anyway."

"That's right, Retta. We're going to take good care of you and we're not leaving until we're convinced you're cured."

"That's what I'm afraid of." She winked at Devonny. "I'll see you soon, honey. Let's go boys."

***

When Luke walked in that evening, Devonny was ridiculously glad to see him. And not just because he had a restaurant takeout bag with him. He set it on the bedside table next to Devonny's unappetizing hospital meal and bent to kiss her. She looped her wrists around his neck and made the kiss count.

He grinned. "Someone's feeling better. Not to mention more energetic."

"And bored." She glanced at the bag of food. "Is that for me?"

Luke unwrapped it. "Chef's salad from the Red Bud Diner, as requested."

Luke removed the hospital fare and arranged the salad on the rolling table, unwrapping the utensils and setting the dressing next to them. "Enjoy." He stepped over to the basinet. "How's Lucy?"

"Dying to get out of here like me, I'm guessing." Devonny dipped a bite of salad into the dressing and started to eat. Luke picked Lucy up, carefully supporting her neck, and nuzzled her head with his chin.

He's going to be great with her.

It no longer mattered to Devonny whether the voice she heard was hers or Jack's. They were in complete agreement.

"Did Mommy tell you she has your room all ready for you?" Luke asked the baby. "And there's a swing set in the back yard. And a big oak tree you can climb in the front."

"In about ten years," Devonny put in.

Luke looked down at Lucy. "I think she's bored. She fell asleep."

"That's because I fed her and changed her right before you arrived."

Luke placed the baby back in the basinet and took a seat on the edge of the bed. "Marcus drove over with me, so I could take the loaner back. I'm driving your car until the Jeep's fixed."

"I didn't know you knew Marcus."

"He and Steve were here visiting Loretta when I was renovating the house. They helped me hang the cabinets and put the closet together. And paint."

"You never mentioned it."

"Didn't I?"

"I'm starting to think everyone in Red Bud has a few secrets."

"It isn't a secret. It just never came up, I guess."

"How's the Jeep? A total loss?"

"No. There's some damage to the rear end. And some of the upholstery and carpet needs to be replaced."

"Send me the bill."

Luke edged closer. With a finger under her chin, he tilted Devonny's head up so he could look into her eyes. "Hey. Dev. We're in this together. Right?"

"Right." Devonny was breathless. This was the commitment she hadn't been sure she was ready for.

A smile spread across Luke's face. "In that case, you can pay half the bill."

Devonny giggled and leaned forward to kiss Luke again. "It's a deal."

***

Late the next morning, Devonny's release came through and Luke came to pick up her and Lucy. He'd installed Lucy's car seat and she slept on the drive back to Red Bud.

"Let's leave her in the carrier and put her in my bedroom," Devonny said. "I'm going to take a nap. Or try to anyway."

"I've got a few things to do at school," Luke said. "But I'll be back to make dinner."

"You don't have to. I made a few meals ahead. They're in the freezer."

"Sounds great." He kissed her and left.

Devonny reacquainted herself with her house. Everything looked a little different to her, but maybe that was because she wasn't the only one occupying it now. She smiled at the thought that soon Luke would move in with her and Lucy. They hadn't talked marriage, but she assumed Luke would want that as much as she did. Maybe in the summer. Maybe on the one-year anniversary of her arrival in Red Bud. The day they'd run into each other outside the diner, even though she barely remembered him from that day.

She undressed and Lucy slept on. Devonny closed her eyes, thinking there was nothing so wonderful as being back in her own bed.

Two hours later her eyes popped open when Lucy began to stir. Though not feeling very well rested, she knew it was time for a feeding. Once she had herself and Lucy situated, she settled on the sofa to nurse and idly flipped through the few items of mail that had accumulated in the past couple of days. Including the most recent issue of the Red Bud Record.

There was a photo of Doug Winston and one of the current mayor, Bart Carmichael. Either it was an unflattering photo of him or he was not well.

Doug was pushing for a town hall meeting where the two candidates could face off and highlight their political agendas. A brief mention was made of Doug's "Clean Up Red Bud" campaign efforts, but not of Devonny specifically. Perhaps support for his mayoral run was falling off. Based on the limited quotes from the current mayor, who'd held the office for thirty years, he wasn't taking Doug's challenge seriously. Nor did it sound like he was interested in participating in a town-hall-meeting type of forum.

Once Devonny stopped working at the high school, the initial local outrage had died down rather quickly. "Maybe everyone's afraid their little secrets will come out," Devonny murmured. Lucy paused nursing as if waiting for further conversation, but resumed when none was forthcoming.

Devonny scanned the rest of the paper, but there wasn't much of interest, other than that the newly appointed state attorney general had undertaken an investigation into methamphetamine manufacturing and trafficking throughout the state.

When Luke arrived later, he wore the grim expression Devonny'd only seen a couple of times before. "What's wrong?" she asked, before he'd even greeted her.

He kissed her before he stepped away to hang up his coat. "Doug Winston's scheduled a town meeting for a week from Saturday."

"With the current mayor?" Devonny asked. "I read about it in the paper."

"I don't know if Carmichael will be in attendance. There's a rumor he's just been diagnosed with liver cancer. If it's true, Doug might be running unopposed and that's not good. He'll think he can do whatever he wants, say whatever he wants, and no one will stop him."

"He's a loose cannon. No doubt about that. I thought he was losing momentum, you know, after everything. It doesn't seem like most of the townspeople are supporting him in his vendetta against me, anyway."

"Most of the town probably isn't. But he has pockets of influence. And a town meeting is a good way to stir everyone up. There's not much else going on this time of year."

Devonny stepped round the counter and slid her arms around Luke's waist. "It'll be okay. You'll see."

"How do you know?"

"Because of what we agreed on yesterday."

"What's that?"

"We're in this together."

If You Knew

Chapter Thirty

"As you all know, we've got a problem, folks. Right here in Red Bud. And I'm here to promise you if you elect me mayor, I *will* keep our town clean. I will keep our town *safe* from those who seek to bring in the kind of smut Devonny Campbell represents.

"A woman like that..." he waited, allowing his audience to consider what kind of woman Devonny was. "Should not be around our young people, should she?"

There were several shouted noes, and murmurs rippled through the crowd.

"She should not be allowed to *influence* our impressionable young people, should she?"

More noes rose up as the crowd grew more agitated.

"Should a woman like that, a peddler of *flesh films*, a woman of *low morals*, be anywhere near the dear, tiny babies of this town?"

Noes were shouted from several directions.

"We're lucky in this regard," Doug went on, once the noise had subsided. "We are able to nip this crisis in the bud, so to speak. Devonny Campbell has resigned her position at Red Bud High School. I've spoken to Sheriff Grady. Ms. Campbell may avoid prosecution for putting her video on display during the morning announcements, if she agrees to leave the county peaceably."

Luke had listened to the entire speech, leaning against the cinder block wall at the back of the room, arms crossed. Disgust was eating him alive. He wanted to believe Doug was grasping at straws to hang onto the support for his mayoral campaign, but the Winstons had a long history in this town and Devonny hadn't even been here a year. Doug still might have enough clout to rally the citizens of Red Bud to run Devonny out of town on a rail, tarred and feathered and shamed, even though she'd done nothing wrong. Nothing illegal. Nothing criminal. Someone else had inserted that disc into the school's broadcast system and Luke knew who had done it.

But if he didn't act quickly, it wouldn't make a difference.

The town meeting was rapidly spinning out of control. The townspeople had begun taking sides after the first newspaper article appeared. And now Doug's outright lies and innuendos had every citizen in the auditorium riled up. Luke wouldn't be surprised if they marched on Devonny's house with lit torches after this.

Without consciously thinking about how he was going to stop it, Luke strode toward the stage.

But before he got there, Petty Winston appeared from the wings and approached the center of the stage, her hand out. There was a smattering of uncertain applause. Luke paused in the middle of the aisle. Doug looked as if he wanted to throttle her.

"I'd like to say a few words, please."

"What do you think you're doing?" Doug hissed. The microphone picked up his words even from a distance. "This isn't an open forum."

"Fine. I'll speak without the microphone." She turned toward the audience. "You all can hear me, can't you?"

"Give her the mike!" Someone shouted from the back. More voices joined in.

Doug didn't look very happy about it, but he handed the microphone over to Petty. "Thank you," she said. She looked out at the audience. "I think everyone here knows me, but in case you don't, I'm Petula Winston, Doug's soon-to-be-ex-wife." The audience didn't react to that, as if waiting for the hammer to fall. "I want to say, much of what's happened, the reason you're all here today, the whole theme of Doug's campaign, is my fault."

"Petty," Doug hissed in a warning tone which she ignored. He reached for the mike but she held on to it and moved a few steps away.

"You see, I haven't been happy with many of the choices I've made in my life, and that includes marrying Doug." She glanced back at him before turning back to the audience. "I shouldn't have married him. I shouldn't have married any man, to be honest, because that's not who I am. But I tried for a long time to be a wife, to be the kind of wife Doug wanted and needed. I thought, if I could see how other couples behaved in an intimate setting, it would help our marriage. That's why I purchased some adult films, including the one that played on the morning announcements at the high school."

Murmurs rippled through the audience. Petty held up her hand. "My actions, my decisions, my poor judgment, caused a chain reaction. Now my husband has all of you riled up against Devonny Campbell. He's made her a target for his own frustration. He wants her to take the blame for everything that's happened recently. He wants you to believe she is a bad influence on our children."

She let her gaze scan the audience from one side to the other. "I know Devonny Campbell. What's more, I admire her. I've seen her interact with children, your children. I've seen her teach them and listen to them when it seems no one else would. I've seen her help them in ways no one else can."

A voice from the audience piped up, "She tutored my daughter on her own time. For free."

"Mine too," came another voice. "She was failing before, but she's getting As in algebra now."

Petty's voice softened. "You may not approve of things Devonny did in her past. But that's exactly what it is. The past. We should make our decision about her on what she's accomplished since she's become a part of our community. If you want to clean up Red Bud, I suggest you look in your own back yard before you decide someone else isn't up to your high standards. Thank you."

She handed the mike back to Doug and left the stage to light applause and more whispering among the audience members.

"Well," Doug said heartily, clearly trying to regroup after the interruption.

Luke took the few steps two at a time and crossed to where Doug stood behind the podium.

He put his hand out. "Thanks, Doug. I think we all appreciate your dedication to the town and to your campaign. Let's give him a big round of applause, everyone. Doug Winston."

"I'm not done yet," Doug said. The mike picked up on it.

"Yes, you are. Time to give the rest of us a chance to speak. You set this up as a town meeting and we're all a part of this town. Right folks?"

There was a smattering of applause and Luke yanked the mike out of Doug's hand, leaving Doug no choice but to step away. But before he did he muttered, "You'll regret this, Bradshaw," close to Luke's ear.

"Let's hear it for Doug Winston, everyone!" Luke held out his hand and the audience applauded with uncertain enthusiasm this time. Unless Doug wanted to make a scene, he'd leave the stage. Luke held his breath but finally, Doug walked off.

Luke stepped out to the center of the stage with the microphone in his hand. He took a moment to organize his thoughts. "In case you don't know me, I'm Luke Bradshaw, the guidance counselor and football coach at the high school. I think we all appreciate it when someone like Doug Winston takes up a cause he believes in. We all want to protect our town and our children and make Red Bud a good place to raise families, am I right?

"I want to tell you a story about a young man. He grew up in a family much like the ones here in Red Bud, but he made a few missteps along the way. When he was in college he and his girlfriend were in a car accident. He was injured. The girl died and so did her unborn child."

"Many of you here tonight have known tragedy like this in your lives, or know someone who has, haven't you?"

The audience murmured in agreement.

"While this young man was recovering from his injuries, his mother passed away. A lawsuit was brought against his family by the girl's parents. His father blamed him. Told him he was no good. Nothing but a screw-up.

"There was a lot of grief and a lot of pain in this young man's life at that time. Pain pills helped. So did alcohol. Eventually he turned to heroin." Luke paused to let his words seep in. People in the audience looked at each other and at their neighbors, wondering if they could figure out who he was talking about.

"This young man was lucky. He got the help he needed. He got off drugs. Stopped drinking. Went back to college and eventually got a degree."

"He's been afraid to tell his story. Afraid he'd be judged and condemned for what happened in his past. Especially in a town like this. And today, after seeing the way many of you have rallied around Doug Winston to condemn Devonny Campbell, maybe he was right to be afraid."

Luke let his gaze wander over the audience before he said, "The accident happened ten years ago, but I'm not afraid any longer." His words fell like feathers drifting into the crowd and he waited to let them sink in. "I'm the same person I was a moment ago. The same person I was last year and the year before. The same coach, the same guidance counselor, the same man I was when you first met me. Except now you know my history."

Murmurs began, but he stopped them by continuing to speak. "And I say to you that Devonny Campbell is *exactly* the same person she was when she arrived in Red Bud last summer. She's the same person who befriended her neighbor Loretta Herman, whom many of you know. The one who drove her to church on Sunday and visited her in the hospital. She's the same one you praised not long ago for volunteering in the church nursery. The one who cared for your babies during church service. She's also the same person some of your teenagers looked up to and sought advice from. The only difference is, now you know something about her you didn't know before, just like you know something about me you didn't know before today. Like you know something about Petty Winston you didn't know before."

The murmuring had stopped. Only the rattling of the ventilation system could be heard.

"A wise woman told me recently life is a journey. We all have mountains and valleys and stumbling blocks. The thing is we don't know what someone else's journey has been or how it's shaped who they are now. So what are we going to do? Dig into everyone's past and run them out of Red Bud if they don't measure up to someone's invisible standard? Because I bet everyone here today has some history the rest of us don't know about. Something they're afraid to share, because if they did they're sure they'd be judged. Is that the kind of town we want to live in? Are these the attitudes we want to teach our children?"

Luke let his question hang there until finally, someone in the back yelled, "No" and someone else hollered, "Hell, no." A smattering of nervous laughter broke out before an older woman rose to her feet. "I've never told anyone this," she said. "I've won the blue ribbon for my apple pie at the county fair for the past three years, but the pies aren't mine. I order them frozen from a bakery in Wisconsin."

A woman two rows behind her stood and said, "I get my daughter-in-law to bake the pies I enter. But I always end up in second place anyway."

A man stood and cleared his throat. "Back in September I told my wife I was going on a men's retreat with the church group. But I went hunting with my cousin." His wife slapped him on the arm.

"I can top that." The wife looked around smugly. "I told Vern I went to visit my sick aunt in Ames last summer. But I was in Las Vegas with my sister playing the slots. And we went to see them Chippendales, too."

Her husband nudged her with his elbow. "Guess that explains why you were feeling so frisky when you got back."

After that it seemed everyone wanted to top everyone else. "I cheated on my husband for years before he died!" "I stole peppers out of my neighbor's garden." "Me and my brothers are the ones that TP'd Miss Fitzgerald's house last Halloween." "When I was sixteen, I gave up a baby for adoption."

The town meeting turned into a free-for-all confessional. Luke stood in astonishment holding the microphone until he realized he wasn't going to need it. He turned it off and replaced it on the podium. The atmosphere in the auditorium had done a one-eighty from anger and outrage to honesty and fellowship.

Luke started down the aisle but was stopped repeatedly by claps on the back and kind words. It seemed everyone wanted to clear the air around them and get rid of the shackles of hidden truths.

Someone turned the microphone back on, which let out a high-pitched squeal and the fumbling sound as someone pulled it off its stand. "Excuse me," said a feminine voice. "Excuse me, everyone. I have something to say."

The audience quieted and turned back to the stage. Luke recognized Emmaline Sanchez. *This ought to be good.*

She looked at the audience, many of whom were already on their feet, until she was sure she had their attention. "I'm Emmaline Sanchez," she began. "Many of you know me. I grew up here in Red Bud, but I left town after graduating. I moved back last year, mostly because I didn't know where else to go."

The audience waited for Emmaline's next words. "In high school I fell in love with a boy. He loved me, too, but...he was under a lot of pressure from his family, especially his father, not to get involved with me. You can probably guess why." The crowd fell silent. "He's a man now and I'm still in love with him. I had hoped our love would have the chance it didn't have the first time. Because, I'm pregnant. Again. And no matter what, this time I'm keeping the baby. And I hope," her voice broke, "this time I hope, his father will want to be part of his life."

"Emmaline." Doug stepped out from the wings. "Don't."

Emmaline looked at him. "I'm not giving this baby up."

Doug's face turned red. Whether from anger or embarrassment it was hard to tell. He shook his head at her, turned on his heel and strode offstage.

Tears fell from her eyes, but she tried to smile as she replaced the mike in its stand.

"Forget him, Emmaline," someone shouted. "We're here for you." She glanced up in surprise. This time the applause reached an enthusiastic, thundering crescendo.

Emmaline made her way down the steps where she was greeted by a crowd of supporters waiting to hug her.

***

Miles knew this was his chance. It was now or never. Brandi was sitting near the back. He'd seen her when he'd first walked in, but had avoided her, taking up a position in the far corner where she wouldn't notice him, and neither would anyone else. Not even his parents.

Everyone in the town, it seemed, was coming clean. His parents were going to divorce no matter what he did. His father had a girlfriend who was pregnant, but he wasn't going to treat her any better than he had his own wife. Coach Bradshaw had been a junkie. The whole damn town had been hiding things they were afraid of everyone else knowing.

He had nothing to lose. And maybe he had nothing to gain, but if he didn't speak up now, he was afraid he never would. He hustled toward the stage and leapt up the stairs and grabbed the microphone, flipping the switch to turn it back on. "Excuse me!" Most of those assembled were out of their seats. There was a buzz of conversation and many had started to leave. "Excuse me," Miles nearly shouted. "Could I have your attention, please?"

The talk died down. Those in the aisles paused and turned back. Miles sought out Brandi and saw her still seated. She was looking at him. He tried to smile. He'd used her. He'd been selfish and cruel. All the things his father had been. He didn't like himself very much. But maybe, just once, he could do something right.

"Thank you." His voice shook. He hoped he didn't start bawling like a baby. That'd be embarrassing. His friends would label him a sissy. Everyone was waiting. He looked out at the sea of curious faces, the townspeople he'd known all his life. The ones he'd continue to be surrounded by on a daily basis as long as he stayed in Red Bud.

He coughed and cleared his throat. "For those of you who don't know me, I'm Miles Winston. And I wanted to tell you, this—" he made a sweeping gesture in the audience's direction, "is all my fault. I'm the one who stole that video, and I'm the one who put it on the morning announcements at school."

He ignored the sounds coming from the crowd. His father stood apart from everyone else, his mouth agape. He probably thought things couldn't get any worse for him, only to see his son get up on stage and do just that.

"All I wanted," Miles said, yanking his gaze back to the sea of listeners, "was to help my dad. He wanted to be the mayor and thought this 'Keep Red Bud Clean' campaign against Ms. Campbell was a good idea. I thought if I helped him, he'd be happy. And maybe my mom wouldn't leave."

He felt every eye on him, but he kept going. "But I found out things don't work that way. I screwed everything up, and I hurt a lot of people. It didn't help my mom or dad and it didn't change what he thinks of me."

He chanced a look at his dad again, who looked crushed. Miles gave him a helpless shrug. But unburdening himself, laying it all on the line, speaking from the heart, had made him feel lighter than he'd ever felt before. As if he could accomplish anything. He didn't have to hide any longer. Or pretend he had a perfect family. He could stop pretending his father loved him. Or that he'd ever earn his dad's approval.

He looked back at the audience. "I'm sorry." He saw Ms. Campbell. She stood at the very back of the auditorium near a side door. "I want to apologize to Ms. Campbell and to Coach Bradshaw. And especially to Brandi." He looked at her. Spoke directly to her. "What I did was wrong. You tried to help me, and I took advantage of it. I'll try to make it up to you if you give me a chance." Miles waited half a beat before he realized he didn't have anything else to say.

***

As the last of the stragglers left, Luke discovered Devonny with a snoozing Lucy tucked into her carrier at the back of the auditorium. A surge of happiness ran through him, as it did each and every time he saw Devonny.

He hugged her hard.

"You were wonderful up there."

"It was time," Luke said. "It felt good."

"Are you ready to go?" Devonny asked.

"More than ready. Want to go get a cup of coffee?"

Devonny laughed. "I would love to."

"Finally." Luke gave her a look full of meaning before he picked up Lucy's carrier.

Outside, Doug, Miles and Sheriff Grady were gathered in a loose circle. A few people had stopped to chat with Emmaline. Miles received several pats on the back.

"Hang on a minute," Luke said to Devonny. He crossed to Miles. "Miles. Just the man I wanted to see."

Doug broke away from his conversation. "I don't think I want you anywhere near my son. Not after what you pulled."

"If that's what you want," Luke said easily. "But I want to tell him how proud I am of him. It takes guts to admit when you've done something wrong. And it takes a real man to apologize in public and try to make it right." Luke stuck out his hand to Miles. Miles hesitated before he took Luke's hand and they shook. "I'd appreciate it if you'd return what you took from me."

"What are you talking about? My son is not a thief."

Luke kept his gaze on Miles. "How about it Miles?"

Doug turned to Miles. "Do you have something that belongs to him?" Doug asked. His tone held no warmth or sympathy at all.

"It's in my car. I'll go get it."

"What are you talking about?" Doug demanded. "What is it you think Miles has?"

"I'd like to know too," Sheriff Grady put in. A few of those leaving the auditorium had found a reason to gather in groups nearby to eavesdrop.

Miles's gaze cut to Devonny. He looked at the carrier Luke held, everywhere but at his father. "The video," he said. "The one I stole out of Coach Bradshaw's backpack."

"The one that played on the school's announcements?" Sheriff Grady asked.

Miles nodded.

"You idiot," Doug hissed. "You let me go out there and make a fool of myself. What kind of a moronic screw-up are you, anyway?"

Tears surged into Miles's eyes.

"He's *not* a screw-up," Luke said, loud enough for everyone around to hear. "He's a kid who wants his father's approval and attention. Maybe even some love. The same way I did when I was his age."

Miles's gaze met Luke's in a moment of understanding.

Luke turned back to Doug. "Probably the same way you wanted your father's approval."

Some of Doug's bluster faded away under Luke's scrutiny. "I don't need to hear any of your psychological bullshit," he snarled.

Luke looked at the sheriff, who nodded. He touched Doug's elbow. "I think the three of us should go back to your house and have a talk. Unless you'd rather come down to my office."

Doug flushed in embarrassment and looked away. They all followed his gaze to where Emmaline was getting into her car.

Doug sighed deeply before he put a hand on his son's shoulder. "Our house is fine. Let's go, Miles. Let's see if we can fix this."

The three of them turned away, but before they got to the outer door Miles turned and came back. "Miss Campbell? I really am sorry. For being such a jerk that time in the parking lot. And for putting your movie on the morning announcements."

"I appreciate a man who can admit he's done something wrong," Devonny said. "And I appreciate your apology."

"Sorry about taking the movie from you, Coach. It was a real JV move."

"It was," Luke agreed. "I see some additional community hours in your future. You talk to Principal Foster about those, all right?"

"All right."

Miles caught up to Doug and the sheriff who looked like they were already discussing possible consequences for Miles.

Luke took Devonny's hand. "Let's go get that coffee."

"You're buying me a muffin, too, you know," she said as they pushed through the double doors to the outside. "Possibly a scone."

"I bet you want one of those fru-fru drinks, too, right? White chocolate and whipped cream? Five bucks a cup."

"You bet. And an extra shot of espresso. Even if it is decaf."

"Dev?" He said when he looked at her. "You can have whatever you want."

"Good. Because there's one more thing I want, but it isn't on the menu at the coffee shop."

"Oh, yeah? What's that?"

"You."

About the Author

Barista by day, romance novelist by night: When not writing fiction, Dr. Seuss-like poetry (for adults) or song lyrics, Barbara Meyers disguises herself behind a green apron and works part-time for a world-wide coffee company.

Her novels are a mix of comedy, suspense and spice and often feature a displaced child.

Barbara is still married to her first husband and has two fantastic children. Originally from Southwest Missouri, (she blames her roots in the Show Me state for her somewhat skeptical nature) she currently resides in Central Florida.

Look for these Titles by Barbara Meyers

Now Available:

Misconceive
Scattered Moments
Not Quite Heaven
Cleo's Web
White Roses in Winter
Training Tommy

The Braddocks Series
A Month From Miami
A Forever Kind of Guy

Coming Soon:
The Red Bud Series
If You Dare
If You Stay
If You Touch

A Family for St. Nick (Christmas Novella)

Barbara Meyers writing as AJ Tillock
The Grinding Reality Series
The Forbidden Bean (Book One)
Cool Beans (Book Two)

Dear Readers,

I hope you enjoyed Devonny's journey. I was told by an editor that a former porn actress would never be accepted by readers of traditional romance. I hope I can prove her wrong, because I love this story and plan to write a series of Red Bud books. My editor, Noah Chinn, suggested giving Doug his own story. "But I don't like him," was my reply. Which, as Noah pointed out, is an even better reason to allow him to redeem himself. Editors, I find, are much like mothers. You don't want to believe they're right, but they usually are. (Except for that first one I mentioned…) Now all I can think about is writing Doug's story which will be titled *If You Dare*. I have plans for Joy to have her own story as well, *If You Stay*. And another mixed-race male friend of Devonny's, Dex, who also relocates to Red Bud and leaves the porn industry behind. His love interest in *If You Touch* will be Melody, who runs the daycare center.

If you enjoyed *If You Knew* I hope you will leave a brief review on the site where you purchased it, on Amazon.com, or on Goodreads. Reviews are so helpful to authors, especially indie authors. I also hope you will tell others about the book.

I love hearing from readers. You can contact me, follow my blog and sign up for my newsletter at barbarameyers.com.

All the best,
Barbara Meyers

Tiffany Preston should have passed out hours ago from the combination of alcohol, coke, and the various pills she'd swallowed throughout the evening. It was a game she played with herself, picking a fat white Percoset, then a small pearly Oxycodone, and later the little gray morphine pills she'd borrowed from her dying grandmother.

Sometimes she'd choose the miniature green anti-depressants, or the cream-colored Xanax. Quite often she couldn't remember which colors of the pharmaceutical rainbow she'd chosen or when. Whatever allowed her to float through her existence, to pretend, to keep her from jumping out of her own skin. Adderall, as a matter of fact, was her new favorite. She had her very own prescription for that because she'd pled with an understanding doctor about her inability to pay attention in class.

Time slowly crept toward dawn and the feeling of nothingness Tiffany craved was as elusive as natural sleep. She wanted to kill somebody. Make that *two* somebodies. Her rage had been why she'd pity-fucked Eric Stranghorn like he'd never been pity-fucked before. He looked surprised and hurt when she told him to get out afterward. He was such a romantic sap he probably thought they'd been making love.

She wasn't attracted to Eric and didn't like him much even though he followed her around like an adoring puppy. He was her brother's friend and the only reason she'd invited him to her party was because he promised to bring Jason Pendell with him. Jason was the birthday gift she'd planned to give herself. Finally, she'd make herself irresistible to him. She'd met him last summer and her very first thought was *mine*. But while Jason was ghost-pepper hot, he was enigmatic and aloof. At least to her. Like a feral cat, acceptance was not important to him. Jason wasn't part of their crowd and he didn't appear to care that he wasn't. Nor did he fall into the category of hanger-on. Which made him that much more intriguing.

When she'd run into him accidentally-on-purpose again on New Year's Eve, he played hard to get, which, even she had to admit, had only fueled her obsession. He wasn't easy to stalk either, since he barely existed according to social media. His phone number was a secret as closely held as nuclear launch codes. She'd swiped Mark's phone only to discover he'd told her the truth when he said he didn't have it.

Still, tonight she'd redoubled her efforts to attract his attention, but Jason pretended to be immune to her charm. When she asked him to dance he refused. Refused! Eric stepped in and told her he'd be happy to dance with her. Tiffany didn't see how she had a choice without dying of mortification. No one turned her down. *No one.* Guys sought *her* out, vied for *her* favor. All of them. Except Jason.

Over Eric's shoulder she'd seen Jason talking to that blond, blue-eyed bitch, Kerrie Huddleston, even after she'd warned Kerrie to stay away from him. Kerrie was a loser. An over-protected only child whose parents doted on her. Everyone loved Kerrie. Teachers. Parents.

Hell, even Tiffany's parents adored sweet, innocent, heart-of-gold Kerrie. Sometimes Tiffany caught them looking at her, their own daughter, as if trying to figure out where they'd gone wrong. If they'd ever cared enough to listen she'd have been happy to tell them. Over the years comparisons had been made between her and Kerrie, and Tiffany had not come out on top.

She didn't even know why she kept Kerrie around. Habit, maybe. They'd been friends since childhood. Two years younger, Kerrie was the dumb little sister Tiffany'd never had. Kerrie had her uses, but stealing Jason right out from under Tiffany's nose at her twenty-first birthday party was not one of them. She'd lost track of Kerrie and Jason when they'd disappeared from the dance floor hours ago and hadn't seen them since. But she had a pretty good idea what they were up to.

Tiffany restlessly roamed the house and the grounds because she didn't know what else to do. Most of her usual asshole party friends had ducked out early and the few who remained were passed out or hooking up in one room or another. She couldn't sleep. She couldn't even sit still. What she needed was a downer. Valium maybe. Or Xanax. Something to smooth away the rough edges. Something to help her relax and forget how miserable and alone she was.

She slid out to the deck thinking she'd make her way down to where the surf pounded against the sand along the Jersey shore. Maybe she'd stay there until the sun came up, let the cool dawn and the sound of the water soothe her. But when she noticed two figures ambling along the shore, nothing short of violence was going to soothe her. One tall and one shorter. One dark head. One blonde. In the moonlight she could see them entwined around each other. Tiffany felt the bile rise in the back of her throat. She wanted to puke. Did she have any pills for acid reflux in her collection? Little purple ones like she saw advertised on TV?

She edged back into the shadows as the couple approached. They wouldn't see her hiding as she was behind the tall beach grass and deck railing.

"I'm a mess," she heard Kerrie say as they came to a stop a few feet away. The deck lights threw shadows but allowed Tiffany to see them both.

Jason fluffed Kerrie's tangled, wind-blown hair. Kerrie looked like she had been lovingly manhandled. Her eyes were huge and soft, her mouth swollen. Her wrinkled dress was damp and sandy.

"You look okay to me," Jason said. Tiffany frowned. Was that sadness she heard in his voice?

"I don't know why, but I feel like crying," Kerrie said.

"Don't do that." Jason pulled her close and held her. "Please don't cry."

Tiffany seethed. *That should be me.* When was the last time anyone had held her so tenderly, spoke to her with such concern in their voice?

Kerrie buried her face in Jason's neck, then in his shoulder. "I won't cry."

"Kerrie, please don't —"

"I'll never see you again. That's what I keep thinking. What if I never see you again?"

It's what you deserve, slut. Tiffany didn't know why she was spying on them. In spite of her revulsion, she was almost enjoying herself. It was like watching a bad soap opera.

Jason rubbed Kerrie's back and rested his head on top of hers. "Kerrie, you don't know that—"

"Are you leaving?"

"I have to."

"Now?"

"I have a job, Kerrie. I'm not like the guys you're used to—"

Kerrie backed away from him. "I'm not 'used to' any of them."

Tiffany almost snorted. Kerrie was unbelievably, revoltingly innocent. Well, she had been until tonight anyway.

"All I meant was," Jason said, "I don't have a lot of free time like they do. I have to work. I have to study and go to class."

"I know. I understand that." Kerrie stepped back into the circle of his arms. "You'll call me, won't you? Or text me?"

"I'd like to, but—"

"Where's your phone?"

He handed her a small gray brick of a phone with a green screen. "Wow. I didn't know they still made these," Kerrie said. He watched while she added her info.

"Kerrie, you need a guy who can be around, take you places, spend money on you—"

"No, I don't."

Yes you do, dumbass, Tiffany mentally argued with her.

"I can't do any of that. Not right now, anyway. You don't need somebody like me."

"Yes, I do," Kerrie said.

For the first time ever, Tiffany saw Jason smile. "Okay, how 'bout this: After I graduate in June, you'll be home for the summer and we'll get together. By then, I should have a decent job and I can afford to take you someplace for dinner where they don't have a drive-thru window."

"I love drive-thru windows." Tiffany was sure Kerrie was smiling.

"Good, because if you start hanging around me, you'll be seeing a lot of them."

Kerrie laughed.

"Kerrie, I've got to get going."

"You need your shoes."

"Wait here. I'll go get them."

Tiffany held her breath as Jason approached the steps. If he came onto the deck he might see her. She wasn't invisible, even though he'd made her feel that way. But he picked up two pairs of shoes from the sand near the bottom step and went back to Kerrie.

They meandered around the side of the house to his car, and Tiffany followed until he stopped next to an old Honda.

"I'll think about you," Kerrie said.

Jason smiled at her again. "Me too." He bent and kissed Kerrie, hard and fast. "You be a good girl, okay?" He let her go and was in the car, backing away almost before Tiffany realized he was gone.

That should have been me. She should have been the one to make him smile like that. The one he singled out and hooked up with on the beach. *That should have been me!*

Tiffany crept back to the deck without making a sound and went up to her room.

Behind the locked door she threw herself onto the bed and punched her pillow again and again and again. Talk about backstabbers. Kerrie had strolled in and stolen Jason right from under her nose after Tiffany had made it clear that he was off limits.

Tonight was to have been Tiffany's night with him. Tonight she'd planned to snare his attention, show him what he had been missing by ignoring her for so long. Instead, her supposed best friend had spent the night screwing him out on the beach somewhere. How could she?

Kerrie was hardly more than a child. Not that long ago, they had been playmates, hosting tea parties in an old tree house for their dolls and bears. Tiffany knew for a fact that Kerrie kept her childhood toys. Her bedroom was still decidedly girlish, with her dolls and stuffed animals adorning various shelves. The special ones took their place of honor on the bed.

How could Jason go for a child like Kerrie when he could have her, Tiffany, instead? Jason *belonged* to her. She had warned Kerrie, hadn't she? Told her to keep her hands off him. Tiffany choked back the rage, fumbling in the dim light for the prescription bottle and twisting off the child-proof medicine cap. She tossed two Valium into her mouth and swallowed, feeling the calm wash over her. Her mind began to clear.

She would find a way to make Kerrie pay. And Jason, too. One day, she promised herself, she would find a way.